CW01468292

KINGS OF WAR

BOOK 2 THE BRUNANBURH SERIES

MJ PORTER

B

Boldwood

First published in Great Britain in 2023 by Boldwood Books Ltd.

Copyright © MJ Porter, 2023

Cover Design by Head Design Ltd

Cover Photography: Shutterstock

The moral right of MJ Porter to be identified as the author of this work has been asserted in accordance with the Copyright, Designs and Patents Act 1988.

All rights reserved. No part of this book may be reproduced in any form or by any electronic or mechanical means, including information storage and retrieval systems, without written permission from the author, except for the use of brief quotations in a book review.

This book is a work of fiction and, except in the case of historical fact, any resemblance to actual persons, living or dead, is purely coincidental.

Every effort has been made to obtain the necessary permissions with reference to copyright material, both illustrative and quoted. We apologise for any omissions in this respect and will be pleased to make the appropriate acknowledgements in any future edition.

A CIP catalogue record for this book is available from the British Library.

Paperback ISBN 978-1-83751-189-1

Large Print ISBN 978-1-83751-188-4

Hardback ISBN 978-1-83751-187-7

Ebook ISBN 978-1-83751-190-7

Kindle ISBN 978-1-83751-191-4

Audio CD ISBN 978-1-83751-182-2

MP3 CD ISBN 978-1-83751-183-9

Digital audio download ISBN 978-1-83751-185-3

Boldwood Books Ltd
23 Bowerdean Street
London SW6 3TN
www.boldwoodbooks.com

For EP, CS and MC who believed in this one from the beginning.

'Never yet in this island was there a greater slaughter.'

— ANGLO-SAXON CHRONICLE, A TEXT, FOR 937

BRITAIN IN THE 10ᵀᴴ CENTURY

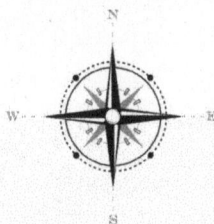

N
W   E
S

ORKNEYS

CAIT

SCOTTISH
WESTERN
ISLANDS

*Atlantic
Ocean*

FORTRIU

DUNNOTTAR

KINGDOM
OF THE
DAL SCOTS
RIATA   SCONE   ST ANDREWS

ATHOLL

*North
Sea*

KINGDOM OF
STRATHCLYDE   BAMBURGH

Tyne   CHESTER
LE STREET

EAMONT

KINGDOM
OF YORK   YORK

*Irish
Sea*

Ribble

Mersey

Don

CLONMACNOISE   DUBLIN

BRUNANBURH

GWYNEDD   NOTTINGHAM

Trent

IRELAND

POWYS

OFFA'S
DYKE   *Severn*   TAMWORTH   *Welland*

LIMERICK

HEREFORD

EAST
ANGLIA

DEHEUBARTH

GWENT

MERCIA

WESSEX   *Thames*

KING'S
WORTHY   KINGSTON
UPON THAMES

EXETER   WINCHESTER   KENT

Tamar

English Channel

0   50   100   MILES

CAST OF CHARACTERS

(ALL HISTORICAL UNLESS UNDERLINED AND
THEN FICTIONAL CHARACTERS)

The Family of Alfred the Great

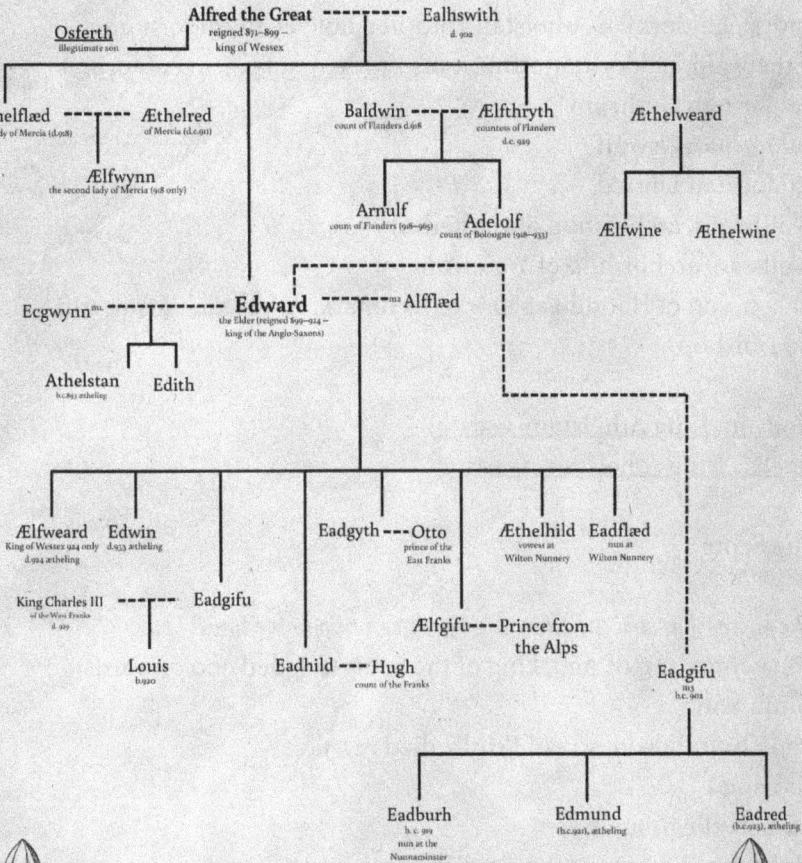

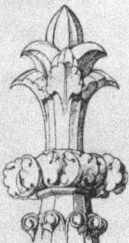

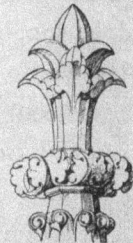

Osferth
illegitimate son

Alfred the Great -------- **Ealhswith**
reigned 871–899 –
king of Wessex

d. 902

Æthelflæd ------- **Æthelred**
the lady of Mercia (d.918)   of Mercia (d.c.911)

Baldwin ------ **Ælfthryth**
count of Flanders d.918   countess of Flanders
d.c. 929

Æthelweard

Ælfwynn
the second lady of Mercia (918 only)

Arnulf
count of Flanders (918–965)

Adelolf
count of Boloungne (918–933)

Ælfwine   **Æthelwine**

Ecgwynn m1 -------- **Edward** -------- m2 **Alfflæd**
the Elder (reigned 899–924 –
king of the Anglo-Saxons)

Athelstan   **Edith**
b.c.893 ætheling

Ælfweard   **Edwin**
King of Wessex 924 only   d.933 ætheling
d.924 ætheling

Eadgyth --- **Otto**
prince of the
East Franks

Æthelhild   **Eadflæd**
vowess at   nun at
Wilton Nunnery   Wilton Nunnery

King Charles III ------- **Eadgifu**
of the West Franks
d. 929

Ælfgifu --- **Prince from
the Alps**

Louis
b.920

Eadhild --- **Hugh**
count of the Franks

Eadgifu
m3
b.c. 902

Eadburh
b. c. 921
nun at the
Nunnaminster

Edmund
(b.c.921), ætheling

Eadred
(b.c.923), ætheling

The English Ealdormen

Ealdorman Wulfgar
Ealdorman Athelstan of the East Angles (from 932), married to Ælfwynn, the lady of Mercia's daughter
Ealdorman Ælfstan of Mercia (from 930–934), Ealdorman Athelstan's brother
Eadric, Ealdorman Athelstan's brother, not yet an ealdorman
Æthelwald, Ealdorman Athelstan's brother, not yet an ealdorman
Ealdorman Guthrum
Ealdorman Oswulf
Ealdorman Uhtred
Wulfheard, archbishop of Canterbury from 926
Wulfstan, archbishop of York from 931
Hakon, son of Harald Fairhair of Denmark, Athelstan's foster son
Oda, bishop

Flodwin, King Athelstan's warrior
Sigelac, King Athelstan's warrior

The Scots

The succession strictly alternated between two noble lines
Constantin, son of Aed, king of the Scots (reigned 900 onwards)
Ildulb, son
Amlaib, grandson, son of Ildulb, died in 934
Aed, son
Cellach, illegitimate son
Alpin, son, hostage at the English king's court
Mael Muire, daughter of Constantin (name is fictional, although we know she existed)
Mael Coluim, Constantin's designated successor, the son of his predecessor, Domnall

Strathclyde

Donald, previous king of Strathclyde (once allied with Constantin of the Scots)
Owain, king of Strathclyde
Dyfnwal, Owain's son

The Welsh kings

Hywel, king of the South Welsh, (Deheubarth) known as Hywel Dda
Owain ap Hywel, Rhodri ap Hywel and Edwin ap Hywel, Hywel's sons
Cadwgan ap Owain, son of Owain ap Hywel
Idwal, king of Gwynedd
Morgan ap Owain, king of Gwent
Tewdwr ap Griffi ab Elise, king of Brycheiniog
Gwriad, king of Glywysing

The independent kingdom of Bamburgh

Ealdred, king of Bamburgh (died 934)
Ealdwulf, his son

The Dublin Norse and their allies

All claimed to be descended from Ivarr the Boneless, the Viking raider who led the Great Heathen Army of the 860s. Some would have been grandsons, others perhaps great-grandsons. The genealogy is particularly complicated.
Ragnall, died c.921, a grandson of Ivarr, claimed Jorvik (York), once allied with Constantin and Donald II of Strathclyde
Sihtric, king of York, died c.926, married Athelstan's only natural sister, Edith
Anlaf Sihtricson, his son, not the son of Edith
Gothfrith, king of Dublin, grandson of Ivarr
Olaf Gothfrithson, son of Gothfrith, great-grandson of Ivarr
Rognavaldr, Olaf Gothfrithson's brother

Blakari, Olaf Gothfrithson's brother
Halfdan, Olaf Gothfrithson's brother, died 926
<u>Gothfrith, Olaf Gothfrithson's brother</u>
Camman, Olaf Gothfrithson's son

Olaf Cenncairech – Scabbyhead, king of Limerick – captured by Olaf Goth-
frithson in 937, fought for him at Brunanburh
Ivarr, son of king of Denmark, Gorm
Gebeachan, king of the Islands (as named in sources of the period)
<u>Snorri the Black</u>
<u>Aodh</u>
<u>Dara</u>

The Irish clans

The Southern Ui Neill, led by Donnchad
The Northern Ui Neill

The notable families of West Frankia

Charles III m. Eadgifu, daughter of Edward and Æfflæd
Louis, their son, king of West Frankia from 926
Hugh the Great, married Eadhild, daughter of Edward and Ælfflæd
Heribert of Vermandois, Charles III captor and jailer

NOTE ON NAMES

The unwary traveller to this period of time will be faced with a profusion of names for the men and women in this story. Names may be given in Welsh, Gallic, Old Norse, Old English or with modern spellings. As such, you may find Olaf/Anlaf/Amlaib and be surprised to discover these are all the same person. You may find the name Eadward used, although the most common form is Edward. Equally, Æthelstan is the correct form of Athelstan. You will find names used interchangeably if you consult different sources, and secondary sources. The choice taken will depend, quite often, on the main sources the writer uses and on their own personal preference. I have attempted to use the names that are most recognisable for the individuals involved. Welsh and Norse convention usually names someone as the son of their father, e.g. Olaf Gothfrithson is Gothfrith's son; Owain ap Hywel is the son of Hywel. Names are often reused throughout the generations in all societies and, in England, families often name all of their children with names that begin with similar letters, e.g. Athelstan, Athelwald, etc.

All quotes from the Anglo-Saxon Chronicle are taken from *The Anglo-Saxon Chronicles*, M. Swanton ed. and trans.

PROLOGUE

SEPTEMBER 934, CIRENCESTER, ENGLAND

Eadgifu, the lady of Wessex

The feast's spectacular. As always, the cooks have outdone themselves, yet the food tastes like dust in my mouth. While I watch all in the hall, my focus remains on King Constantin of the Scots. The ealdormen, bishops, and those of the king's household warriors honoured with a seat in the king's hall, remain on the periphery. Occasionally, I summon a servant to my side with a hasty word or remonstrance for something not done to my satisfaction. But it's King Constantin that I gaze at, time and time again.

He's an old man, grey and haggard, more monk-like than a warrior king; even his fine clothes seeming tarnished, as though he spends his days on his knees and not ruling a kingdom. But I know his bearing masks much. As soon as I laid eyes on him, a shiver, not of triumph but of foreboding, rippled through my body.

King Constantin isn't at all the image of my late husband, Edward of England, and yet, had Edward lived and not died a decade ago, the two would have been of age. Seeing Constantin brings back unwelcome reminders of my, thankfully short, marriage but makes me realise that this enemy of King Athelstan isn't to be lightly dismissed. My husband, along-side his sister and brother by marriage, fought their entire adult lives to reunite the part of their kingdoms lost to the advance of the Viking raiders, the Norse, as it's now easier to name them. The kingdom of the East Angles, the lands to the east of Mercia and, of course, my birth kingdom of Kent, were all handed over to the Norse by King Alfred, who some laud as saving the Saxons from being overrun.

King Constantin has done the same. Athelstan, my husband's son but a man older than me, has picked up his father's warrior-helm and accomplished even more, intending to drive the Norse permanently from Britain. And yet, in doing so, it seems apparent that Athelstan has created a new enemy for himself. King Constantin. King Constantin was meant to be an ally, but instead he's been brought to his knees after the battle at Cait, in the far northern lands of the kingdom of the Scots, his punishment for meddling in the succession to the northern kingdom of Bamburgh. Athelstan is victorious. Constantin is here, at Cirencester, to bend the knee.

This worries me, but more than anything, the part that my beloved son has played in the expedition to the land of the Scots concerns me more. I didn't embrace Edmund riding to war with his much older stepbrother. I welcomed the news even less upon receiving word that Edmund is forging battle renown for himself. Not just any battle renown either. No, my son killed King Constantin's grandson in a fair fight.

But the young lad's dead whether it was fair or not.

While I'm grateful that it wasn't Edmund who bled his last on that faraway battlefield in the northernmost region of Cait, one of the ancient kingdoms making up the land of the Scots, I know more than any other about the unending bond that's formed between my son and King Constantin. I know what it is to crave revenge. To need it more than anything. The Norse killed my father before my birth. For all that, I hold dear to the memories others share about him, even if they come from my detested mother and uncles. I know my father was a great man, a firm ally of the House of Wessex. And now, I fear for my son because I understand what it is to be driven by vengeance.

Again and again, I pull my eyes away from the craggy face of King Constantin of the Scots. Again and again, I try not to look at my son, seated beside his stepbrother, the king, at the feast. Athelstan couldn't have made it any clearer that he holds young Edmund in high regard.

Again and again, I try to quell the thudding of my rapidly beating heart and enjoy the labours of the cooks for this fine feast, in Cirencester, deep in the core of the English kingdom. And yet, my unease won't dissipate.

The battle has been won against the kingdom of the Scots. King Constantin's here, in the middle of England. But there's no solace to be found in that. If King Constantin can be here, in the heart of England, my son will never be safe from those seeking vengeance against him. While Constantin might be old, his son, Ildulb, the father of the boy Edmund killed, isn't.

Raising a hand, as a thought strikes me, my servant hastens to my side.

'Ensure the king's especial warriors, Sigelac and Flodwin, know I wish to speak to them as soon as the feast's concluded,' I whisper into the ear of my faithful servant. The woman bows deeply, no hint of surprise in her stance at receiving such an unexpected order when she can have expected to be told to bring more wine or ale.

'My lady,' is all the confirmation I receive, her words lacking all inflexion.

I reach for my goblet and drink deeply of the tart wine. I savour the sensation over my tongue, as King Constantin meets my eyes from his place to the other side of King Athelstan. He sits beside one of his other sons, Alpin, who has been a hostage in Athelstan's court to ensure his father's good behaviour since the Treaty of Eamont ten summers ago. He's lucky to still live after his father's defiance. I can't see that either are comfortable in one another's presence.

Constantin might be a wily, craggy old man, a warrior of fierce renown in his younger days, when he beat back all contenders to his kingdom, including the Viking raiders, but I've been at the king's court for many summers. King Constantin won't win this time. He'll never win, but perhaps it's important that he thinks he might.

I meet his eyes, raising my wine goblet in greeting, and for a moment I detect something more than grief for his grandson in the tight stance of the defeated man. He remains defiant, a man who hasn't been brought easily to his knees. A man who's used to winning and not losing. When the spectre of the defeat, not two months ago, leaves him, he'll be troublesome and bold. He'll want to overthrow Athelstan. He'll want to kill my son. He'll want to counter the humiliation of being brought before the English king's witan to repledge his allegiance to the peace treaty of Eamont.

King Constantin's capitulation could portend trouble for the House of Wessex. But I'm alert to it already. I'll ensure my young sons and stepson, the king, are protected as best I can.

I smile, straining my tight cheeks at the other man.

King Constantin's white tufted cheeks rise in reciprocity.

He'll not remain conquered for long. I'm sure of that.

PART I

AN UNEASY PEACE

1

OCTOBER 934, DUNNOTTAR, THE KINGDOM OF THE SCOTS

Constantin, king of the Scots

'I'll kill him,' my son, face puce with rage, menaces. I nod along with him. Ildulb's likely to rupture if anyone utters a word in denial of his decision. I want nothing more than to revel in delight at being home, even if the loss of Amlaib, my grandson, murdered by Prince Edmund of the English, is felt keenly whenever I glance at my remaining collection of grandsons.

I feel soiled by my time at Athelstan's court in England. I shudder at the recollection of it. I'd been paraded as a slave before the court of the upstart English king. I was defeated, but I'll rise above it. Those jeering looks of the king's ealdormen and thegns, his archbishops and bishops, won't last long. No. I'll gain my revenge and my battle renown, even if I die doing so. All I need is the opportunity. And that opportunity exercises my mind, even while my son, Ildulb, rants and rages.

Ildulb disappeared from the English king's court, and I don't know where he's been. Not that I don't have my suspicions. Neither, I consider, do I think that King Athelstan allowed Ildulb to leave without him being watched until he left England's vast kingdom.

Revenge. It burns white and hot inside me. I must have it. I must. I've ruled my kingdom for over thirty winters. Never in all that time has someone vanquished me as Athelstan has done. Not for the first time, I rail at my failure to triumph over the English king. I should have been better prepared. Equally, I shouldn't have enticed King Athelstan into my kingdom. I'm not fool enough to appreciate that I don't shoulder some of the blame for this.

I can feel the power of Mael Coluim's delighted smirk from where he sits before the hearth. The man, my acknowledged heir but not my son, thinks to gain from my failure, and that can never happen. What I need is to reassert myself and bring Athelstan to his knees as he did to me. Now that I know the correct roads to take, I can envision myself at the English king's royal palace in Cirencester. I can, if I close my eyes, imagine riding at the head of my brave Scots warriors along their ancient road, Ermine Street. I'll urge my men to take their revenge, not just for the death of Amlaib but for all the English have done to the proud kingdom of the Scots.

King Athelstan has thought to unite every kingdom against the ravages of the Dublin Norse, and any other stragglers who think to try their luck along the many rivers and coastlines of the English kingdom. But in doing so, he's made another enemy. And one that's much closer to home. The Scots will take revenge for their humiliation at the hands of the English. Yes, the English have now receded, and yes, King Athelstan has graciously restored the terms agreed upon at Eamont a decade ago, but that's not enough. We've been disgraced. We're a proud people and will not accept it.

Not that I think it'll be possible to gain my vengeance alone. No. The battle at Cait assures me that the English king has far superior numbers to mine. I need an alliance, just as he did to counter the might of the people of the kingdom of the Scots. He brought his Welsh kings with him to Cait. I need to do the same when I overawe the English.

'Are you listening to me?' The hot words of Ildulb cut through the image of the future playing out before my eyes when I'm ruler over England and the kingdom of the Scots.

'Sorry, son, I was thinking of King Athelstan.'

'And I was thinking of his stepbrother, Edmund. I'll kill him,' Ildulb hisses, his face so close to mine that I can smell his rankness. Ildulb needs to stop drinking and discard his desire to drown his sorrows and gain some vengeance. 'I'll kill him,' he repeats.

Lightning quick, I grab my son's arm, pulling him closer. 'Don't let anyone hear you say that,' I order harshly. 'They can't know of our plans.' I cast my eyes around the room. There are men and women here spying for the English king. I'm sure of it, but I don't know who they are. Not yet.

'Our plans?' Ildulb's incredulous. 'Our plans. Yours are little more than a tale to tell children and those lucky to live through battles. Your plan involves that useless scop and his dry words, which are impossible for most to decipher, and nothing further. It's been many winters now, and I hear no outcry from the Welsh kingdoms. If Hywel was any closer to King Athelstan, they'd share clothes. Where are the swords, seaxes and warriors? My plan, Father, will bring Athelstan's death and that of his bastard brother. I'll kill all the surviving sons of King Edward, and then I might turn my attention to his daughters as well.'

'My plan,' I reassert over his harsh whisper. If he weren't my son, I'd have him killed for speaking to me with such disdain. I'd have him killed for even speaking of the scop and his words. I can't allow anyone to know how I've been slowly and carefully unravelling Athelstan's peace accord by stirring up problems with the Welsh.

'Will be nothing compared to mine,' Ildulb almost shouts triumphantly. 'While you allowed the English king to feast you, parade you before his minions, I, Father, I have been working on a means to finish them all, once and for all.'

I just manage to suppress the derision from showing on my down-turned face. My son's questioning me, bringing my proposals into question. How dare the little git! I am the king here, not him.

'And what have you been doing?' I force through tight lips, determined not to allow others to see the spurt of fury I feel towards Ildulb. If Mael Coluim realises we're at crossed purposes, he'll seek to undermine me. If others realise that Ildulb blames me for the death of his son, then my future plans for him will be curtailed.

'I, Father, have been sounding out allies.'

'Olaf Gothfrithson of Dublin,' I counter calmly. 'It's yet to be seen whether he can hold his kingdom, let alone strike out against the English. And anyway, how have you made contact with him?' I'm curious. If there are those in my kingdom communicating with the Dublin Norse then I need to know their identity. I'll not allow any dissent. All communications will be at my command. Not my son's. Once more, I cast my eyes around the room, not paying any attention to Mael Coluim and his collection of allies. For this, the threat won't come from him but from someone who thinks to hover beneath my attention. Who thinks their loyalty should be to the Dublin Norse, not to me and the kingdom of the Scots?

'Father,' Ildulb growls, attempting to yank his arm free from my grasp. 'You're not the only one with a collection of spies and informants.'

Slowly, I release my grip, attention entirely focused on my son. Perhaps some who conspire are more than servants looking to make extra coin for their troubles. But my son? I'm sure he'd never act against my wishes. Would he?

'I'm the only one who'll treat with the Dublin Norse,' I intimidate, only to be met with the wild eyes of Ildulb, triumph on his flushed face, saliva dripping into his beard, the smell of sweat emanating from him.

'And you are, Father. You are. All is being done in your name. Even if you don't yet bloody know it.' He laughs, and I fear the death of his son has made him half-crazed. How dare he begin negotiations with the Dublin Norse! How dare he threaten the life of Alpin, still held captive by the English king in order to ensure my compliance to the peace treaty! And yet, I consider, calming myself, who else is there to combat Athelstan? Perhaps it's only with the help of the Dublin Norse that I'll bring Athelstan to his knees? After all, Alpin still lives. The English king has shown his weakness in that regard.

2

934, IRELAND

Olaf Gothfrithson, king of the Dublin Norse

'My lord.' The man bends low before me, his nose almost scraping the muddy ground beneath our feet.

'What?' I glower. Now isn't the time to be distracted with news from anywhere other than Limerick. That bastard, Olaf Scabbyhead, will be mine. I just need to kill the upstart, and then my rule over the Dublin Norse, and those Norse from Limerick, will be secure.

The man flinches from me but doesn't move aside. I shrug, admiring him for that. Few would risk my wrath, my brothers amongst them, especially when it's clear I mean to battle against one of my enemies.

'I bring you a message.'

'A message? What use do I have for a message? I speak in deeds and actions, not bits of parchment that the Christ-men insist on using.'

'From the king of the Scots,' the man speaks into the mud, for all his words reach my ears clearly.

'Who?' I huff. I don't know whom he speaks about.

'Constantin, the king of the Scots,' the man reiterates.

I try to conjure up a face to the name. Which bloody tribe are these 'Scots'? Where do they live? Who's their high king? Are they part of the Ui Neill or some other clan? Then I growl. The Scots aren't an Irish tribe. They're from over the sea, a part of the island of Britain. I remember who they are now.

'The man who refused to help my father capture Jorvik from the English king after the death of Sihtric?'

'Yes, my lord.' The man doesn't hesitate to agree with me. I admire him afresh for such courage in the face of my growling fury. How I've forgotten the man, albeit briefly, I don't know.

'Oh, stand up.' I glower, thinking if he doesn't, I can't kick him to the mud for the audacity in thinking I'll listen to anything he has to say. The man, older than I expect, slowly lumbers to his feet. He's no great warrior. Or if he was, those days are so long behind him that all of his fighting prowess has drained away, along with the hair that must once have covered much more of his head. Yet I recognise him. He's one of those men, I'm sure of it, who's made Dublin his home for more winters than I have. Did he serve my father? I wish I could recall. 'Tell me what it is and get away from here.'

'My lord,' the man offers once more. I'm trying to think of his name. He must be a Halfdan, or an Ivarr. One of the names that seem to fit everyone. I'm sure he has some other title. Skullsplitter? The Black? Hmm, I find my mind wandering as he composes himself to deliver the message from this Constantin, king of the Scots. 'The king of the Scots has heard of your great victory against the Irish tribes, and he's eager to assist you in claiming back Jorvik from the English king.' The man sneers as he speaks of the English. He's old enough to have fought those warriors when they were merely from the kingdom of Mercia, Wessex, or even the East Angles. Before they were all English.

'And why would I want anything to do with him?' I jab. Since my father lost Jorvik, I've done little but fight. First at my father's side to retain his hold on Dublin, but since his death, alongside my brothers, forging our destiny. What need do we have for an ally who turned tail on our father?

'He's a powerful man, filled with a thirst for vengeance,' the man offers, his bushy grey eyebrows bouncing high. Well, one does, the silvery glint of a long-ago wound revealing itself over his left eye.

'How do you know this?' I counter, intrigued, despite myself. I'm sure that Constantin is filled with a desire for revenge. But after what I heard about the English king, I don't believe that Constantin has anything to offer me. He's a weak man. He's an old man. His warring days are far behind him. I hear he didn't even face the English, but allowed his sons and grandsons to stand in his stead. I'd sooner not ally with someone who might drop dead at any moment.

'I've been to the kingdom of the Scots.' The man juts his heavily bearded chin forwards. 'I've spoken with those who'd forge this alliance. They know I'm a man to be trusted.'

'Do they now?' I drawl. I'm unconvinced. This man. Ah, there, I have it. He's Snorri the Black. He fought with King Sihtric of Jorvik. I remember the tales surrounding him. He's always been a lucky warrior. He's also as likely to want vengeance against Athelstan of the English as King Constantin. Snorri the Black lost much when the English took Jorvik after Sihtric's death.

'So, you've spoken to this Constantin?'

A flicker of uncertainty over the man's face, and I know he hasn't. Bloody fool for staking his life on such an easily disproved claim.

'Not him, but his son. The mad one. The one who will be his heir when that Mael Coluim is dead.'

'What?' I snarl. 'What are you talking about?'

'The Scots. Constantin's son isn't his heir. Mael Coluim is. And then, when Mael Coluim's dead, Constantin's son can rule. It's him I've spoken to. Ildulb. The English killed his son. He thirsts for revenge. He can barely speak a sentence without mentioning how he'll enact it.'

'So, you spoke to the son of the Scots king, and he told you of his father's desire for an alliance?' I'm trying to get everything straight in my mind. I can't deny that the more I hear, the more I believe this might not be a bad idea. I want Jorvik back. I've endured near enough a decade of men taunting me for all my father lost. Once I've triumphed over Olaf Scabby-head of Limerick, and with my brothers holding Dublin secure, I can finally reassert our family's hold over Jorvik.

I can even think of a way I might countenance this alliance.

'I did, my lord, yes.' A look of relief touches Snorri's cheeks at my reasoned words.

'And?'

'And, he suggests an alliance.'

'And what are the details of this alliance?' I huff, frustrated once more. It's taken too long to get to the point of the conversation, and now Snorri has no details.

'Ah, now, that's open to negotiation. Ildulb offered no particulars. But he made it clear. Everything's open to negotiation. Everything.'

'I doubt everything,' I counter, licking my lips all the same. An alliance with this Scots king could give me a level of permanence in the eyes of the Irish clans, and those of Norse descent who think to take Dublin from me. It would mean I was acknowledged as the king of the Dublin Norse by those outside Ireland. That's worth a great deal, as would be the aid of others to win back Jorvik. When my father lost the settlement, he lost half his wealth and many of his oath-sworn men. I'd welcome more warriors to fight on my behalf, especially if I weren't the one shouldering their cost. 'I need details,' I huff. Snorri nods so vigorously that I think his few remaining teeth might shake loose.

'A meeting will be arranged,' Snorri concludes. 'Who will you send to speak on your behalf?'

I feel my lips twist at this. I want to go. I do, but I can't, not when I need to counter Olaf Scabbyhead's claim over Limerick.

'One of my brothers,' I exhale. But which one will depend on whom I trust the most and what the Southern and Northern Ui Neill are doing at the time, and that remains to be seen.

3

934, THE KINGDOM OF THE ENGLISH

Athelstan, king of the English

'Tell me.' I listen with half a smile. I can understand young Eadred's desire to hear everything of our journey to Cait in the kingdom of the Scots. Equally, I understand Edmund's reticence to speak of it as often as his younger brother wants to hear it.

Beneath the byrnie, my chest heaves as I struggle to suck in much-needed air. I've been practising for much of the morning, facing my loyal warriors, Sigelac and Flodwin, Athelstan and his brother, Eadric. Eadric's a mean fighter. Mean and devious. Yet I admire him. It's good for me to fight against men I've not grown used to. Sigelac and Flodwin's movements are almost as well-known to me as mine.

Not that Eadred's alone. Louis is at his side. The pair of them, wearing tunics, and trying to look as magnificent as the fighting men, are at least as sweaty as the rest of us. It's a cold day, but we've all been working hard to ensure, should the need ever arise again, that we'll be ready and prepared to face England's foe. The Norse.

'He fought valiantly,' Eadric booms over the higher-pitched voices of

the youngest of our party. I'm surprised the boys haven't been recalled by
their mothers, but then, perhaps they welcome having them away from
beneath their feet for a moment or two to themselves. Not, I think, that
Lady Eadgifu, my father's third wife, will be taking her ease. But my stepsister, the exiled queen of the West Franks, is probably gossiping with her
women. Perhaps she attempts to find out news of how Eadhild fares in
West Frankia with her husband, Hugh, count of the Franks. But perhaps
not. I'm unsure if the childhood rivalry of the pair has healed or if they
would still fight if positioned in the same room as one another. I'd also
listen, but I have clerics who'll succinctly inform me of new developments
as they receive the information from their ears in East and West Frankia.

'He ate well before the battle, mind,' Eadric continues. I find a smile on
my lips to match that of Eadric's broad one. It's good to be here, surrounded
by my family and allies, some of whom I hope are my friends.

'Please don't.' Edmund's face winces at the reminder of how he vomited
after the battle at Cait. He's no cause to be embarrassed. I know of no man
who can say they didn't. It either comes out the mouth, or the arse, when
the battle is won.

Æthelwald, Eadric's brother, isn't smiling, but his eyes dance with the
joy of recalling a fight won well.

'And with all that food in his belly,' Eadric continues to recount, Eadred
and Louis hanging on his every word, 'young Edmund here slew the Scots
scum. He slit their throats open. He turned their innards to outtards. He
took the life of every one of the twenty Scots who dared lay about him.'

I chuckle. The telling gets more outrageous each time it's told. Eadric is
wasted as a warrior. He should be a scop.

'Twenty?' Louis gasps, his lips aquiver. Louis and Edmund are the same
age, but Louis didn't travel to the kingdom of the Scots. His fight doesn't lie
to the north of England, but rather to the south, across the Narrow Sea, in
the kingdom he's been exiled from since no more than a babe.

'With that sword?' Eadred questions simultaneously, pointing to the
blade in Edmund's hand. Eadred is the youngest of us all. He's barely a
man. Yet he must learn to fight for his kingdom.

'With this very sword,' Eadric continues, bending to grip Edmund's
right arm, where he holds the blade. I glance at it, almost expecting it to

flash with the maroon of shed blood, but it's merely dulled by the sweat of those who've fought today. Edmund allows his arm to be raised high, a rueful look on his face. 'He killed the Scots king's grandson. With this very sword, he nearly killed the Scots king's son as well.'

That's not true, but legends of battle prowess must begin somewhere. Eadric's working hard on Edmund's. None of us is about to cast doubt on Eadric's words. Especially to Louis and Eadred. Their faces are a balm to any troubled soul, even Edmund's. He's become a warrior, but realising what it truly means has been hard on him. He's spent much time praying, trying to find comfort in knowing that he acted to protect his kingdom. I can't say taking the life of another will ever be easy, but he'll come to accept it for what it is. A king must kill to protect his kingdom and his people. So my aunt and uncle taught me, when I was a similar age in Mercia, learning to fight and defend Mercia from the Welsh and the Norse. And, of course, with every kill made, there are merely more warriors who wish to seek their vengeance against you. That I've also learned well.

'Will you kill the Scots king with it as well?' Louis exhales, only for silence to fall amongst us all. I can feel the eyes of others on me. Will I kill the Scots king, wily old Constantin? No, I don't believe I will.

'King Constantin is our ally now,' Edmund speaks hastily. Louis must belatedly realise what he's said. Worried eyes look my way, and they aren't just the eyes of Alpin, Constantin's son, who's a hostage at my court. Younger than Ildulb, but older than Constantin's grandsons, Alpin is a lively man, for all he's a hostage to ensure the good behaviour of his irresponsible father.

'There'll be no more war with King Constantin,' I offer quickly. 'We're at peace with the kingdom of the Scots now. We have a peace accord with every one of our neighbours on the island of Britain.'

'And yet we still train to kill?' Louis isn't to be easily put off. I nod, considering his words. He makes a fair point, and equally, for him to reclaim his kingdom of the West Franks, from which he was rescued as a small baby when his father was captured and his kingdom stolen, he'll probably need to fight. And, if he does manage to reclaim it, he'll have to fight to keep it. The kingdom of the West Franks is far more violent than the English kingdom.

'Peace is always the answer,' I speak into the growing stillness. 'But to ensure it, we must be prepared to give our lives to protect our kingdom, whether it be England or that of the West Franks. Or Denmark,' I add as well, noting that young Hakon has joined the growing group of sweating warriors. 'To be a king means accepting that our foes may wish to desolate us,' I caution. What started as a jovial conversation has become anything but, and I'm reminded of the words I spoke at my consecration as England's king.

'Then there can never be an end to war,' Eadred challenges, his eyebrows furrowed so tightly on his slight face that it makes him look even younger than his twelve winters.

'There can never be an end to the threat of war, no,' I confirm. 'But that doesn't mean there'll always be war.'

'And anyway.' Eadric raises his voice above the silenced men and boys. 'If there was no war, then how would we get to see what Edmund ate to break his fast on the way back up?' He chortles. The sound is deep and infectious. I join him, reaching over to ruffle Eadred's soft blonde hair now that the wind has dried it from the sweat of his exertion. I'd hope that Eadred and Louis need never know war. I'd hope that my peace accord would accomplish that, and yet, as the actions of King Constantin have shown, peace can never be assured.

But I'll do all I can to keep England safe from the pretensions of the Norse. And if, in doing so, I prevent my youngest stepbrother from ever bloodying his blade in rage, then that's all the better.

4

934, THE KINGDOM OF THE SOUTH WELSH

Hywel, king of the South Welsh

'Tell me again,' I ask softly, 'what it is that you've heard?'

I eye my grandson, Cadwgan. He's little more than a tottering child, and yet my son has brought him to me, concern on his face and also a hint of amusement in his eyes.

'It's probably nothing,' he prevaricates, but Owain hasn't summoned his son before me, as his king, for no good reason. The child, trying to stuff his thumb in his mouth, only to find his father's hand gently holding it away, looks at me with confusion and stubbornness. The stubbornness I recognise only too well. The fear turns my stomach. He's my grandson, after all. I don't want him to dread me.

Or, perhaps, I do.

'It's a song,' Cadwgan stutters. 'I've heard them singing it.' He hiccups. His face is red and splotchy. I think he's been crying, and I glower at Owain over his son's head. He shrugs a shoulder in a 'what could I do?' sort of way. I can think of many other ways he could have questioned his son, but I hold my tongue. He's the boy's father, not me. I can't tell Owain how to treat his son. I know only too well that I'd not have taken any interference kindly. No, if he made Cadwgan cry, then he can live with that grief for the rest of his life. And it'll pain him, I could assure Owain of that if he asked the question.

'I was singing what I've heard,' Cadwgan continues, his words lisping but just about clear enough to understand. I want to reach out and rustle the soft thatch of pale hair above his head that makes him seem hallowed in gold. He appears just as the monks achieve with their precious manuscripts for our kingdom's saints, and as I saw only too many versions of when I travelled to Rome. But I don't touch him.

'And what did you sing?' Behind her son, Owain's wife waits frantically. She fears me as well, but that's probably for the best. After all, she has the raising of my grandsons. I must ensure she doesn't encourage them to rebel against me.

Cadwgan's voice is pure and filled with light. All eyes in the hall turn towards me, a soft expression on many of my most hardened warriors at the sound. 'Warriors will scatter as far as Cait. The Welsh will reconcile as one.' The tune is pleasant, although, from how he nods in time to the words, I think it perhaps contains more words than my grandson sings.

I find a smile on my lips, and consider why Owain thinks I need to hear this child's story of uniting the Welsh under one king. It's a story we've all been told since childhood. The actions of my grandfather, Rhodri Mawr, have reinvigorated this dream of unification. I can't say it doesn't drive me onwards, but then, Idwal of Gwynedd, my cousin, would no doubt say the same from his kingdom to the north of mine. Only one of us can triumph. I want that one person to be me.

'It's a beautiful song,' I console my distraught grandson. The tune's bright and easy enough to recall, even having heard it only once. Cadwgan's eyes brighten as he rubs a grubby hand across a streaming nose. I turn to Owain's wife, a pleasant enough woman, and nod. Eagerly, she grips her son's shoulders and steers him away, soft words flowing from her mouth as she consoles him. Only when Cadwgan's gone does Owain glance at me with some evident frustration.

'Why did you do that? We need to know who's spreading such tales amongst the populace. I believe he heard one of the servants singing the tale, perhaps while she did the washing in the river. Other than that, I can't think who would believe it.'

'Why do you think they believe it just because they sing it?' I query. It's just a few words. I replay them in my mind. *Warriors will scatter as far as Cait. The Welsh will reconcile as one.* I'm reminded of my journey with Athelstan of the English to defeat the king of the Scots. I consider why the Scots would feature in a tale about uniting the Welsh? All the same, I'm unsure why my son has made such an issue of the lilting tale.

Owain's scowl broadens. 'My brothers said you'd dismiss it. They said it was just another in a long line of such tales that occasionally ripple through our people. But, Father, this one is different.'

'How so?' I ask, beckoning for wine and food from one of my servants.

'This is coming from the mouth of babes,' Owain rumbles. Now I pause, and glance at him. Is he right? Is this tale, of some long-forgotten and mythical man, normally given the name of Cynan, different to these others?

'And so?'

'Whoever is doing this has decided to have children act as their mouthpiece. Parents will listen to these gentle songs. I mean, how sweet does it sound? It'll harden their resolve and make them want to do as these innocent faces demand. They'll be acting for their children, not themselves.'

'But it's only a tale of the Welsh together?'

'Perhaps that's all he knows it to be,' Owain urges. 'I fear it's more than just that.'

I pause again, considering the urgency in Owain's words. 'Then, son, track down the rest of this child's song and bring it to me. I can do nothing with half a line.'

'So, you think it's important?' he demands, eyes alight with pride at forcing Cadwgan before me. I can well imagine how that conversation will play out when he returns to his wife's side.

'It might be, it might not be, but yes, it's right that you're alert to all possible threats and conspiracies, even if they spring from your son's mouth.' He nods, evidently missing the hint of reproach in my voice for upsetting Cadwgan as he has.

'I'll have the servants listened to. I'll have my sons tell me all they learn at their knees.'

'Indeed, son, but carefully does it. I'll not have complaints that the king's son spends his days with the washerwomen and the servants. That would be beneath you.'

This does stop Owain, and the slash of a smile lights his face.

'It might, yes. I'll let you know as soon as I hear more.' Owain skips from my side in such a parody of his son that my cheeks twitch in amusement.

Out of babes' mouths, I muse when Owain is gone. What might that be all about? I'd suspect Idwal of being involved in any conspiracy to unite the Welsh, but I can't believe he thinks so far in the future. No, if this is more than just the soft singing of a child, then I don't know where it originates. But I'll have to find out.

5

935, SHAFTESBURY, THE KINGDOM OF THE ENGLISH

Edmund, ætheling and prince of the English

Louis is at my side, my brother beside him. I try my hardest not to fidget. I can feel them both doing the same. I dare not look up to feel the glare of my mother. She needn't speak for me to hear the admonishment for our antics.

But Bishop Ælfheah's words have been ongoing for far too long. It's almost as though he knows we need the service of remembrance to be short and has determined to make it as long as possible as punishment. Not that we did anything too wrong. Well, I didn't. Well, maybe I did, but it was long overdue that my brother, Eadred, knew what it was to drink until he was sick. I make no apology for that. Nor, I believe, will Louis, or Hakon. Indeed, even Eadric, the brother of Ealdorman Athelstan, was involved in some of it. He laughed and laughed, tears rolling down his cheeks until he fell off his stool, and the next noise to be heard was his loud snores.

Not that my mother sees it in the same way. And I can understand her anger, for all my head pounds with the excess. My stepsister, the exiled queen of the West Franks, has made it clear that her son, Louis, couldn't possibly have been involved. Her cross words with my mother are why our foolish escapade is to be punished with more than just the usual flurry of admonishment.

My mother hates my stepsister. I do as well. But Louis is my friend, so I try not to complain about his mother too much. And he does the same to Eadred and me. Hakon has no memory of his mother, so he watches the interplay between our mothers with fascination and, perhaps, I appreciate not a little jealousy. In which case, he's welcome to my mother. Sooner she was chastising him than me.

And on the words of the bishop drone. I've never known a mass of celebration to take so long. This place, Shaftesbury, was founded by the House of Wessex. Here, my grandfather's sister was abbess until her death. Even now, Athelstan takes an interest in it. He's keen for the establishment to thrive. My long-dead great aunt isn't revered as a saint, although perhaps one day she might be. All the same, Athelstan has made a grant to the nunnery, the charter signed by the king, and his allies, although not my mother, something I don't overlook. The nunnery is to receive land at Tarrant Hinton, Dorset, to enable them to continue their work of praying for the abbess' soul and also that of the other dead members of the House of Wessex.

I've no problem with that, but I'm sure the bishop need not stress it so much as he speaks. And the archbishop hasn't even begun his sermon yet. I shake my head, trying to force my eyes open. I can feel myself swaying. We stayed up too long drinking. I'd barely shut my eyes, or so it seemed, when a cold bucket of water rudely woke me, with my mother's acerbic tone telling me to wash and dress for the king's service.

Perhaps, had the king been involved, we'd have been treated more kindly. But, as I turn to look at Athelstan, majestic in his finery, I think not. The king doesn't drink to excess or, indeed, do anything to excess other than govern well. I can't think that he'll be best pleased by our display. Once more, I hear my mother's words from earlier.

'Do you want the king to think of you like he did your stepbrother Edwin?' The argument had been a hiss of outrage, directed at me, but not at Eadred, for Eadred had his head in a bucket, the sound of his retching turning my stomach. I'd swallowed hastily, not wanting to embarrass myself further.

'It was...' I'd begun, but no further words had come forth.

'We're at the royal estates close to the nunnery of Shaftesbury. Did you want everyone here to know you're no better than your little-lamented older stepbrother? You'll be king one day, my son. You'll rule here and the whole of England, and yet you drink yourself into this state and, worse, drag your young brother into it as well.'

'It was...' I'd tried once more when she paused her pacing to take in a much-needed breath.

'And Eadric should know better. He's a man grown. What was he thinking? Not that it matters. It's you and your brother that everyone will be watching today. The nuns in the nunnery, and the bishop and archbishop. They'll smell you from ten hides away,' she continued to rant.

I shake my head to clear the conversation from my mind, only to swallow convulsively once more. The scent of vomit that pervades my brother reaches my nostrils. I gag and swallow down any urge to void my stomach. Bad enough to be found unconscious in a pool of saliva in the royal hall close to Shaftesbury. Should I vomit here, in the nunnery church, my mother would never forgive me.

A lull in the service has me glancing up, hopeful that the bishop and archbishop have concluded their sermon. But there's no such luck. Bishop Ælfheah might have completed his task, but now Archbishop Wulfhelm replaces him. He settles himself and then meets my gaze, a quirk on his lips before he begins to preach. This part of the service is at least in the tongue of my people. I can understand everything he says. Not that the Latin of the Mass is entirely lost on me. I've been taught in the school at Glastonbury monastery. And I've been listening to the same since I was no more than a baby. The tenor of the Mass is easy enough to follow. The words of the archbishop are, at least, far from as admonitory as Bishop Ælfheah's.

Archbishop Wulfhelm instead praises Abbess Æthelgifu, the daughter of King Alfred, and the abbesses and religious women since her death. He also speaks of King Alfred and all he accomplished before turning to my father, King Edward. To hear my father spoken about, a man I've nothing but vague memories of, is always strange. The men and women of the witan knew my father as more than just a figment of their memories. They spoke with him and carried out his orders and instructions. They believed in his vision of Wessex, and then Wessex and Mercia combined to become the kingdom of the Anglo-Saxons. It took many of them much longer to be convinced of my stepbrother's vision of England.

I listen, my nausea forgotten, as Archbishop Wulfhelm lists the accomplishments of my father and his sister, Lady Æthelflæd of the Mercians.

'Following the wishes of King Alfred, King Edward and Lady Æthelflæd pushed back the boundaries of the kingdoms of the Saxons. Initially with small steps and then with more assured ones. First, Bremesbyrig, Scergeat, Bridgnorth. And then Tamworth and Stafford, Derby, Brunanburh and Nottingham. At the same time, King Edward reclaimed Northampton, Leicester and Thelwall. And then the prize of all, the allegiance of York, if not York itself.'

Here the archbishop risks a glance at Athelstan. I appreciate once more that the battle for the north that my stepbrother undertook has been ongoing for many years. Indeed, the Treaty of Eamont was only the latest in a long line of alliances and peace accords agreed with those of the kingdoms of the Scots and Strathclyde. Of what, then, does the archbishop speak? Is it praise, or is it a call for caution? One I don't believe the king needs.

Athelstan is cautious, I'm sure of it. He has what he wants, but doesn't expect it to be easy to maintain.

King Athelstan inclines his head towards the archbishop, acknowledging those words. While I'm grateful to allow the final sentences of the Mass to tumble over my sleep-deprived and ale-addled mind, I consider those words, perhaps more than I should.

My mother's correct. One day I'll be king, but I pray it'll be many years in the future. I don't wish to have to replace my stepbrother when his task is only just completed. And I'm sure there are those who'd think to undo it. No. I need Athelstan to rule for decades yet. Perhaps I'll only be king when I'm old and grey. The thought doesn't upset me as others might think.

6

935, SCONE, THE KINGDOM OF THE SCOTS

Constantin, king of the Scots

Ealdwulf, son of Ealdred of Bamburgh, still hasn't learned to make himself scarce. And more, I see him too often in the company of my successor, Mael Coluim. That turns my lips, but not as much as the whispers brought to me by men and women I trust that Ealdwulf has reached out to Owain of Strathclyde as well.

Owain's my underking. He has no remit to make allies with anyone I don't believe he should. It's not passed me by that Owain was slow to respond to my request for support when the bloody English king rampaged through my kingdom. I already have reservations about his future without this complication of Ealdwulf of Bamburgh. If Ealdwulf were any sort of a man, he'd have slunk from these shores long ago. He has no one to support him in any attempt to reclaim Bamburgh from the English king. He should have remained there with the warriors he did have rather than come mewing to my side when Athelstan threatened him following the death of his father.

And then there's my son. Ildulb should be the most loyal of them, but a flicker of unease now touches our every interaction. He speaks with my voice to potential allies, yet he's not asking my opinion. I growl low in my throat. I feel beset on all sides by those who should be my allies but whose true allegiance I doubt.

Next there's the English king. I know to doubt him, but since he came to my kingdom with his army, including the Welsh kings who submitted to him, his actions have been nothing like a conquering king. My son, Alpin, still resides at his court. My submission has been made before the English. The independent kingdom of Bamburgh is part of Athelstan's England. But all Athelstan does to remind me of all that is to send the occasional messenger and ensure I make payment for warring against him.

Even the restitutions he demands aren't onerous. All I must do is accept Athelstan's presence on my southern border, his detaining of Alpin, and of course, the reparations due him for bringing me to my senses for threatening to interfere in the running of the kingdom of Bamburgh.

It seems that Athelstan is truly a benign force when not roused to anger. I should have learned that sooner and then I'd not have suffered such an ignominious defeat. When – and it is when, because for all his magnanimity, I know there can only be war again – I triumph over him and rewrite the outcome of his Scottish campaign, I'll not be as soft-hearted as he is. We might share a God, but mine is more brimstone than his. Revenge must be taken. Vengeance will be mine. No matter my age, I'll take my place on the shield wall. I'll conquer him just as surely as he's taken control of me.

'Father.' The annoyed voice of my oldest son permeates my thoughts. I look to Ildulb, for the first time, truly seeing him as my son as opposed to someone who thinks to circumnavigate my resolve to get his own way.

'Son,' I acknowledge.

'Were you even listening to me?' he queries. I shake my head.

In all honesty, I wasn't listening to him. I've not heard a single word since he reminded me of the battle at Cait. Damn the English king.

He sighs and begins to speak again, taking me back to the battle at Cait once more, only this time, I hold my thoughts in check as words rumble from his mouth, thrumming with conviction. 'Those of the Outer Isles have tentatively agreed. All the lord demands in exchange is a wife for his son.'

'They were no use to us before,' I counter quickly. The thought of turning once more to the Outer Isles for assistance is unpalatable. If they'd come to our assistance last time, then Athelstan would already be rotting in his family's royal mausoleum, far to the south of England.

'They will be this time.' Ildulb speaks with conviction, his eyes bright with fervour. I don't believe that. 'Anyway, they aren't the only ones keen to ally with the great king of the Scots.'

'Who else is there? The Welsh kings? King Owain of Gwent? King Idwal of Gwynedd?'

'The Dublin Norse, as I told you,' Ildulb interrupts me impatiently. I believe we should ally with the Welsh, but Ildulb has been slow to adopt my suggestion. He doesn't have faith that the Welsh will aid him. He believes my scop song, hoping to rouse the Welsh alongside the Scots, has been a waste of good coin.

'That young fool isn't even proclaimed as their king yet. What can he possibly commit to? I hear he almost lost his kingdom to Olaf Scabbyhead of Limerick.'

'No, Father, he didn't. He's victorious.'

'He isn't, my lord.' Somehow Mael Coluim has joined the conversation, his words unctuous. I flash him a glare but allow him to remain. Even he knows more than my son, and right now, Ildulb needs to understand the limits of what he proposes. We must test our allies before they become our allies.

'He will be soon,' Ildulb retorts, the colour high on his cheeks for being gainsaid, and by Mael Coluim of all people. The two detest one another. One day, when I'm cold and dead, the two will violently clash. I would almost wish to live to see that.

'And what does he demand?' I query. This I'd know. What would a Norse lord want from me?

'My sister.'

'A wife?' I glower. I'll not send her from my side. She's precious to me. I have many sons. Daughters are in short supply.

'A wife is all he demands.'

'But surely he has one?'

'Even if he does, he'll cast her aside. He's very keen to ally with the king of the Scots.' Ildulb speaks with little regard for his sister, and that infuriates me. I have one son at the English king's court. I lost a grandson fighting in Cait. Would Ildulb so lightly barter away his sister?

'So keen that he lies about his holdings and influence?' Mael Coluim snaps. I eye him then. Does Mael Coluim think he should wed my daughter? Yes, it would unite our two clans and perhaps do away with this need to alternate kingships between the two ruling lines, but it can't be denied that he and she would share a common ancestor. The Church wouldn't approve of that.

'He doesn't lie.' Ildulb's face drains of colour, his anger growing every time Mael Coluim breathes beside him.

'He doesn't tell the truth,' Mael Coluim interjects. 'He has what? A handful of men, and many of them are his brothers? These cursed Norse families always have sons growing out of their arses.'

I watch as Ildulb's entire body judders with the effort it takes him to retain his temper. I'm just grateful that it's Mael Coluim who questions my son.

'He'll be king of the Dublin Norse by the time this damn conversation is over,' Ildulb huffs, dangerously soft. 'And if he's not our ally, he'll look elsewhere for one.'

'And who'll have him? The English king won't,' Mael Coluim provokes.

'There are more kings on this blighted island than just the English one,' Ildulb snarls, his eyes pleading as he holds my gaze. But I can't give him what he wants.

'Once he's truly the king of all he believes, I'll discuss this further. Until then, we've more important concerns.'

'What's more important than defeating the king of the English?' Ildulb howls.

'Keeping the kingdom united is always more essential than defeating the king of the English. Mael Coluim, I need you to journey to Strathclyde and see what that weasel, Owain, is up to. Ildulb, you'll go south to our borders with the English king. I must know everything that's happening at Bamburgh. Don't be seen,' I caution Ildulb. Mael Coluim stamps from my presence, furious to be given the less enviable task. It's much harder to keep Owain of Strathclyde pliable than it is to scout the border with the English.

Ildulb glowers at me, but he'll thank me for this. Just not any time soon.

7

935, DUBLIN, IRELAND

Olaf Gothfrithson, king of the Dublin Norse

I wince at the sight of my brother, Rognavaldr. His nose is bulbous, and the cut that's threatened to carve it clean through infected.

'You need to get that looked at,' I urge him, snapping his filthy hand away as he attempts to run it over the wound.

'Those bastards,' he growls low in his throat. Rognavaldr is bloodthirsty. 'They came at us, hidden in the undergrowth beneath animal skins. They stank of death even before we sliced their throats open.' I nod. This incessant warfare with the Northern Ui Neill clan threatens the relative stability we've achieved since our father's death. Which side is the dirtiest in battle is impossible to determine. The Northern Ui Neill and we, the sons of Gothfrith, will do everything that needs to be done to triumph.

Urgently, I beckon forward the old crone who has some skill with ensuring men I thought would die can live another day and continue the fight. She tuts on seeing Rognavaldr's nose. Her hands, nails clean and short, contrast to his. She fights her battles in different ways to Rognavaldr.

'Go,' I urge him. 'Have that tended to before it falls off, and we're left looking at your damn skull even while you live.'

He thinks of nodding but changes his mind and follows the woman, like a child trailing their mother.

'Tell me the truth,' I direct to Blakari. He's also my brother, of a slighter build than Rognavaldr, but lethal all the same.

He shrugs, the movement rattling the weaponry around his weapons belt. 'They attacked us, and we were unprepared. The scout's dead. He knew of the coming attack and didn't warn us. We stumbled into it, and were lucky to escape with only nine dead.'

I grimace to hear that. The loss of every single one of my warriors is unwelcome. The death of a further nine will do the morale of my warriors little good. This was intended as little more than a scouting mission to see where the Northern Ui Neill were. It wasn't to be a battle. Certainly, no one was meant to die.

'And they're closer now?' I demand, just to be sure. My other brother, Gothfrith, unfortunate to share our little-lamented father's name, nods and then drinks deeply from his beaker of ale. Already he has bruises forming on his cheeks, and one eye is puffing up nicely. He'll not be able to see tomorrow, either because of the ale he's consumed or the wound he took.

'Yes, but not much, and we did kill eighteen of theirs,' he huffs with annoyance. Blakari should have told me this before he told me of our losses.

'Eighteen. That's a good number,' I confirm. I rub my hand through my long beard, feeling the weight of the trinkets there, clattering softly, one against another. I didn't go with my brothers. I took my warriors towards Limerick, and that other bastard, Olaf Scabbyhead, who causes as much trouble as the damn Northern Ui Neill. On this occasion, I fared the best. No casualties, but equally, no sight of the slippery bastard.

'Then we're no further forward,' I announce despondently. I should like to declare Dublin safe from attack, but it's not. Until it is, I can do nothing further to regain Jorvik. It's as unobtainable as when my father was alive. Angrily, I thump the wooden table beneath my hand.

'No, we're not,' Gothfrith admits too easily. I glower at him. He merely arches his eyebrows high as if daring me to counter his honesty. Moodily, I reach for the jug of ale and splash more into the beaker. It tastes sour, and of my thwarted hopes and wishes. My father was a fool being so far from Jorvik when Sihtric died. He should have been there, just waiting to march into the kingdom and claim it as his own. Sihtric should have sent word of his impending death, or my father should have left one of us, his sons, to stand in his place. The succession should have been assured. All know it.

'Why not ally with Olaf Scabbyhead of Limerick?' Blakari queries. This had been my father's intention before his death. Blakari is keen to pursue it, mostly because he was to be wed to one of Olaf's daughters.

I snarl in reply. 'Because, Blakari, as you know, Olaf Scabbyhead of Limerick is a prick and can't be trusted.'

'But, if Limerick and Dublin were united, we could overpower the Northern Ui Neill.'

'If Limerick and Dublin were to be united, it would be because Dublin conquered Limerick, and not because we allied with them. Our father was foolish to consider such an option. You need to forget about it. It's never going to happen. Olaf Scabbyhead of Limerick will die a slow and painful death alongside the leader of the Northern Ui Neill clan. There's to be no further talk of marriage and an alliance.'

'But you've been talking to this Scots king about a marriage alliance?' Blakari spews back at me angrily.

'That's different.' I'm tired of explaining this. 'He'll help me regain Jorvik. Marrying Olaf Scabbyhead of Limerick's pox-riddled daughter will do nothing but bring the bloody pox here.'

'She's not pox-riddled,' Blakari shouts, scraping back his chair as he stands abruptly.

I shake my head watching him stride through the mass of warriors in our father's hall. Men call jovially to him, others moan and complain of their wounds, but Blakari ignores all of them, even shoving one of the slaves to the side when she gets in his way. I wince as she clatters to the floor, ale and beakers smashing into pieces, as many of my warriors shout their acclaim for the disturbance.

I shake my head. Blakari's an arse. But he's my brother. I can understand his desire to be wed, but now isn't the time to think of such things. He can have any woman he wants. Any child born to such a union will still be his son, and in turn, our great grandfather's great-great-grandson. Being wed is not a requisite as it is for others.

No, I need to counter the threat from the Northern Ui Neill and Olaf Scabbyhead of Limerick, and only then can I press on with my plans for Jorvik. It will be returned to my family line. My great grandfather didn't spend his entire life at war just for his bloody grandson to lose it by being in the wrong place and failing to plan for the succession.

'We going to proper war then?' Gothfrith asks me conversationally. He has the right to it, as so often is the case. Gothfrith is a fine warrior, and he can do more than think with his sword or his manhood. Gothfrith can see what needs to be done.

'No doubt to it,' I confirm.

'Then, brother dearest, when you have Jorvik, what will I get?' Now I eye him, noting the rampant ambition in his eyes for the first time.

'You'll be well rewarded, brother, never fear,' I assure him, but already I'm adding him to the list of men and women whose allegiance is only contingent on how I recompense them. He's my bloody brother. Couldn't he just do something for me out of brotherly love? I grumble beneath my breath and reach for my ale once more. No, he can't. And if our situation were reversed, I'd want to know what I was to gain as well. We're not that different.

I raise my ale cup high towards him.

'We'll all get exactly what we deserve,' I assure him. 'We are all, after all, great-grandsons of Ivarr.' My brother nods, clinking his ale cup against mine, but the smile on his lips doesn't touch his cheeks. I appreciate that I need to keep a firm eye on him. Just another one to add to the endless list of potential troublemakers.

8

935, THE KINGDOM OF STRATHCLYDE

Owain, king of Strathclyde

I eye Mael Coluim with barely suppressed loathing. I don't miss that King Constantin hasn't even deigned to send one of his many sons to converse with me. No, the miserable old goat has sent the one person he despises above all others, Mael Coluim.

I don't know what all this is about, but it's an evident show of strength from Constantin. Not only is he my overlord, but he has the authority to send the little-loved Mael Coluim to do his bidding. I growl low in my throat, eyeing the man. He's about my age. His hair has lost its bright colour, and a man crueller than I would note that on top of his head there's almost no hair at all. But his eyes are bright and filled with malice. He has next to no authority within the kingdom of the Scots, but here he can rule over me with the voice of King Constantin, and that boils me. I'd like nothing more than to send the man back to his king, perhaps in a few pieces.

'That's no way to greet your overlord,' he intones as I beckon him towards me. I pretend not to hear those words.

'My lord,' I offer, keen to see if such a simple courtesy will wipe the scowl from his face. How he expected me to greet him, I'm unsure. It's not as though he sent word of his intentions. No, Mael Coluim has just appeared and now looks around with disdain.

'Don't "my lord" me, Lord Owain. I'm here at the king of Scots' behest, which means I speak with the authority of the entire Scots people behind me.'

I hold his gaze. For a moment, I consider what I've done to deserve the arrival of Mael Coluim. I wrack my mind, but I can think of no true slight foisted on the king of the Scots. I don't do half the things I'd like to do to King Constantin, especially not in light of all the unpleasant tasks he's involved me in.

I wish I'd been there when King Constantin was finally forced to bend the knee to King Athelstan of the English. Now that I wouldn't have minded the weeks-long journey to Cirencester to witness.

'And of what, pray, does King Constantin wish to inform me?' I ask, my tone ingratiating. I'd sooner that it was Ildulb here before me. He might be a mouthy sod, but at least I know he does genuinely speak with the voice of his father. Mael Coluim might have determined to make trouble for me. Yes, it might be King Constantin who means to show me the true nature of our relationship, but Mael Coluim could still force his interpretation on his king's commands. I need to be wary and yet respectful. I'd like nothing more than to thrust my seax through the swine's open mouth.

'King Constantin deserves more respect than that,' Mael Coluim voices. In those words I actually hear, *When I'm the king of the Scots, there'll be none of this disrespect*, but that day is still, hopefully, many years in the future. I might not like King Constantin, but I respect him far more than I do Mael Coluim.

'My lord.' I lower my head once more, wishing this meeting was taking place somewhere much more private. I don't like knowing that others can see me being subdued by Mael Coluim.

'Now, that's better,' Mael Coluim replies languidly, stretching his legs out towards the hearth fire, and peremptorily beckoning for food and wine from my servants.

I snap down on my thoughts about that. I won't give Mael Coluim the satisfaction of knowing how much his actions anger me.

'Your overlord, the king of the Scots' – again, although Mael Coluim doesn't say it, I know he's thinking of himself – 'requests that you remember where your loyalties lie in the coming months and perhaps years. He also suggests that you prepare for war, for there will be war with the English, and soon. In the meantime, you're to listen carefully for any and all signs of unease from the English and the Welsh, especially from the former kingdom of Bamburgh. Oh, and the Scots king also seeks to ally with the Norse of Dublin. He expects your assistance.'

I don't like that idea. An alliance with the Dublin Norse will mean war between King Constantin and the English will be inevitable. And, in all honesty, I don't feel that Athelstan is enough of a threat for me to risk my men and my warriors.

'But we made a peace accord at Eamont,' I counter angrily. I was forced to that peace, and now it seems I'll be forced to war. I played my part in Constantin's plot with the scop. I faced the anger of King Idwal of Gwynedd and King Owain of Gwent. That little has resulted from the scop's tale is hardly my fault.

'And King Athelstan has since overstepped himself.'

I laugh then. I can't help it. And the affront on Mael Coluim's face only makes me laugh all the more.

'The English have overstepped themselves?' I chuckle, thinking that Constantin and Mael Coluim are both delusional. 'How did they overstep themselves when they rode through the kingdom of the Scots to Cait? When they beat the Scots force that finally lumbered to its feet to meet their attack. How is that overstepping themselves?'

Mael Coluim's on his feet in a heartbeat, heat suffusing his face as he glares at me. This reaction surprises me. I'd have expected Mael Coluim to be eager to see King Constantin fail at something.

He lifts his hand as though to strike me. I focus on his fist, opening and closing, as he tries to decide whether to lash out. I wish he would. How I'd like that tale to be told at the court of the Scots king. Should Mael Coluim abuse me, then I might just gain some much-needed support from my nobility and warriors, those who might have had enough of the Scots king's pretensions. But Mael Coluim collects himself.

He sits slowly, never taking his eyes off mine. He nods before reaching for the blood-red wine and swilling it down his throat.

'I'll not give you the satisfaction,' he grunts on drinking deeply. 'You're the creature of King Constantin, and so, for the time being, am I. But you'll do what you're told. There's no future where you're free to act as you want. Not like me. One day, I'll be the king of the Scots, and you'll be subservient to me, and then, my friend, we'll finally resolve this little argument from today.'

I'd think it mere hot words, but the threat is real. Mael Coluim has won the argument for King Constantin. Now I need to ensure that old bastard lives, for I won't survive to fulfil the orders of Mael Coluim. He's made that clear.

9

936, WINCHESTER, THE KINGDOM OF THE ENGLISH

Athelstan, king of the English

'Tell me again the words of my cousin?' I've had my stepsister and her son summoned to my hall to hear this. After all, it concerns them more than anyone else here.

'My lord king.' The messenger bows low, his accent making it only a little difficult to understand what he says. 'I bring word from Count Arnulf of Flanders. He has, in turn, been approached by Count Hugh of the Franks, your dear brother by marriage.'

I risk turning my eyes from the messenger to gaze at my stepsister. It's been many years since we heard directly from Count Hugh. He wed Eadhild, but alas, and as far as I know, no child has been born from the union. Yet, contrary to opinion, Hugh's English and West Frankish kin haven't been forgotten.

'The king of the West Franks is dead. Count Hugh, and Count Arnulf, working in unity, are determined to ensure that the next king will be Louis, son of King Charles III.'

I see the exiled queen of the West Franks, Eadgifu, shift at those words, her mouth hanging open in shock. My stepsister has been embittered by the failure of her marriage. Is it possible that all of that is at an end?

It's Louis' expression that I watch most avidly. Does the boy want to be a king? Does he wish to claim his father's birthright, or would he be more content remaining in England? He's my foster son. I've taken him under my wing, as I have other lost children, but this is the first of those boys who might be restored to their patrimony. The news has me thinking of my father's death, my stepbrother's acclamation as king of Wessex, and how I felt abandoned and forgotten by my father banished to the kingdom of Mercia. At least Louis can't think like that. His father was a prisoner, and then he died while in captivity. His father didn't abandon him. His father had no choice in the matter. If anything, Louis is lucky to be alive. It could have easily ended for him when he was still a babe in his mother's arms.

Now I count Louis as one of mine. I'll not send him to West Frankia if he doesn't wish to go, and yet, if he does go, the ruins of my stepsister's marriage will once more be victorious. This is what my father wanted when he agreed to the union with Charles III of the West Franks. Equally, this is what I believed would happen when I wed my sister to Sihtric of York. Luckily, his death proved to be the most convenient. But Charles' was not. I can no sooner march on West Frankia with my army than I can turn water into wine. But others can support Louis if I trust them enough.

Louis looks perplexed, and then he stands taller, widening his stance, almost as though he can make himself a man grown when he's still a youth of sixteen winters. He looks shockingly similar to my stepbrother, Edmund. I've determined that Edmund will one day be king in my place. I hope that's many years in the future, but even as young as Louis and Edmund are, both of them know their worth. They're æthelings – throne worthy. It's just whether either of them would take their kingdoms now. Is Louis brave enough to leave behind all that he's known and venture to a kingdom which is his to rule but in which he's not stepped foot for the vast majority of his life?

'Tell me more,' I prompt the messenger, whose words have faltered, perhaps because he's waiting for some expression of joy to fall from the lips of the exiled queen of the West Franks and her son. I know that both are well in control of their emotions. Even Eadgifu has snapped her mouth shut. I imagine what tumbles through her mind. Does she wish to return to West Frankia? She's always made it clear that was the intention, but I know there's a huge difference between wanting something and having it given.

'It's proposed that Louis, the fourth of his name to rule West Frankia, will be met at Boulogne-sur-Mer, by his dear cousin, and his dear uncle, and many of the great ruling men and women of West Frankia, including the archbishop of Rheims. From there, he'll be escorted to Laon for his coronation. His dear cousin will stay at his side, and his dear uncle, and aunt, will assist the new king in learning all that must be learned. A steadying hand, if you will, while his kingship is given time to grow roots and branch out.' I breathe deeply at the florid words of the messenger, wanting to force a smile on my lips but finding it impossible. All the same, I nod at the words.

'And what requirements would my nephew's dear uncle and my dear cousin place upon the House of Wessex, the English king?'

'My lord king?' the man exclaims as though the thought hasn't occurred to any of those plotting this return to West Frankia for Louis. 'Ships, my lord king, and an armed guard, of course, to ensure that Louis is safely returned to Laon where he can be proclaimed king of the West Franks.' The man is quick enough to say this that I know my involvement has been carefully considered.

'Yes, yes, but what of an assurance that Louis won't be subjected to over-mighty subjects, as his father was before him? What of the traitorous House of Vermandois who kept Charles III captive for almost a decade?'

I don't miss the sliver of unease that crosses the man's face. In this, I confess, I would have expected my cousin to appear before me. If he could make the journey across the Narrow Sea to discuss the marriage of my step-sister to Count Hugh, then surely he could come in person to discuss the return of Louis to his kingdom. But perhaps I'm unfair. West Frankia has no current king. What might happen without such could make it impossible for Arnulf to leave his kingdom of Flanders.

'The House of Vermandois are eager to accept the rightful king of the West Franks in his return to the kingdom. They are, as you must be aware, allies of Count Hugh.' I absorb this information, not wishing to look at the exiled queen of the West Franks. Her thoughts on that family aren't hard to determine. She'd happily allow the entire edifice to crumble and feel no remorse for a single member. I don't blame her. I'm grateful that here, in England, there are none eager to topple the ruling House of Wessex. But if there were, I'd counter them.

'And when is this fine meeting arranged to take place?'

'Nothing is yet agreed, my lord king. Of course, we can't force young Louis to return to West Frankia. We're just hoping that he'll do us all the honour of claiming his birthright and the kingship.'

Such honeyed words cover a whole host of crimes committed against his father, an anointed king. I'd like to discuss the matter in some privacy, and seek the advice of my bishops and archbishops. But my stepsister draws the eye of all as she walks towards me. Her head's held high, her back rigid. She wears the clothes of a queen, for all she's not one in England.

'My lord king.' She curtseys before me. I detect the wobble of her chin and the wild look in her eyes. As I said, there's a huge difference between wishing for something and having it handed to her.

'My dear sister,' I reply, the messenger watching us avidly. I'm sure word of what's said here will wind its way back to Count Hugh and Count Arnulf.

'I am grateful for the words from our dear cousin and our sister's husband.' Her voice remains firm, despite it all. I hold her gaze, not looking at Louis. 'In this matter, my son and I are yours to command,' she informs me. I close my eyes, just briefly. She asks me to decide for her after all this time. Should I send my foster son away, hopeful that the nobility of the West Franks will be honourable? Should I refuse and keep my stepsister and her son at my court?

'I'll take advice,' I inform everyone in the great hall. 'I'll summon you when all has been decided.' I incline my head to the messenger. He's no dust-stained rider but rather a man wearing rich finery and with an escort of twenty mounted warriors, all gleaming and bristling.

'My lord king.' The man bows again, and I bid him rise.

I know my sister wishes to return to West Frankia, although how she'll fare I don't know. Her sister is the wife of Count Hugh, one of the most powerful men in West Frankia. Will they become allies and work together, or will such action really pit sister against sister?

Of the desires of my foster son, I've no idea. And, I confess, I've heard much about Count Hugh. Will he have my foster son's best interest at heart, or is Louis merely the means for Hugh to rule West Frankia but without himself being proclaimed as king, which is what I actually suspect? Hugh's sister was married to the previous king. Had a child been born to that union, I'm convinced Hugh would have ruled through him. But there was not. And so, he looks to Louis.

Perhaps, had I known more of Count Hugh's rampant ambitions, I wouldn't have allowed my stepsister to be wed to him. And yet this could be the only means by which Louis can safely return to the kingdom that is his by birth.

And, after all, there might be no need for Louis to long continue the alliance with Counts Hugh and Arnulf, not if he finds it stifling. I glimpse Louis, observing the flood of emotions that roll over his face. Louis was once in awe of Edmund's battle prowess. Is it perhaps time that he was able to earn the same acclaim for himself, as king of the West Franks? I wish I knew.

10

936, CLONMACNOISE, IRELAND

Olaf Gothfrithson, king of the Dublin Norse

I grip my war axe firmly, eyes focused on the settlement coming into view ahead. This is Clonmacnoise, the church of the Southern Ui Neill, and my intentions are simple. I'll take the vast wealth stored inside this church and claim it as mine. Only then, when the Southern Ui Neill clan are assured of my resolve to govern Dublin firmly, will I switch my gaze to finally bringing Olaf Scabbyhead to his knees. The Limerick king. Pah. He calls himself a king, but he's little more than a leader of a handful of men. He's a pestilent boil on my arse in need of lancing. The settlement of Limerick, with its position on the River Shannon, gives too easy access into the heartlands of Ireland, and Olaf Scabbyhead uses it to meddle in affairs that are none of his concern.

But first, it must be the Southern Ui Neill who face my wrath. Their overking, Donnchad, son of Flann, thinks himself a big man in Ireland. He's no such thing. I'll prove that to him today.

'My lord.' I turn to meet the penetrating gaze of my brother, Rognavaldr. His eyes gleam with the promise of the coming attack, a wide grin showing the black maw of his mouth. I see the glimmer of his stitched nose as it wrinkles. He has fewer teeth than a toothless crone who's lived for near enough a hundred winters, but then, he shouldn't bite his enemy as he does. Some of them are more solid than he anticipates.

'Will we kill the monks?' Rognavaldr demands to know, eyes wide with the prospect.

'A few. Not all of them. They bring us nothing, and neither do they make good slaves,' I growl in return. It's the wealth and the audacity of the attack that's important. Yes, we must win, but equally, we must leave enough for Donnchad to know I'm responsible for what's about to happen. I want Clonmacnoise's wealth. It will finance my return to Jorvik. I also want the damn Southern Ui Neill to appreciate that I'm not to be easily cowed. I am not my father.

Rognavaldr's smile dims a little, but he's never been one to complain about what he can't do. Instead, he'll focus on what he can do.

The structure ahead is impressive, smoke billowing from more than one hearth fire. I've three ships of my warriors, more than enough to overpower the holy men of Clonmacnoise, and those who support it. The smell of smelting iron ripples through the air and I scent it, drawn to it almost as much as to that of blood.

Blakari is also with us, as is Gothfrith. We four, the great-grandsons of Ivarr the Boneless, will make our mark on Clonmacnoise together. My remaining brother, Halfdan, has been dead for over a decade. A pity. I would have liked him at my side.

'Steady,' I order my warriors. Rognavaldr isn't alone in delighting in a touch of bloodshed to accompany the plundering. I find myself grinning along with them. I know full well that our attack's entirely unexpected. No one's seen our approach. No one has run to Donnchad to tell him of my intentions this day. I hope it's this easy to take Limerick from Olaf Scabby-head and then I don't see that anyone will be able to stop my brothers or me. And once that's accomplished, well, then Jorvik calls to me. I'll hold the Irish Norse under my command and, united, we'll reclaim Jorvik, all the while holding Dublin and Limerick. The Southern Ui Neill will be forced to acknowledge my influence. After all, they'll have no wealth to counter it once I've stolen the church's priceless artefacts.

'Steady,' I urge my warriors once more. I can smell their anticipation, which only increases as the settlement finally comes fully into sight. Frightened eyes of those working along the wide riverbank meet mine. I arch an eyebrow beneath my helm, offering them a few moments to decide whether to run towards the dubious safety of the monastery or dash into the surrounding countryside. I'd tell them which way to go, but that would deflect from the amusement of observing their panic.

'Nearly there, boys,' I holler, the shrieks of those soon to be under attack causing my body to thrum with the anticipation of what's to come. I spy the wooden houses of the residents and artisans, the stone crest of the church, only recently completed, and the stark stone crosses for which this place is so famous. This is an ancient religious site and, as such, rich in all that I desire.

'Now,' I order, and as one, the three ships bounce against the riverbank, and my men are running towards the settlement. Men, women and children scatter from the approach of near enough two hundred heavily weaponed men. I'm in the forefront, determined to be the one to take first blood, but already I can hear the shrieks of those who've fallen beneath the blade of one of my warriors.

All these people needed to do was step aside from our advance. We came for the treasure, not to kill the general populace. A few bloodied bodies are all that's needed to rouse Donnchad's fury and to make him understand that I intend to hold what I have in Dublin and that I'm not to be toyed with. It's the church's wealth that's so important to me.

Ahead, I see a hastily assembled collection of men and monks carrying anything from a seax to a scythe in their hands. I grin, licking the sweat on my lips, and rush at the bravest of them. He's tall and lithe, a determined expression on his tanned face, his brown robe covering him only as far as his shins. He carries a scythe and swings it towards my legs. I don't even break my stride to jump over it, plunging my seax into the exposed area between his shoulder and neck. His body judders beneath my blow. I think him dead, only for his fist to emerge and punch my nose. I gasp against the sudden pain, yanking my seax clear so that blood gushes, shockingly maroon, and he falls in a crash of bone and cooling flesh.

He's not alone. These men, monks and artisans alike, and I notice some of the women as well, all plummet beneath the blades of my brothers and me as we continue, dismissing them from our concerns. We came for treasure, not to kill men and women who have nothing but farming equipment to protect themselves. Once or two deaths, that was all that was needed.

Where before the smell of smouldering iron was ripe in the air, now thatch burns and there are other less palatable smells as well. One of my men, or perhaps many of them, have thought to fire the homes of these people. Above the thickening smoke, my eyes alight on the stone-built church, the holy crosses rising proudly from the sheep-cropped grass. I amble once more to a run.

I cast a glance to either side, my warriors escorting me. At the church doorway, I expect to find the monks, barring our passage, but wherever they are, they don't mean to die for these treasures.

'Hurry,' I urge my fellow warriors, breathing deeply of the incense-infused air only to be forced to cough it from my body. The stink is cloying. I don't know how they stand the smell day after day.

The church itself is smaller than I anticipated, and yet it glows with light from the small windows, high on the stone walls, seeming to illuminate the path I need to take to the treasures. There's more gold inside the church than I've seen in my life. And not just gold. Silver as well, and precious gems adorn the crosses and other statues within the church itself. Hastily, I direct my men, pointing them to what I want to plunder.

I lick my lips again, and Rognavaldr is at my side, a splash of bright blood covering the parts of his face visible beneath his helm. He breathes heavily but, as far as I can tell, has no wounds.

'Bloody hell,' he whistles.

'Daft bastards, keeping it all on display like this,' I acknowledge, wincing at the sound of something heavy hitting the floor. 'I hope you haven't bloody broken that,' I call to three of my men, desperately trying to fit a huge golden cross into one of the hemp sacks we've brought with us in preparation for today's task.

'Just a bit,' one of the men calls cheerfully, holding a glowing ruby upwards. I shake my head, but really, it's not as though I intend to keep the cross complete. No, I'll be melting this down, hacking it into sections, and gifting it to my warriors in payment for our coming attack on Jorvik.

More and more items disappear into hemp sacks, some too large for them, and so held over shoulders or under arms. My men breathe heavily, but not one looks fearful at our desecration of this holy site. It means nothing to us. We don't share these gods.

'Quickly,' I urge four men, busy bickering over some heavy object. I march towards them, aghast at what it is. 'We've no need for their books,' I glower, turning the word over my tongue in disgust.

'It's not the damn book I want.' I meet the eyes of Blakari. 'Look at it.' And I do. This is no book that I've ever seen before. It shimmers with gems and inlaid gold work.

'Hurry up then,' is all I offer, turning my back on Blakari and his comrades. This attack is to be quick. We take what we can carry.

From beyond the church, I hear the howl of my warriors and the shrieks of those who think to stop or avoid the slashing blades of my men. I hasten outside, temporarily blinded by the brightness of the day and the sun streaming through the grey clouds of smoke. I sniff and cough, the smoke replacing the cloying incense, and then my eyes alight on the tall stone structure. I know it's a cross, but not a Christian one. With Rognavaldr at my side, I stride towards it, pushing those who throng to it for protection, even here, beside a Christian church, aside. I want to see it with my own eyes.

'What is it?' Rognavaldr queries with interest. We're people of stone. We know of such power as this, and I confess, I'm a little in awe of the symbols etched on it.

'An ancient stone that tells tales of the past,' I offer, running my hand along its heavily carved surface. I can hardly tell what the carvings are meant to represent. One must be a beast of some sort. Although a beast of what I don't know. Yet the people here, who profess to their Christianity, believe in the power of it. I almost wish I could unseat it and take it with me. It means more to me than the gold and silver. But it's stood for centuries. Two hundred men will not topple it.

'Ugly thing,' Rognavaldr responds. I laugh to hear him speak with disgust, while others still sob and wail.

'Come on,' I urge him. I notice that Blakari has run from the church, and I mean to follow him. I don't wish to be left behind when the ships depart back towards Dublin. We have limited time. That was the intention all along.

'Aye, my lord,' Rognavaldr agrees. As we run back the way we've come, dodging the leaping flames of burning buildings and those bodies abandoned along the path, I think this was really too easy. I can hardly wait to see Donnchad, son of Flann, bending his knee before me as I take his submission, and after that, Olaf Scabbyhead will be next, and then, Jorvik.

11

936, THE KINGDOM OF THE SCOTS

Constantin, king of the Scots

'He says war must be in the north, close to Jorvik.' I scowl as I listen to the words of Ildulb. I'm not enjoying determining on war when I've never even looked Olaf in the eye. Indeed, Ildulb has only spoken to this Snorri, acting as our intermediary. I'd sooner send anyone else to barter with Olaf Goth-frithson, but my son wishes to arrange this alliance. He is determined. It's taken near enough two long years to arrive at his moment. It's been a long and trying period, my resolve for revenge as bright as Ildulb's, for all I'm also wary of relying on a man I've never met.

What sort of man is Olaf? What sort of warrior will he be? I've already agreed that he can wed my precious daughter, against my better judgement. I'd still rather see the man for myself and test him before my eyes. If he's no good and his battle prowess little more than the inflated words of other men, then he can't give me what I need: a strong ally to counter the reach of King Athelstan of the English. I fear my desperation has made me too keen to accept my son's plan for redressing the balance between my kingdom and that of the English. I was against the alliance, but after careful thought, and prayer, I've realised that this is my chance to be victorious. The Viking raiders have always been vicious bastards. I can't imagine that Olaf, descendant of the mighty Ivarr the Boneless, will be any different. And news from Ireland is hopeful. Olaf has triumphed over some of his enemies. He's gathered the coin to finance his expedition.

'It'll be in the north but far from my kingdom,' I counter quickly. Ildulb's eyes flash with incredulity as he realises what I mean.

'So Jorvik?' he persists.

'No, not Jorvik. The kingdom of the English is weaker in other places. To the north-west, the hold on the populace and the land will be easier to exploit, and it'll be simpler for the Dublin Norse to journey there.'

'And it'll keep Olaf from Jorvik.'

'For now, it will, yes. I'll not support him in his endeavours until I'm assured he can accomplish what he intends. I've had more than enough weak allies.' Unbidden, an image of Lord Ealdred of Bamburgh enters my mind. In the end, he was a disappointment. He wasn't at all the man his father was. And his son is even worse. 'How will he get to Jorvik if that's where he wants it to be?' I muse, suddenly curious as to just what Olaf was thinking.

'There was talk of boats and Bamburgh.'

'So, he means to sail around my kingdom and join me?'

'Perhaps.' Ildulb is less than reassuring. I pause and truly look at him.

'And you meant to agree to this?' I try to keep the heat from my tone, but it's impossible.

'I thought it was what you wanted,' Ildulb counters, angry at having me question him.

'I never want to allow an enemy, let alone a supposed ally with a host of warriors at their back, anywhere near my kingdom. You should know that.' I allow my words to fall slowly, to drive the heat from them and replace it with the ice of my resolve. So far, to counter Athelstan, I've been forced to agree on a marriage union between my daughter and a man I've never met. And all the while, I imperil my other son, Alpin, hostage at the English king's court. I don't believe Athelstan will have him killed. He didn't last time. And yet. Well, I'm extremely aware that Athelstan can only be pushed so far. Look at what happened to his stepbrother, Edwin.

I never intended to allow my family to suffer to gain my vengeance. It pains me. It makes me weak. Mael Coluim watches all and knows that for every part of my family I give away, I weaken myself. Damn the man. And damn King Athelstan of the English.

Ildulb, his eyes downcast, reminds me too fiercely of his son, Amlaib. I swallow against my grief at the unwelcome reminder of his death in Cait.

'You'll march to meet him and his allies?' Ildulb questions.

'I'll take the force of the kingdom of the Scots, and ally it with that of Olaf of Dublin, but I won't leave my kingdom undefended. Not all will join the battle.' Another flash of fury, and I follow Ildulb's thoughts easily. 'You'll command in the battle, I assure you.'

'Good,' is his satisfied response. 'So where then?' he continues. Ildulb has been instrumental in bringing about this alliance with the Dublin Norse. I might well have been uneasy at first. I might even remain uneasy, but Ildulb is deeply invested in its success. Should it falter, I fear what it'll do to him.

'To the north-west not far from Chester and the land that Athelstan foolishly gave to the archbishop of York before invading our kingdom.'

'So, close to the Welsh kingdoms as well?'

I nod and offer my son a smile of appreciation. For all his fury and anger, his mind is sharp. One day, when I'm dead, and Mael Coluim is as well, Ildulb will be a fine king for the Scots. 'Not far from the Welsh kingdoms, indeed. It might be enough to have some of them join us, fearful that when we overpower Athelstan, all they hold will be lost to them as well.'

'I don't believe King Hywel of the South Welsh will ever abandon his alliance with Athelstan,' Ildulb interjects sourly.

'King Hywel is strong to the south of the Welsh kingdoms. He'll not come running to us, regardless. I saw him at Eamont. I know that he honours the English king too highly. He won't be parted from Athelstan, but if we can make him uneasy about what his people think then that'll have to suffice.'

'And how will we do that?'

'We don't need to do more than ensure our friend, the scop, continues with his work. Word of mouth, the faint stirrings of a possible rebellion, and Hywel will look to his kingdom, not outside his borders. He can hardly emulate his grandfather if he loses what he currently holds.' As I speak, my confidence begins to grow. Yes, I've not met Olaf of Dublin, but everything Ildulb has told me about the negotiations speaks to me of a man keen to reclaim his lost inheritance. When he weds my daughter, he'll become like Owain of Strathclyde, just another man under my firm control, whether he realises it or not. It might cost me my daughter, but I don't plan on allowing her to leave my kingdom when she's married. She can remain here, at my side, and her husband can visit her, when he desires to.

'Then I'll ensure the message is sent to Olaf of Dublin,' Ildulb confirms, standing taller, his face twisted with a grimace of the promise of his vengeance.

'Good, and then we must discuss timings. I don't want King Athelstan to have a warning of our approach. If our forces meet close to Chester, and the English king is safely ensconced in Wessex, then we can march through Mercia and take those parts of his kingdom that never fell to the Norse raiders, the west of Mercia and Wessex itself. The shock waves of such betrayal will fracture the English king more violently than if Olaf simply strode into York.'

'Father, your ambitions are immense.' My son grins. I meet his eyes and nod. They are huge. I don't deny that.

'I fully intend to march on bloody Wessex and raze Cirencester to the ground. I just need the opportunity.' And if it costs me my son, Alpin, and my daughter, then that is what must happen, not that I say as much. I've already lost a grandson. To show reticence now would infuriate Ildulb. After all, he has paid the ultimate price already.

12

936, WINCHESTER, THE KINGDOM OF THE ENGLISH

Eadgifu, the lady of Wessex

My son's unhappy, in fact, both of them are unhappy, but I can barely contain my delight. My namesake, the exiled queen of the West Franks, Eadgifu, is departing from England's shores. I only hope I have no course to see her again in this life. While we might have worn our sharp edges smooth over the intervening years, I'm sure we'll both feel better when we're no longer forced to occupy the same halls and royal palaces.

King Athelstan sought the advice of his bishops and archbishops, his ealdormen and other royal officials, and all agreed that it was only right to accede to the request from Count Hugh and Count Arnulf. Louis will return to the kingdom of the West Franks. He will become a king, as his father was before him.

I feel some sympathy for Edmund and Eadred. They've been great friends with Louis since childhood, and now it's highly unlikely they'll ever see each other again. And they know it.

They've spent the last month taking their leave of one another. One more ride. One more visit to the alehouse. One more hunt. It's been elongated and not good for any of them. But now they will finally part. It's more than just the forced separation. Despite Edmund earning himself a name as a warrior, this departure will truly drag them into unwelcome adulthood. No more games. No more retreating behind their mothers when too grumpy or angry. Now they all, and I include young Eadred in this, must become the men they're destined to be. It's a heavy burden for the three of them. One perhaps not helped by the fact that Athelstan is a mighty and great king.

Edmund and Eadred might not relish living up to their father's reputation, but it's nothing compared to Athelstan's. And likewise for Louis. His father is remembered as a man who fathered only daughters for many decades. No sooner did he produce a legitimate male heir to inherit the kingdom of the West Franks than he was apprehended and imprisoned for years so that another could be king in his place.

'My lady, I bid you go with God.' I curtsey before the no-longer-exiled queen of the West Franks, Eadgifu. She meets my eyes, and I see a whole host of emotions cover her familiar face, all quickly stifled so that her expression is a mask once more. We're more alike than either of us would like to believe. Both wed to old men. Both wed to men who had more than enough children already. Both wed to men with children older than ourselves. I've made the best of my ordeal. It remains to be seen if Eadgifu manages the same, but I've done my best to show her how to succeed. Now she merely needs to do so.

'And you, my lady mother,' she replies, dropping a curtsey as well. I might think there was some spite in her words, but actually, I hunt for it and find it lacking. Perhaps, after all, and at our moment of final goodbyes, we can cast aside our disdain of one another.

She turns sideways then, gesturing for Louis to hurry. A brief smile touches my cheeks, seeing the mutiny on his face, mirrored by that on my sons'. This is a fine thing for young Louis, but West Frankia is a place he's only heard about. It has no meaning for him. His home has been England for much of his life. And those parts when he didn't live in England are far beyond his memory. It'll be very different for him. I know a moment of pity for the task that lies ahead.

He was asked for an opinion, but Louis had little choice other than to accept the inevitable. He was born to be a king. He must become a king whether he wants to or not.

My sons have encumbered Louis with many fine gifts. A new shield. A new weapons belt. A new tunic and cloak. A new saddle for his horse. All of these and more my sons have gifted to their cousin and foster brother. Not that Louis has been slow to reciprocate. My sons have many new items to their name as well. I only hope that they've not forgotten about Athelstan. While he's not a petty individual, even he must feel overlooked at the rabid gift exchanges.

'Louis.' I look to Athelstan now, finding him speaking with his foster son. 'I'll miss your presence,' Athelstan begins, and embraces the slight youth. Louis is desperate to own Edmund's reputation. I don't know if the West Frankish king will be called upon to fight with his warriors. Not that I can see how that won't happen eventually. The kingdom of the West Franks is more akin to a fox running amuck in the henhouse than an orderly kingship. I wish the boy luck. I'm afraid he'll need it. I doubt the integrity of Count Hugh and my sons' cousin, who beckon Louis and Eadgifu to return. Not that I fear it will lead to imprisonment and death. But I do suspect that Louis won't be the king he wishes to be. I think he'll be a figurehead. I don't believe that's what he wants.

Louis accepts the embrace of his king, but his cheeks suffuse with pink at the unexpected display of affection. 'I've sent chests with gifts for you,' Athelstan continues, aware that many are watching this official leave-taking between one king and a future one. 'I've also arranged for this to be made for you.' With that, one of Athelstan's closest attendants steps forwards, head bowed, a seax in his hand. I didn't know about this. But it doesn't surprise me to see Athelstan gifting such an item to Louis.

'It has the wyvern of Wessex on the hilt,' Athelstan continues. 'A reminder, should you ever need to lift it in rage, that you're descended from a long line of warrior kings on your mother's side. Such knowledge will give you the resolve to succeed, no matter what.' Athelstan's words thrum with intensity. There's more at work here than just gift exchange. Athelstan is making something very clear to his young foster son. The West Franks might have asked for Louis to return, to take his rightful place as king, based on the marriage of his father to his mother, but Athelstan offers something else. He reminds all here, and there are messengers from the West Franks, that Louis isn't just a king in the making, he's a member of the powerful House of Wessex. While the West Franks have fallen over one another in their attempts to come out on top, the House of Wessex has triumphed and excelled.

The House of Wessex has lost no land or influence. The House of Wessex has grown and expanded, so much so that even the mighty Constantin of the Scots and Hywel of the South Welsh have been forced to their knees.

I nod along with Athelstan's intentions, noting how Louis' eyes open wide, understanding his uncle's words as well. Louis might be returning to West Frankia, but he's not being abandoned to his fate.

I swallow the sudden lump in my throat. Athelstan will never be able to make such a statement for my sons. My sons can only be king once Athelstan's dead. Such knowledge pains me. Athelstan is a mighty king. His intentions are clear. To assist his foster sons to claim what's theirs, not just Louis, but Hakon, son of the Danish king, and indeed, Alain of Brittany. Athelstan will support the new generation of kings, giving them the support they need to succeed, but in his absence, my sons will need to find someone new to reinforce them, and I don't know whom that might be.

I close my eyes and offer a swift prayer, both for Louis' safe passage and also for Athelstan. He must live for many long years to come. I don't wish to see such terror, as I've seen on Louis' face, emblazoned on that of Edmund's or Eadred's. Terror of the unknown. Terror of the weight of responsibility. Terror of failure.

13

936, DUBLIN, IRELAND

Olaf Gothfrithson, king of the Dublin Norse

It's the smell that comes to me first, and only then the shrieks.

'What's happening?' I demand of no one, striding from my hall, my jug of ale and beaker abandoned and dripping to the floor. I sense a hound rushing to lick the liquid but leave it to its task without rebuke. 'Is someone attacking Dublin?' I demand, again, from no one.

I look around, but my hall is strangely devoid of people. Where are my brothers? I glower as I emerge into what should be bright daylight but is anything but.

'What?' I snap my mouth shut, where it hangs open in shock. My settlement burns. I can hardly see through the thick grey smoke, but I can see ships bobbing on the water, and they weren't there when I went inside my hall earlier. I can't see the sails, but they must be those of my enemy.

Now I truly hear the shrieks and cries of those under attack, and my rage explodes.

'Get my brothers,' I roar, even as my son halts in front of me. His face is soot-streaked, and I wince to see the mark of a livid burn on his left cheek. 'Camman, what's happening?'

My son sucks in air, hands on his knees before he speaks. 'They say it's Donnchad, son of Flann, the overking of the Southern Ui Neill.'

'What? Here?' I hear the shriek of outrage in my voice and wish I could take back that moment. Donnchad wasn't meant to come here with his warriors. He was supposed to bend the knee and bring the Southern Ui Neill under my compliance, if not my command. I didn't believe him capable of retribution for us stealing the wealth of Clonmacnoise. 'That bastard,' I hiss.

'What are your orders?'

'Summon my men, have them meet me at the quayside. We'll fight back,' I urge my son, and only now see my brothers appear, Rognavaldr already armoured as though he knew this was coming, Blakari wearing a bewildered expression, Gothfrith hastening to gather what he needs to fight for Dublin. Behind them, I see the men of their ships waiting for their commands. 'To the quayside,' I urge Rognavaldr and Gothfrith. 'Blakari, you stay here and guard the hall and our plunder.'

All three men growl at such orders, but Rognavaldr and Gothfrith are the men to fight our enemy. Blakari is the one to protect everything should we falter. I know who'll make the better king of the Dublin Norse should I fall in battle against Donnchad. Not that I have any intention of doing so.

Hastily, I return to my hall, reaching for weapons and shield, shrugging into my heavy byrnie, tightening my belt and jamming my helm over my head. The scent of old sweat makes me grimace, but outside once more, it's impossible to smell anything over the cloying smoke.

As I hurry towards the quayside, my band of warriors surrounding me, frightened men, women and children surge upwards, making their way to the safety of my hall. I'd batter them aside, but these are my people. These people pay me taxes to protect them. These people provide me with food and clothes, iron for my weapons, and I'll keep them safe. Still, the smell of so much humanity on the move brings tears to my eyes.

And then I'm close enough to the quayside to hear the crash of iron on iron. I'm not the first to engage our enemy. I've not seen the sails on the ships, depicting them as the Southern Ui Neill, but I can tell from the mangled cries of the warriors that these men aren't Norse. I'd decry my stupidity in attacking Clonmacnoise, but when this battle ends it'll be Donnchad cursing. I'll make sure to exact my vengeance against him.

Rounding a smouldering building, the flames leaping merrily in the bright thatch of a new roof, I curse the recent good weather. Had it been raining incessantly, as it often does, then the roof would be too wet to burn. My eyes sweep the force, trying to forge a path through the clustered street-way. I notice with disgust that even the ground beneath my feet is hard-baked. There's no mud for the Southern Ui Neill to slip and slide in. Not yet. I'll make it muddy with the blood I shed.

I can't determine how many enemies there are, but I'm confident that my numbers will overtop any that Donnchad has summoned to this fight. What he hopes to achieve, I'm unsure. He'll not win Dublin. And even if he did, what would he do with it? The people here are Norse, they're not Irish. They won't accept an Irishman to rule them. But there's no time for more thought. Pulling my seax loose, I test the grip on my shield.

'Shield wall,' I roar, lifting my voice to raise it over the continuing fight and the crackle of the burning building.

Around me, I sense men falling into line. There are enough of us, and it's not by chance, to fill the streetway, the men of either edge struggling to stand tall where the drainage ditches funnel downwards towards the sucking water of the sea.

'Advance,' I command. But we only take two steps before the Southern Ui Neill counter our attack. Shields crash, one against another, the smell of sweating men filling my nostrils so that I have to cough aside sweat and smoke combined. But my seax is already busy, jabbing against my enemy. Behind me, men with spears thrust them against our foes. I want to kill all these men and then get my hands on Donnchad.

Thrusting and slashing, blood quickly coats my arm to the elbow. I can feel reciprocal spears trying to stab at my legs and trip me. I keep my feet, but the man to my left falls with a shriek, quickly replaced by another as we push our opponents back towards the water. Mouth open, I shout commands that echo back to me in the confined space and slowly feel some movement forwards. Missiles strike above, no doubt fishing equipment thrown from the quayside, or even the ballast from ships, and I duck more than once, only to feel my head flung back as one finally finds its target.

I taste blood, my nose streaming beneath its nose guard. I lick it aside, almost gagging on the rich taste, and then, between one heartbeat and the next, the enemy's gone. I don't even hear the word for retreat, but it must be given. I gasp air into my body, gazing at the scene around me. Ahead, my adversaries scamper back to their ships, the sails quickly lifted as a gentle breeze begins removing them from Dublin, my settlement. Through narrowed eyes, I watch. Through the drifting smoke, I catch sight of my enemy showing me their naked arses and pissing over the sides of their ships, but it's the final ship that truly captures my attention.

There, for all to see, is the very golden cross my brother plundered from Clonmacnoise. Forgetting my exhaustion, I dash back towards my hall, hasty orders instructing others to follow the enemy and ensure they leave Dublin's shores, but my thoughts have turned to Blakari, forced to defend the hall, the place where my plunder was kept, including the golden cross. Have they retrieved it all? Are my hopes for reclaiming Jorvik in ruin?

Blakari better still live, or I'll kill him myself.

14

936, YORK, NORTHERN ENGLAND, THE KINGDOM OF THE ENGLISH

Hywel, king of the South Welsh

I ride into York with interest. It's a settlement that's caused so many problems over the last nine summers, and I fear still does. It seems no different to any places I've visited on my travels to Rome and Britain. I wonder what the special lure of the place is because, at a moment's glance, I can't see anything that would make me want it so much that I'd kill for it as Athelstan and the Norse have done.

The rumours coming from the Dublin Norse are that Olaf Gothfrith-son's close to becoming both king of Dublin and overlord of Limerick. He has men falling to his knees to pledge their allegiance to him, keen to be seen to be the ones that backed the ultimate victor in the contest of would-be kings that's been played out over the last five years between the sons of Gothfrith and Sihtric, whose death allowed Athelstan to claim York.

I can't see that it'll be too many more years before Olaf turns his sights on York. He's made no secret of his plans to regain the land he feels King Athelstan stole from his father. Such thinking makes me uneasy. I joined Athelstan's alliance at Eamont for peace. I needed harmony to travel to

Rome, and to instigate my legal reforms. But such tranquillity has been in short supply for the last few years. And now that I've made my trip across the seas, I'm not convinced that staying such a close ally of Athelstan serves my people well if the Dublin Norse, and perhaps the Scots, mean to undermine his kingship. Yet neither do I want a war with the king of the English, for if I make war on Athelstan, my ambitions, held close to my heart, to unite the Welsh peoples as my grandfather did before me, will fail even before they've begun.

Added to which, Athelstan is more powerful than any other king on this island, of that I'm sure. Even King Constantin, though he wouldn't take kindly to being told that.

My decision to come here today to speak to Athelstan as he surveys his domain is threefold: to sound Athelstan out on his plans for the future, to make him aware of the situation within Dublin and, also, the one brewing in the myriad kingdoms of the Welsh. My son, Owain, as much as I don't like to admit it, was right. Out of the mouth of babes, still more words come, calling for the Welsh to rebel and not unite with the English, the descendants of the Saxons who forced the Welsh into the extremities of the west when they invaded Britain over four hundred years ago. No, the English are the enemy in that sweet-sounding song, and unease within my kingdom grows.

A day of reckoning is coming. I need to know as much as possible before I decide which side of the divide to stand on.

King Athelstan presides over his royal court in the old hall of the Dublin Norse kings. It's a building needing some repair work, but on a bright summer's day, as this is, it's a stunning building, huge and dominating with its ancient stone walls from a time even before the Saxons. I consider what it'll be like inside.

My horses are led away, while Athelstan comes outside to greet me. It's still early in the day. I've travelled all night to get here, hopeful that Athelstan will speak with me before the day's business is conducted.

He's aged since I last saw him, but he walks with the strength and vigour of a younger man. The irony of his hair turning grey isn't lost on me. It gifts him with the gravitas of the ancient, while his vigour assures all that he's far from frail.

Athelstan's blue eyes light up when he sees me. A smile tugs at his solemn face.

'King Hywel,' he calls, 'I wasn't expecting you to arrive until much later.'

'Well, my lord, Athelstan, the night was light, and I needed to speak with you, so here I am.' I try and sound jovial but fail.

His face clouds at my serious tone, but the rare smile remains firmly in place.

'Then come, we'll eat and talk in what privacy we can muster.' As he speaks, he indicates the chaos of the forecourt. As I said, it's still early in the day, but already people rush to complete tasks.

The few men following Athelstan, I recognise some of his warriors, stop a reasonable distance away and then start to file back indoors. My escorts stand around, unsure what to do next until one of Athelstan's men realises their predicament and comes to their rescue. With an open face, he talks to my second in command, gesturing him toward one of the stables.

The inside of the stone-built hall is much the same as the outside. A little tired in places but full of warmth and people. A reminder that York is now a part of England evident in the wyvern and eagle banners hanging from the dusty eaves. A handful of men huddle around the open hearth. They watch Athelstan and me with sleepy eyes. I think they must be the nightwatchmen, eating before they sleep.

A servant observes Athelstan and picks up some signal that I don't see, for we're barely seated behind the table at the top of the hall before food and drink are placed before us. I reach for my goblet greedily. I've ridden nearly all night, dissecting the land of the English, the promise of a safe passage from Athelstan not quite enough to prevent the English I've encountered from demanding to know who I am. I'm hungry and thirsty, and have had more than enough of explaining my intentions.

Athelstan watches me eat, but his gaze is on a small collection of men and women. I wonder who they are, only for the voice of one to rise higher than another's. I recognise the language of the Norse, and yet Athelstan shows no concern. I imagine that here, in York, there are many languages spoken, just as there were at Athelstan's courts in the south when I visited him at Exeter. Only when I've eaten and drunk my fill does he asks what he must have been contemplating ever since I arrived.

'What brings you here so early?'

'Rumours, my lord king, Athelstan, and worries. And a desire to share these with you.'

'Regarding Olaf Gothfrithson of Dublin?' he queries, picking at a piece of bread and chewing slowly.

'Yes, and unease in the Welsh lands. King Idwal and King Owain are at one another's throats over some perceived slight.'

That news surprises him, not the rumours concerning Olaf of Dublin.

'Again? I thought the problem dealt with.' I detect a thread of annoyance in those words.

'And I, but since Constantin's defeat, there's been a resurgence in discontent. My men keep coming to me with stories and half-formed tales, even my son about a song my grandson sings, heard from the servants. I believe someone is working to undermine the alliance of the Welsh with the English. And, if I know the Welsh, it'll be a scop working against us all. I've heard the words in full, finally, and would share them with you.'

Athelstan's intrigued. I can tell by the light of interest in his eyes. He draws his gaze away from the youngsters just walking into the hall, yawning wildly, scratching at armpits, and instead meets my gaze.

'A scop? What does he say?'

I nod quickly, looking back at my food. The bread's good, the cheese even better, and my stomach's slowly settling. But I must share this story with Athelstan, and I do so. The words are emblazoned on my memory.

'And after peace, commotion everywhere,
Brave, mighty men, in battle tumult.
Swift to attack, stubborn in defence.
Warriors will scatter the interlopers as far as Cait
The Welsh and the men of Dublin, the Scots and the Norsemen,
Those of Cornwall and Strathclyde will reconcile as one.
Kings and nobles will subdue the interlopers, drive them into exile,
Bring an end to the dominion, and make them food for the wild
    beasts.
There will be no return for the tribes of the Saxons.'

'You think that someone has instructed the scop?' Athelstan quickly surmises, having heard the words.

I'm relieved that the king retains his wits and understands their intent so quickly. 'This is my thought. I believe that King Constantin is the one who's directed the scop. I wish I'd managed to find the man, but he's staying far away from my lands for the time being. He's taught children his song, and now, no doubt, Idwal of Gwynedd is protecting him just for the pure fun of it. My cousin relishes in causing trouble. And if not Idwal, then one of the other kings.' Perhaps, I consider, I just want it to be Idwal so I have a good basis to hunt him down and claim his kingdom to add to mine.

'You think King Constantin has?' Athelstan muses. I nod. 'The conniving bastard,' he murmurs. I smirk at Athelstan's obvious respect for the ploy. 'Well, I never heard anything like this,' he continues. 'Although it's an ingenious device to cause unease. All know that the Welsh love their tales of a future where they evict the Saxons, or rather the English, from this island.'

And there it is, the thing I like most about Athelstan. Even now, even here, when I've just told him of my fear, he can still admire the man who's the cause of so much unease. He's not a man who'll undermine another by trying to belittle their accomplishments. No, he's the opposite. He'll laud and admire them, even when they might harm him.

'And what would you like me to do about him?' Athelstan continues, going to that next step I'd hoped he would.

'The scop must be hunted and caught. His incendiary words need to be defused.' Athelstan nods in agreement once more, and I realise my words are too rushed. He detects my worry and fear, even though I meant to be much calmer when I approached him.

'I could have one of my scops devise a counter to those words. Do you think it was the man who came to my witan at King's Worthy a few years ago?' he abruptly asks. 'When the other Welsh kings were in attendance, alongside Owain of Strathclyde? I remember they seemed uneasy. I thought it merely because they were at my court.' I nod once more. Athelstan has deciphered all the tafl pieces in a matter of moments. It's taken me at least a year for my niggling worries to coalesce and take form and to decipher how it's all been brought about without my knowledge.

'I do, yes, and equally, it would be a good idea to find the man and offer a counter. I suggest one of my scops should assist, ensure it sounds patriotic enough to the people of the Welsh lands and not just the English.'

Athelstan's tight lips split into a smile. He inclines his head. 'Of course, you're correct. I shouldn't have my poets laud me too greatly or speak of the English in too complimentary a tone, as it'll turn your people even more against me. Perhaps you'd like some of my men to join yours in the hunt for the man?'

'Again, I do, and my thanks for your offer, but they must be men who can blend in well in my kingdom.'

'Yes, men raised on the border and used to the ways of all our people. And you, my lord king, Hywel, what do you say to this attempt to undermine our alliance?' His eyebrows quirk at the question. I'd think he was testing me, but instead, I know it's asked only out of interest.

My face turns serious. I'm unsure how to respond, even after the days of thought I've given the matter travelling here. 'My lord king, Athelstan.' He shudders at the use of his proper title, knowing that it means I've gone from his friend to his subordinate in the blink of an eye. 'If the scop and the scop song continue to work as well as they've been doing until now, and if Olaf Gothfrithson of Dublin comes to claim York, and if Constantin of the Scots continues to work against you, then we'll have problems. I'll need to stand aloof from our alliance.'

Athelstan's humour evaporates. His mouth forms an angry red line. I press on regardless.

'But honestly, I find it difficult to imagine all those things happening, one after another, and falling into place so that you're left fighting for this great settlement.' I indicate York by sweeping my hand behind me.

Athelstan stands abruptly and paces back towards the doorway that's just opened and admitted my men from the stables. Athelstan turns back before striding outside.

'You have my greatest thanks and support for your words, King Hywel. I hope we remain allies. But now I need to pray.'

And with that, he's out of the door, probably returning to his errand that I interrupted earlier. I can't say I'm delighted with our conversation, but I know that Athelstan will work hard to keep my kingdom as his ally. In this strange world of rumour and battle, where one scandal can lead to bloody battle, and bloody battle can lead to further rumour, I'm not sure I could have achieved more than I have.

Like Athelstan, I can admire King Constantin for this tactic, trying to turn the Welsh against the English, but I don't have to bloody like it.

15

936, DUBLIN, IRELAND

Olaf Gothfrithson, king of the Dublin Norse

I eye my brother where he lies, his chest rising and falling languidly. He needs to heal and do it quickly, or he'll miss out on the opportunity to take his revenge for Donnchad's attack on us.

Blakari was wounded in the fight at Dublin, protecting the plunder that was supposed to finance our expedition to Jorvik. Now I have no funds to pay my men and, worse, I'm the laughing stock of all Ireland. Not just Donnchad and the Southern Ui Neill, but the Northern Ui Neill also know of my defeat.

'Father.' Camman lowers his head before me, but I urge him to stand. He wears a thick cloak, determined to keep the chill from his limbs. His face is pale, apart from where he carries the scar of his burn, and I realise he doesn't bring me news I wish to hear.

'Out with it,' I demand.

'We must wait.'

'What?' I glower at him, and he flinches from the fury on my face.

'We must wait,' he resumes. I look for Rognavaldr and Gothfrith, but no doubt my brothers are drowning their sorrows in one of the taverns, sending my son to do a man's work. Damn them.

'Explain.' I march from Blakari's side, and the healer bows low and returns to her ministrations. Her hands are busy as they rest on his chest, assuring herself that he still breaths. And then she daubs him with foul-smelling herbs that would rouse the dead, let alone someone in a stupor. Blakari needs to wake.

'Our enemy did much damage to the ships in the short time they were here.'

'What?' My voice is dangerously low. I should have known of this as soon as it happened. Why has it taken two days to reach my attention? Which one of my foolish ships' commanders has been too craven to speak the truth to me? While I've been ordering supplies and preparing to attack Olaf Scabbyhead at Limerick, others have been evading the reality of my current situation.

'They need repairing. One of the ships needs to be lifted from the harbour. Others need holes patching, and one is entirely missing a sail.'

'And why do you tell me this?' I growl, but shake my head. I know why they've not told me. It's not that they're scared to do so. But I've been like a bear the last two days, determined to kill every other wolf in the woodlands. They've not wanted to risk adding to my fury. 'Then, return to those ships' commanders and inform them I need to know how long the repairs will take. The winter is coming. If we must wait, then that's what must happen. I won't like it, but sooner I was assured of a victory than worrying the ships and my warriors would sink before we reached Limerick.' My son nods. His face twists, and I'm reminded of how young he is. He's barely a man, no more than fifteen winters to his name.

'Those old fools owe me a lot of coin now.' Camman smirks.

'You were paid to tell me?' My fury returns.

'A game of chance. I lost or, rather, won. And the prize was to face you.'

'And I imagine that Rognavaldr put them up to it.' Camman has the good grace not to deny my words. 'Bloody arse,' I huff. 'He should be here, beside Blakari and me, as should Gothfrith.'

'You know Rognavaldr doesn't like to be with anyone who's sick or wounded.'

'And that's why I'm the king of Dublin, and not him.'

'Perhaps, Father, but the men love him for it.'

'The healthy men do. Those who are wounded quickly realise they've been abandoned.'

'I think we should wait for the better weather to attack Limerick,' my son offers, feeling surer of himself. 'Our enemies will be expecting us to retaliate immediately for what Donnchad orchestrated against us. Better if they have the entire winter to worry about it. Perhaps they might even grow lax and think you won't seek your revenge.' My lips turn down at his words, but not in disgust. I think Camman might have the right of it.

'If we wait until the better weather, all of the ships will be repaired, and Blakari will be healed as well,' I muse, deciding if I can afford to allow so much time to elapse following the attack by Donnchad. I'd ask Blakari, but he's beyond me. There's no point asking Rognavaldr. He plans nothing. Rognavaldr has only to think of something, and then he wishes to do it. Leave it a day or two, and he'll forget all about it. Gothfrith is more far-sighted, but overly ambitious.

My plan was to attack Limerick after the triumph at Clonmacnoise and bring Olaf Scabbyhead to heel. I must still attack Limerick. The revenge attack by Donnchad, as embarrassing as it is, might even work in my favour. Most will expect me to lash out against Donnchad, but the Irish would never aid me in reclaiming Jorvik whereas the Norse of Limerick will. Especially if their leader is subservient to me. I'll allow Donnchad his triumph and turn my attention elsewhere, for now. Once I'm king of Jorvik as well as Dublin, Donnchad will face my wrath. I was kind enough just to attack the monastery. Next time, I'll set my sights on one of their strongholds instead.

'Then we'll wait,' I confirm, only for Rognavaldr to appear in the doorway. He sways a little, clearly having enjoyed himself in the alehouse. Behind him, another figure strides into my hall. I'm not sure I know who he is, and immediately my hand reaches for my seax, but then I relax. I know who this man is.

'It seems I may have better news today, after all.' This time, it's my son who grumbles.

'Good day.' I beckon the man closer. He comes, a smile on his wind-reddened face, bringing with him the scent of salt and dampness. The man hasn't long extracted himself from a ship. 'A rough day for sailing?' I sneer. Only a damn fool would be out in a boat on a day like this, let alone attempting to cross the stretch of water that divides Dublin from the kingdom of the Scots and that of Strathclyde.

'It was fair when we set sail,' the man offers. If his cheeks were less bright, I believe his face would be entirely white.

''Tis the time of year.' Rognavaldr staggers to a bench and sits with a shriek of wood on wood.

'It was worth it, anyway, my lord. All is as discussed with the king of the Scots.'

'Is it now?' I smile, beckoning for ale and cups, and settle beside my brother. My hall is still bereft of my warriors. We've burnt those who died, sending them to Valhalla in a swirl of grey smoke, and the rest drown their sorrows or escape my wrath in the collection of alehouses that lead from my doorway down to the quayside.

'And what did you bring me, from the king of the Scots, to prove that I am indeed in negotiations with the king of the Scots himself, Constantin, and not his damn son?'

'This, my lord.' And the man reaches into a sack at his feet and hastily pulls forth a brooch of shimmering silver.

'What is it?' I demand, taking it from the man's hand, trying not to notice his filthy nails.

He shrugs, his thin shoulders cracking with the movement. 'He said you'd know.'

Now I turn the item over in my hands. It's both heavy and small, and yet it could be a lump of iron for all I know. I run my left hand over it, feeling the rippling surface beneath my oar-roughened hands. And then I stand and take it to the light of the hearth fire.

'Ah,' I exclaim. 'Indeed, I do know what this is,' I announce, but offer nothing further, even when Rognavaldr glowers at me with his ale-fussed eyes, and my son comes to stand at my side. I snatch the object into the palm of my hand. I don't need to show this to them, but one thing is sure: it does come from Constantin of the Scots. 'I believe we have a marriage to celebrate,' I chorus, looking on to the raised dais, where my son's mother glowers at me. I feel the heat of her rage and dismiss it just as easily. She can be my wife here, in Dublin. When I capture Jorvik, the Scots king's daughter will be at my side.

16

936, YORK, NORTHERN ENGLAND, THE KINGDOM OF THE ENGLISH

Cousin Athelstan of the English, King Athelstan's ally

'King Hywel says the Scots king means to undermine my imperium.' The news hardly surprises me. I grunt softly on hearing the king's words. We sit together in the hall. I'm aware that Hywel has already spoken to the king, but I've not long since arrived in York.

'I've heard similar reports,' I confirm, wishing I hadn't sought the king to tell him the same. 'Lady Ælfwynn was keen you knew of it.'

'Then there's a great deal of truth in it,' the king confirms. I eye him. He's aged since the battle in the kingdom of the Scots. I don't know what weighs on him, but something does. 'No doubt that accounts for Idwal of Gwynedd and Owain of Gwent's recent belligerence.' I hardly call their refusal to accept the king's messengers or send their agreed tithe belligerence, but the king has a way with words.

'It has been nearly a decade,' I try and console. Even taking into account the foray into the kingdom of the Scots, the English king has maintained his rigid hold on the island of Britain well. No one before him was able to ensure peace for such a long time.

'It must endure for longer than that,' he grumbles unhappily. 'The Dublin Norse have only just found their arse from their elbow. What good is the peace we've achieved if, now that there's a credible threat, Constantin has sewn such discord amongst my allies?'

'You have new allies now.' I think to cheer him, my thoughts on Louis in West Frankia. He'll be king there now. He will have warriors at his beck and call to command.

'Louis will be unable to assist me should war come. He has more than enough enemies of his own.' I consider whom the king means with such a statement, but it's hardly a secret. Hugh, count of the Franks, means to bend Louis, his nephew, to his will. I don't believe such attempts will last. The no-longer-exiled queen of West Frankia, Eadgifu, no matter that Count Hugh is married to her sister, won't countenance it for long.

'Hywel is still your ally?' I press. It's unusual to see the king so disillusioned.

'He is, yes, for now. If he and those of my men I've sent to assist him don't manage to hunt down this damn scop, then who knows how much longer he will be? Constantin is a clever man.' The king meets my gaze then. He understands the importance of words just as much as I do.

'Constantin is old, and his heir is in disagreement with his son. I don't believe you have much to fear from the Scots.'

'I wish that were so.' The king twists his lips in thoughts, and my eyes alight on his moustache. I know that Lady Ælfwynn hates the thing, and that no doubt accounts for why her cousin refuses to remove it. 'Tell me of more pleasant events. How is your wife? Your sons?'

'All are well, and thriving in the kingdom of the East Angles. It might have been ravaged by the Viking raiders, but most there don't even consider themselves Norse.'

'It pains me to remember your brother following his death, for all he could be a difficult man.'

I shrug my shoulders. It's painful to realise that while Ælfstan is dead, Eadric, Æthelwald and I yet live. 'He was taken too soon, that's for sure.'

'No man lives forever,' the king counters, and now I furrow my eyebrows.

'Why would you say that?' I demand to know, fear turning my stomach leaden. The king's grandfather and father hardly lived to a grand old age, but they were older than the king is now.

'Lord Osferth,' he surprises me by saying. 'Lady Eadgifu has sent word that he's succumbed to his illness.' Now I understand Athelstan's introspection. He and Osferth, acknowledged by all as Alfred's illegitimate son, even mentioned in his father's will, for all no one ever openly named him as the king's son, has long been a firm ally of the king's.

'He'll be missed,' I confirm. When I think of Osferth, I more often than not imagine him beside Lady Eadgifu. Following her husband's death, they were usually of similar mind. I realise now why his thoughts have tumbled to Ælfstan. Osferth has reminded him of those he's lost.

Visibly, the king shakes himself, and offers me a wry smile. 'I'm not good company, even to myself,' he offers softly.

'You're the king and you carry the weight of the kingdom on your shoulders.'

'I do, yes, and indeed, other kingdoms as well.' But still, the king's face carries a flicker of unease. 'Tell me, my friend and cousin, did I do the wrong thing with the kingdom of the Scots?'

'No, Constantin was the one who overstepped. You offered him peace and he refused it. He shouldn't have meddled after Lord Ealdred of Bamburgh's death.'

'Perhaps I should have been less keen to ride to war,' the king states, as though testing me.

'You're a warrior king. You only went to war when there was no alternative. Constantin couldn't be allowed to exert control over Bamburgh. Bamburgh is Saxon. It should have been reunited with the rest of the Saxon kingdoms. Don't doubt yourself, Athelstan. You've brought a decade of peace. *A decade of peace.* This island hasn't known the same for over eighty-odd winters.'

'Maybe,' he mutters, but I can tell he remains unconvinced.

'What would you have done instead?' I demand, deciding to play devil's advocate. 'If you'd allowed Constantin to hold Bamburgh, then we'd be at war even now. York would have fallen to the Dublin Norse, and the English would be under threat once more. The Norse, they sense weakness. They sniff it out, and make haste to overwhelm the people of those places. The

English need a strong king, as your father was, as your grandfather was, but more importantly, as your aunt was. She saved Mercia, and you must continue her good work.' I find I'm gasping as I near the end of my tirade. If my wife heard her cousin speaking, she'd be dismayed. And yet, she'd also understand. The Mercians broke her with their betrayal. But Athelstan doesn't face an internal threat, not since Edwin's death. He's the acknowledged king, and Edmund will one day, in the distant future, be king in his place.

'You're right, Athelstan,' he admits, reaching for his wine and drinking sparingly. 'Hywel's visit and the news of Osferth's death have made me melancholy. But I've accomplished a great deal, with the aid of my loyal followers. I won't forget that. And yet, I believe Hywel's correct to be cautious. Before we return to the south, the defences must be inspected, the loyalty of the archbishop ascertained, and even then, more can be done. Our warriors must be instructed to resume their training and to be prepared for when England's enemy does attack us. I don't much mind if it's next year or ten years from now; we must not anticipate peace. We should always be prepared for war.'

'My lord king,' I murmur, pleased to see the resolve returned to his stance. I don't hunger for more war, but I'll fight at my king's side when the need next arises. He ought never to doubt that.

17

937, NEAR LIMERICK, WESTERN IRELAND

Olaf Gothfrithson, king of the Dublin Norse

It's too dark to see, but I know the way easily enough. It's not as though we've not followed this route before.

Ahead lies the settlement of Limerick, and a wolf grin touches my cheeks. Once bloody Olaf Scabbyhead is brought to heel, I can begin the next part of my plans to recapture Jorvik. I might have lost the treasure from Clonmacnoise but Limerick will recompense for that. My alliance with the Scots king is firmly in place. I'll be his son by marriage, and he'll be my father by marriage, and between us we'll hold the kingdom of the Scots, Jorvik and Dublin.

But first, my enemy in Limerick.

Blakari's recovered, and he leads his men in one of the ships. Rognavaldr, sober for once, leads the men in another, Gothfrith in another, and my son, Camman, commands yet another of the ships. But there are more than just five ships. Together, I've ten ships at my command now, Anlaf Sihtricson, son of the man who wed the English king's sister, has brought his ships to join with mine. He dreams of reclaiming Jorvik as much as I do. Not that he can have Jorvik, but he, like me, is a descendant of Ivarr the Boneless. Between us, we'll reach an accord, in time. All of the men, including Anlaf, know the task that lies ahead.

Limerick will become subject to the Dublin Norse. And Olaf Scabby-head will either be mine or mine to command. I think I'd prefer it if he lived through the attack. Such a triumph will be more rewarding. Once I have Limerick and Jorvik, I'll seek my revenge against Donnchad. But there's time for that yet. He beat me with his hasty retaliation. I'll over-whelm him with my much slower one. Revenge doesn't have to be dealt quickly.

'My lord.' I turn to face my ship's commander. 'There, we should disem-bark. The water's gentle. It'll ensure the ships don't grate against the quayside.'

I nod and then softly agree, in case he can't see my small action. It's a cloudy night – well, dawn really. We've travelled in the blackness of night from our base of yesterday evening, somewhat to the west of where the ships now wallow in the water. We'll attack with the coming daylight. I grin once more, checking my blades are in place around my weapons belt. My shield's with the rest of the shipmen's equipment. Soon, it'll be in my hand.

Ahead, a scattering of light assures me that the people of Limerick are asleep in their beds. We could have enticed Olaf Scabbyhead to counter our attack outside Limerick. But Donnchad of the Southern Ui Neill attacked my people inside Dublin, and I'll revisit that ploy on Olaf because I've learned it's a powerful weapon. It undermines the confidence of those looking to others for protection. When Jorvik's mine, I'll take my revenge against Donnchad of the Southern Ui Neill for stealing my valuable plunder and delaying my advance on Jorvik throughout the long winter that we've been holed up inside Dublin.

There are many things I hope to accomplish once I've reclaimed my lost settlement. King Athelstan of the English has no comprehension of my ambitions. Neither do others of his allies, King Hywel amongst them. But first, I must accomplish this.

With a gentle thud, the forward momentum of the ship ceases, the salt tang of the ocean being replaced with the smell of too many people living together in one small enclave. With oars hastily brought inside the ship, my warriors hurry to grab their shields and spears and step onto the quayside. There should be a watchman, or maybe even a handful of them, but they're not in sight. Perhaps they believe Limerick is invincible. Maybe they accept, as I've heard others murmur, that I'm too weak to make good on the attack by Donnchad, having waited so long to do so.

The damn fools, all of them. They've not thought that my ambitions might be counter to the initial desire for revenge.

Leading my men, and with a swift backward glance over my shoulder, I jump onto the quayside and begin the run towards dry land. Other ships bob on the water, but only soft snores, and some not so soft, from the other ships birthed on the quayside, witness my actions. I hold my shield tight to my side, seax loose in my hand for when I encounter some resistance, but my eyes are on Olaf Scabbyhead's hall.

Donnchad stole through Dublin and murdered my people. I've every intention of offering the same to Olaf's people, but that's a task for my warriors. My focus is on Olaf Scabbyhead himself. I know he's been collaborating with Donnchad. I know that he assisted the attack on Dublin. For that, I despise him all the more. We are the Norse. We shouldn't allow the Irish to attack us. Not, I admit, that I wouldn't have done the same, had I thought of it first.

I feel my men divide behind me, some running along the foreshore, others streaking along the streets that lead towards the great hall of Limerick. I continue onwards. I sense, more than know, that my brothers and son have joined me.

I've been to Limerick many times in the past. I've traded slaves and furs from the quayside, having made the journey around the coastline of this island. I know the way, even in the almost impenetrable darkness. Random cries reach my ears. I wince as a lone shriek splits the air. I pause, chest heaving, hopeful that the sound occasions no response. When not even the barking of a crazed hound answers the cry, I continue, rushing my steps. My men know to be as quiet as possible, but in the darkness, anyone might happen upon them about their grizzly task.

'Hurry,' I urge my brothers and son. Sweat beads down my back as I try and evade the slick mess of the drainage ditches, the smell impossible to mistake. I can hear the slap of their feet on the wooden walkways over my ragged breathing and, for a moment, fear that all can hear us. If we find Olaf's hall and he's standing there, armed men ensuring his survival, our endeavour will have failed. The thought drives my feet, and they pump beneath my body. I've waited too long for this.

And then I see it and abruptly stop. There are guards on duty at the front of the hall. One of them is visible in the glow from a guttering brazier. I hear his elongated yawn, even over the hammering of my heart. The other guard appears to be asleep on his feet. Either that, or he's so still it's as though he sleeps.

I look to my brothers and my son. We've discussed this. We know what to do. On silent feet, Blakari and Rognavaldr take the lead. To them falls the task of silencing the guards. My son, Gothfrith, and I will then slip into the hall and find Olaf.

From far away, the whine of a hound is quickly silenced, even as Blakari rears up before the yawning man, having scampered almost on his hands and knees to avoid his eyeline. With a soft shush, the man crumbles to the floor. But Rognavaldr isn't so lucky.

I see the guard, far from sleeping, move with lightning-fast reflexes to hold his seax against Rognavaldr's neck, even as a loud cry rips from his mouth. But Blakari's quicker, and he plunges his shimmering seax through the man's throat so that the cry cuts off. I stay my ground and listen, but no one has heard. These fools truly think themselves safe. Such arrogance.

I hasten onwards, Gothfrith with me. I slip in the lifeblood of the dead men and just about come to a stop before the still-closed door. The smell of old mead and ale is ripe in the air. I doubt the inhabitants have yet to throw open their doors and cleanse the building from a winter of feasting and sleeping. I wrinkle my nose. The sharp smell of spilt blood adds a metallic scent to the scene.

'Hurry up,' Rognavaldr grumbles.

Eagerly, I reach out, my hand hunting for the door catch to allow me entry. The lock's heavy. I know it'll shriek when I try and move it, but if I want Olaf Scabbyhead alive, instead of being burned in his bed, I need to get inside.

Wincing at the too-loud sound, I lift the catch and let the door swing inwards. The smell of pork and fat assails my nostrils. I gag but keep my head up and seek out my enemy.

I've been inside this hall before. I know that while the men sleep where they fall, Olaf and whichever thrall he's taken to his bed will be in a smaller room to the left. Glancing down, I see a sleeping man, his arms flung to either side of him as though in mockery of the Christian God's death. I bend and stab through his throat. He dies with a gurgle, the sharp stink of spilt blood lost in the general aroma of cooked meat.

Without speaking, I gesture for Camman to stay close. Two of my brothers remain outside the hall, pretending, should anyone come this way, to be the original guards. If I cry out, they'll come running, as will my shipmen, who've taken a more circular route to the hall.

Reaching up, I push aside the curtain, screening the small room, and a pile of pale flesh greets me. It's impossible to tell where Olaf starts, and his women end. I rush forwards, a gasp from Camman assuring me that he's never even imagined such a sight, but Olaf Scabbyhead has vociferous appetites. All know of them. Gothfrith, I imagine, smirks at what he sees.

I beckon Camman to the far side of the bed and bend to peer over the mass of flesh. Here, a light would be welcome, but any brightness will awaken everyone, and even the naked and weaponless will put up a fight. A shocked breath assures me that we've been seen, and I reach out and grab the cheeks of the woman who tries to close her eyes to cover the fact she made a sound on seeing us.

'Stay quiet,' I urge her just about audibly, my seax held close to her throat. 'I came for Olaf, not you.' I feel the action in the darkness as she swallows and nods.

To the far side, I detect movement and see that Camman's busy trying to determine which body belongs to Olaf, but I already know. His meaty hand is cupped around the breast of the silent woman. I follow the arm upwards and find him watching me with a glint in his eye.

'You bastard,' he huffs, but it's too late for him to put up a fight. Camman has his blade levelled against his belly, I have mine at his throat, and Gothfrith is there should either of us fail.

'If you do what I say, I won't kill you,' I offer him. 'Now, get out of that bed. Gothfrith, ensure the women stay silent.' The women – I realise there are four of them, aside from the one who's already awake – are slowly rousing, their eyes fearful. 'Stay quiet unless you want to die,' I urge them, taking the time to notice that Camman hardly knows where to look. Perhaps it would have been better to bring Blakari inside with me, but Blakari wants to kill Olaf, as does Rognavaldr, and I desire him alive.

From beyond the hall's walls, I hear the movement of more and more men and the cries of those being woken to find cold, hard iron at their throats.

'I have him,' I call through the thin curtains and slightly thicker wooden walls. The sound's greeted with a cry of triumph from my allies and one of dismay from Olaf Scabbyhead's warriors.

Olaf stands before me, naked and shivering. He opens his mouth, but I'm forcing him forward. I need his men to see him so they won't fight my warriors.

In the main hall, men are quickly coming awake, all of them reaching for weapons they don't have to hand, other than an eating knife. My brothers have moved indoors and taken command of the cache of weapons not allowed inside their lord's hall to prevent bloody fights. Now they look like arseholes.

'Tell them not to fight us,' I instruct Olaf. He stands proud, not at all ashamed of his nakedness. I'm in half a mind to leave him like this, but I don't want to face his flaccid manhood every time I look at him. 'Get him some clothes,' I call to the women, slowly slinking their way from behind the curtain.

Olaf's warriors growl their anger, but none look set to defend their lord, not when my ship's crew are there, holding blades directed at throats and cocks.

Blakari's shipmen busily tear up the wooden floorboard under the dais. I imagine that's where Olaf keeps his plunder, and in no time at all, exclamations of satisfaction fill the air. With the growing light of dawn sneaking through the cracks in the wattle-and-daub walls, I see treasures of gold, silver and priceless gems.

With Olaf covered in a long cloak and a pair of trews forced over his legs by one of the women, I have his hands bound, his legs as well, while I settle in his chair at the front of the hall.

'Your lord is now my captive,' I inform them. 'You'll keep your lives, provided you don't take up weapons against us.' I watch as one of the men leaps forwards, his hands encircling the neck of one of my warriors. I shake my head as two others rush to my ally's aid, and the enemy warrior is slashed to pieces before the eyes of all.

Blood flies through the air, landing on two of Olaf's women, making them shriek.

Olaf Scabbyhead hasn't spoken, but he winces to see his warrior cut down in his prime.

'Anyone else?' I call into the sudden silence after the man's thudded to the floor and his death throes have stilled. 'Good. We came to replace our lost plunder and to take your lord captive. Limerick is now mine to command. You'll prepare your warships and your weapons. We're going to Britain to fight the English king, and if you win the fight for me, you might just keep your lives. Those who survive the fight.'

A muted acclamation greets my words, and even Olaf Scabbyhead stands a little taller.

'You only had to ask,' he huffs, but the glint in his eyes assures me that's far from true.

18

937, THE KINGDOM OF THE SCOTS

Constantin, king of the Scots

'He's done it.' My son sweeps before me before I've risen from my bed. I try to banish the wince from my face so he doesn't see how weak I've become.

'Who's done what?' I demand, knowing I sound grumpy and not truly caring. He should have waited until I was dressed to come and speak with me. Just the act of getting upright after a night in bed is enough to make me irritable. That, and the fact I've slept poorly, needing to piss more and more often. I've even taken to restricting how much I drink before going to sleep, but it makes little difference.

My son is far from perturbed by my response.

'Olaf Gothfrithson. He's overpowered the king of Limerick, another man called Olaf, and he sends word of his intention to travel to the north-west of Britain.'

'Already?' Suddenly, I'm standing upright, the ache in my back forgotten, a slow smile curving my lips.

'Already, yes,' my son confirms, and I note the gleam in his eyes. It seems that Ildulb has been awake for far longer than me.

'And he will meet us where I suggested?'

'Snorri assures me that Olaf Gothfrithson, his ally Anlaf Sihtricson, his prisoner Olaf Scabbyhead, and his brothers and son will meet you to the north-west, yes. But Snorri also said Olaf expected to meet his bride at the same time.'

'We must overwhelm the English king first,' I growl. I know I've agreed to this union between my family and Olaf's, but I don't wish to take my daughter to war.

'Snorri is adamant that Olaf is determined on this. He wants a new wife for when he claims Jorvik as his own.' Ildulb assists me in shrugging a cloak around my shoulders. I can feel the excitement for the coming attack thrumming through his entire body.

'The English king remains unaware of our intentions?'

'As I understand it, yes. His ealdorman, Guthrum I believe he's named, has visited Bamburgh recently on the king's orders, but as the people of Bamburgh don't know our intentions, seeing as they're now part of England, and have no allies in the kingdom of the Scots, he remains in the dark, as does the English king.'

'Then we'll take your sister with us. Have the orders given for my warriors to join us at the border to the north-west. From there, we'll ride through the English king's land, and he'll have no idea. We'll be in Cirencester before he can so much as mount a defence.'

My son nods but then grips my arm. 'What of Owain of Strathclyde? He's ignored all communication regarding your intentions.'

'Send Mael Coluim to rouse him to war. Mael will get under his skin.'

'And if that doesn't work?'

I fix Ildulb with a frustrated stare. 'If that doesn't work, then I'll do the work myself. And Owain won't be long for this world. If the git won't accede to the wishes of his overking, then he'll not remain my puppet for long. He has sons, doesn't he?'

'I believe so. Indeed, one of them is due to marry some jarl's daughter from the Outer Isles soon. It might even be happening now.'

'Is there only one son?'

'No, there are at least two.'

'Then I'll have the one who's not married. I can find him a wife to bind him to me.'

'That's agreed then.' Ildulb speaks as though he's the king, and not me. I feel my shoulders tense.

'This alliance might have been forged with your assistance, but remember, son, I'll be in command on the battlefield, me and Olaf Gothfrithson. You'll do as you're ordered. I can't have you running off to fulfil your vendetta.'

Silence falls between us, punctuated only by Ildulb's heavy breathing. Now I grip his arm. I need him to understand this.

'We will triumph through unity, you, and your brothers, and my grandsons. We'll gain victory by following the plan. And the plan is to kill as many of the English as we can and, if possible, infiltrate deep into England before Athelstan is aware of our intentions so that we can retrieve Alpin as well.'

'I understand that, Father.' Ildulb's words are colder than winter.

'Do you, son, do you? I'm giving up my daughter to this alliance, and I'll have victory for such a cost.' I see a flurry of emotions cover his furious face. I know what he thinks. That Amlaib wasn't given as much concern, but Amlaib wished to be a warrior. I don't believe my daughter wishes to be saddled with a Viking raider for a husband, even if Olaf does name himself as a king. Amlaib made his choices. My daughter hasn't. Neither did Alpin when he was taken to the English king's court.

The silence between us elongates, but I don't speak into it. My son must give me his assurance that he understands our intentions. Should the English king hear of our alliance, he'll mount fierce resistance. If he does so, the fighting will be bloody. If he doesn't, Ildulb stands more chance of getting his wish of holding a blade to Edmund's throat.

'I do understand, Father, my lord king, I assure you,' Ildulb eventually capitulates. 'We must undo the harm that Athelstan caused your kingdom, and at the same time, ensure the alliance with Olaf Gothfrithson is strong enough to endure. But we will triumph, Father, I assure you of that.'

'Good, as long as you understand,' I inform him and only then turn to find my boots and clothes so I can dress and address my warriors and noblemen.

'And, Father, Olaf Gothfrithson has netted himself some other prizes as well.'

'What prizes?' The news unnerves me. We should be equals in this alliance. Indeed, I would sooner be the one with more warriors to their name.

'Ivarr, the son of the king of Denmark has arrived in Dublin and made an agreement with Olaf to join the expedition, as has another, with a name I can hardly pronounce. Gebeachan, I believe.'

'Snorri told you of this?'

'He did, yes, with a chuckle of delight. He thinks Olaf's alliances are akin to the amassing of warriors who descended on Northumbria, East Anglia, Wessex and Mercia seventy years ago.'

'As long as all they want is a part of Jorvik, then he can bring every bloody king he knows to the fight. But it's only Jorvik that'll be his. England will be mine,' I growl, not wanting Ildulb to see how much the news unsettles me. I thought I had a good idea of my role in the alliance, but Olaf Gothfrithson is changing the dynamics.

'You'll have Owain of Strathclyde,' my son counters, but we both know that's not the same thing. Olaf has men pledging their support to him in the hope of finding treasures and land for themselves. But Owain of Strathclyde is my man, and that's far more dangerous. He could refuse to fight. He could decline to send his men south. I'll have to ensure he doesn't do that, or I'll have my family and my warriors, but no other ally, while Olaf Gothfrithson has them coming out of his arse.

'Come.' I beckon Ildulb. 'Let's begin our preparations. The sooner that Athelstan of the English is either dead or wedged back inside the confines of Wessex, the better.' And, what remains unsaid, is the sooner I can strip Olaf of his allies then the sooner I'll be the overking of Britain, not Athelstan, and certainly not bloody Olaf Gothfrithson of the Dublin Norse.

PART II

NEVER GREATER SLAUGHTER

19

937, THE KINGDOM OF THE ENGLISH

Olaf Gothfrithson, king of the Dublin Norse

The three-day journey has been almost pleasant, but now, with my ships at my back, I turn to face my new ally, Constantin of the Scots. He'd better have my new bride with him, or I may just forget our alliance. I might then turn my force not into the reaches of the English kingdom, but northwards, to Jorvik. After all, it's Jorvik that drives me. It's for Jorvik that I first plundered Clonmacnoise, and then, when Donnchad took his vengeance, overawed Olaf Scabbyhead and Limerick instead to once more steal the wealth I needed to purchase the allegiance of the Norse of Ireland.

And such triumph has brought many more warriors to me. I think little of Ivarr, son of the king of Denmark, and his vast wealth and showy equipment. But he has men who look to him who do know how to fight. Equally, Gebeachan, a man with a name to try the very best of our tongues, has also brought his warriors to me. They all mean to triumph from our rampage into England, and if not into the heart of England, Mercia and Wessex, then they'll take what wealth they desire from York when it is once more known as Jorvik, and under my rule.

There are many others as well, some joining my fleet of ships at the Isle of the Manx, others coming to me even as our ships sped towards the distant shores of the English kingdom. I find a smirk on my face, as I catch sight of the force the Scots king has brought. It hardly outnumbers mine at all.

Snorri, in his guise as an intermediary, walks sedately at my side, as do my three brothers, and my son. Olaf Scabbyhead and Gebeachan have also been accorded a part to play in this meeting, for all they're my underlings. Still, it pleases me. I know of Constantin's overkingship of Owain of Strathclyde. I bring two men to his one.

'The king is keen to meet you,' Snorri announces. He came in my ship from Dublin, but he's already made his presence known to the Scots king. He, of us all, knows both sides of this alliance, whereas Constantin and I know only of each other.

'And I'm keen to meet his daughter.' Blakari chuckles at my words, but I don't miss the fury descending over Camman's face. His mother has been left in Dublin. He knows I'm to wed again, and he doesn't like it. I imagine she's poisoned his mind against me, but he'll come to understand why I've determined on a new wife. I'll get much more from Constantin's daughter than I ever did from my first wife. It helps that she's old and lined, whereas Constantin's daughter is much younger. I don't care if she's pretty or not, provided I can swell her belly with another son. Having just the one is somewhat precarious, as Ealdred of Bamburgh learned to his dismay.

'Yes, I've seen her. She's here,' Snorri confirms, his tone as smug as mine. Snorri will be a rich man after today. Not only will he be accorded respect for being instrumental in bringing Constantin and me together, but I don't doubt that both of us have also promised the man wealth in response to the risks he's taken.

'Tell me more of this place, Snorri,' I demand, as we stride onwards. The Scots camp is further from the river than I'd have liked. Indeed, the Scots camp is to the north of the river. While it might still be in England, the wily old fox has ensured that, should the English king suddenly appear, he can easily pull his forces back before the English can navigate around the river.

'This is a land long in conflict with those around them. Some say it's part of Northumbria, others that it isn't. For now, I believe that the arch-bishop of York claims it as his, gifted to him by King Athelstan.'

I nod. I've seen some of the local inhabitants, most of them running from my ships, southwards before we could stop them. That frustrates me. It means the English king no doubt knows we're here already. But then, for all my journey here has been quick, a terrible storm delayed the start. The Scots king has been waiting for me, perhaps for as long as seven days. That may be the reason he's encamped to the north of the river.

'Then these people will welcome a Norse king to rule them,' Rognavaldr interjects. 'Not a man of their God, or a weak English king, but instead, the great-grandsons of Ivarr the Boneless.'

Snorri doesn't so much as misstep at the announcement. He remains as committed to the alliance as I am. I find I approve of that.

Ahead, I see a line of warriors, all of them standing ready and to atten-tion, blocking much of my view of the Scots king's camp. I feel a flicker of unease, but again, Snorri doesn't break stride as he rushes to meet the man leading these warriors in protecting their king.

'My lord Ildulb, it is good to see you again.' Snorri's voice rises above the clank of iron and the shuffling of men bored and overheated from waiting in the midday sun. I squint against the sudden glare of the sun and receive my first view of Ildulb, the son of King Constantin and another of those who've pushed for this alliance.

He's a fine-looking man, for all his face is twisted in a scowl.

'I thought you said first light,' Ildulb retorts. 'My men and I are hot from waiting all morning long.'

'We were a little delayed, no more than that,' Snorri counters. 'You could see we were here.' He indicates behind us where my encampment stretches on the far side of the river.

I force myself towards him.

'My lord, my lord.' Snorri quickly takes control. 'Ildulb, this is King Olaf, and his brothers, Rognavaldr, Blakari, and his son, Camman. Gentle-men, this is Ildulb, the son of the king of the Scots.' Snorri sounds alto-gether too pleased with himself as he makes the introductions. I'd sooner the king had come himself to meet me, but Snorri's warned me that he's old and frail these days. Certainly, he wouldn't have been able to stand all morning waiting for our arrival. I don't ever wish to grow old and frail. Constantin was once a mighty warrior, I know that. What he is now remains to be seen.

'Well met.' Ildulb is quick to reach out and grip my forearm. His strength thrums through his body, his eyes taking full note of me. If his father is weak, then his son is certainly not. A pity, I think, that the way of the Scots is that Constantin's son can't succeed him. If he could, I reason that perhaps Constantin would have stepped aside long before now.

'Well met, indeed,' I reciprocate, gripping him just as tightly, although my eyes are focused behind him. I want to see my new wife, and the king of the Scots. I'm also curious to see just how feeble Owain of Strathclyde is. I've heard many rumours about him.

'Come, we have a feast ready for you.' As Ildulb speaks, he signals the commander of the king's warriors, and they relax their stance. All the same, I don't much welcome having to walk through such a vast force when I have only twenty men at my back, and one of them is Olaf Scabbyhead, whose loyalty is predicated on the fact that I claim Limerick as mine to rule. 'And of course, the king, and my sister.' Ildulb's words end with a growl, and I consider he doesn't approve of the marriage part of the alliance. Mind, if her children are going to look like some of the Scots warriors I can see, I might not approve of it either. I wouldn't wish to father a child as ugly as some of these men.

As we make our way through the ranks of warriors, I spy a collection of canvases, raised to house the Scots contingent. Not all of them look like they'll withstand the day's gentle breeze blowing from the river, but the one Ildulb strides towards is elaborate and held upright by almost as many planks of wood as go into building a king's hall. Only this has the advantage of being built of cloth that's been dyed a vibrant purple. Surrounding it are yet more warriors, alert to our presence, their eyes tracking our every movement.

And in front of the canvas, an old man stands, waiting for us. At his side are a number of iterations of himself, his sons and grandsons, I must assume. They have the look of Ildulb about them. Neither do I miss that while most of them are male, there is a woman as well. She's much younger than I anticipated, perhaps Constantin's last-born child. She wears a thick cloak of deep purple, with a white fur collar keeping her neck warm.

'Your wife?' Blakari speaks from the corner of his mouth, and I feel a thrum of desire for the auburn-haired beauty. I hope she is my future wife, and not Constantin's wife.

'My lord king.' I greet Constantin, calling over the short space of a horse's length, which it appears I'm not to cross, as I follow Ildulb's example of stopping.

'My lord king.' Constantin's voice is hale, for all he appears fragile. Where, I consider, is the great warrior I've heard so much about? But, with so many sons, perhaps he doesn't need to fight in the many ranks of warriors.

He sounds much like Ildulb, his words a little more weighted, but it's easy enough to understand the Norse he uses. I'm grateful. I can't speak the language of the Scots well. It's similar to that of the Irish, but there too I only know the basics.

'This is my daughter, Mael Muire, soon to be your wife.' The woman eyes me curiously. I consider what she sees on looking at me. I'd like to think I was a good-looking man, but I carry the scars of a life spent fighting the Southern and Northern Ui Neill as well as the men of Limerick. All the same, she offers me a demure curtsey, and I cross the divide to take her hand and raise it to my lips, as I've seen others do. I don't miss the hiss of anger from Camman, or the low whistle of Rognavaldr. It's good to know he approves.

'I'll make you a good husband,' I assure her, turning to point out my son. 'This is Camman, my son. He's strong and fearless, as your sons will be.'

'Indeed, my lord king.' Her voice remains clear. The knowledge that I have a son already doesn't concern her.

'When will we be wed?' I demand from Constantin, for all I can hardly take my eyes from Mael Muire.

'I think we should at least eat and drink together once,' he counters, his words rich with amusement. 'But I'm sure there'll be time for you to bed her before we must march on England.'

I incline my head. Even from these few words, I think I might like Constantin. My actions don't dismay him, and as I gaze out at the force he's brought to this part of England, I appreciate that he has a vast army to hand and at his command. He might, as I realise, be old. Some say he has over sixty winters to his name, a vast age when men must fight to hold what is theirs. But he's a powerful individual, even with the failure against the English king as a stain against his long career.

Quickly, claiming the arm of my soon-to-be wife, I introduce my brothers and allies.

Constantin watches with something akin to relief on his face as Ildulb is the one to introduce me to Aed and Cellach, Constantin's sons, as well as a host of grandsons, too many to remember their names.

'And this is Owain, king of Strathclyde,' Constantin announces when it seems we've run out of introductions to make. Owain is not much younger than Constantin, and I notice he's surrounded by his own collection of allies. I take one of them to be his son, for all he's younger than I think he should be. Perhaps Owain wed late in life. Perhaps he has already lost older sons on the edge of a blade. The others, attired for war, are more difficult to place. Indeed, one of the men looks to be older than Constantin but seems sprightly enough.

'And these men are Olaf, Lord of Limerick, for now. Lord Gebeachan and Lord Ivarr, son of King Gorm of Denmark. And I think you know Anlaf Sihtricson.' It's Ildulb's eyes that note the growl when naming Olaf. Constantin merely nods and mutters soft words of welcome to the remainder of my allies, recognition in his eyes as he looks to Anlaf. He knew his father when he was king of York.

'Now we all know who we are, we should eat and drink, arrange a wedding, and then, of course, we can talk of our real purpose. The attack on England and the reclamation of York.' Constantin's taken control of the conversation, and I bite down on my angry retort. I'm not to be told what to do. Admittedly, I'm in his camp, but he must remember I'm his equal, not an underling, as Owain of Strathclyde is. I must remain master over Olaf

Scabbyhead, Lord Gebeachan and Lord Ivarr. They're tricky individuals at the best of times.

Still, as we're led into the elaborate tent of the Scots king, complete with banners and shields hanging from the structure of the building, I can't say I'm disappointed with my ally.

Now, we simply need to win, and I will be entirely content.

20

937, WINCHESTER, THE KINGDOM OF THE ENGLISH

Eadgifu, the lady of Wessex

I struggle to keep the unease from my face as I listen to the barrage of words exchanged within the witan. King Athelstan seeks advice following the rumours of the alliance between the Dublin Norse and the Scots, and whether it should be countered with military might. But that's not what worries me. No. It's that my son will once more be at the forefront of any fight for the future of England. I thought it enough when he went with Athelstan to the land of the Scots. He came back to me, at Winchester, on that occasion, with the reputation of a warrior. That should have been enough to ensure he was acceptable as England's king when the time arose. But what Athelstan hoped to achieve with his war against the kingdom of the Scots, in bringing them under his dominion, has had the opposite effect. Athelstan was too kind to the Scots. He should have enforced one of his ealdormen over the realm, perhaps Ealdorman Athelstan and his wife, Lady Ælfwynn. The daughter of the Lady of the Mercians would have imposed her control over that wayward kingdom.

King Constantin of the Scots, even as old as he is at sixty winters, hasn't ceased his politicking. Despite being humiliated at Cirencester, he's allied with the very enemy that Athelstan hoped to protect Britain from, and Constantin has done so willingly and flagrantly. King Constantin doesn't care about those he kills in the process of getting what he wants. He lost a grandson at the battle of Cait. Now, if the roar of the witan is to be believed, he'll also lose Alpin, his son, a hostage in England for the last decade. And I pity the poor daughter who'll be wed to one of the Dublin Norse. I know what that means for her. Athelstan has told me of all his sister, Edith, suffered when she was wed to the short-reigned Sihtric of York.

For months now, messengers have rushed to and fro from Athelstan's palaces, informing him of every rumour or confirmed fact as Olaf Gothfrithson has fought his enemies, been overwhelmed himself, and then claimed a triumph over the lord of Limerick. I had hoped, when Donnchad countered Olaf's aggressive stance, that Olaf would be cowed by his enemy. But no. Olaf isn't the same man his father was before him. Olaf Gothfrithson might have his father's name, but he's a warrior. And he means to fight as his great-grandfather, Ivarr the Boneless, once did.

I shake my unease aside and try to focus on the words being spoken by the men and women of the witan. I can see Lady Ælfwynn, her face troubled by the prospect of more war. She, like I, must hope that one day there'll be peace for our children. But her husband, Ealdorman Athelstan, is one of those most vocal in encouraging King Athelstan to fight. I'd curse him and his two brothers for their bloodthirsty natures. But they're far from the only men. Even, and this staggers me, the archbishop of Canterbury demands that King Athelstan declares war against the alliance of the Dublin Norse and King Constantin of the Scots. I thought holy men would preach only harmony and reconciliation, but perhaps, knowing how hard Athelstan wished the peace agreed at Eamont to persist for many years, if not decades, the archbishop is alert to its eventual failure.

While King Athelstan craves peace, those who surround his kingdom don't. They hark back to the days of the Viking raiders' attacks, and to the days when the kingdom of the Scots controlled more land than it currently does. The Treaty of Eamont has been cast aside by one of its signatories.

'My lord king.' I hear King Athelstan's cousin, Æthelwine, calling upon him. 'We'll fight at your side. We'll protect the kingdom of the

English with our lives if necessary. But we'll beat back the pretensions of the Dublin Norse.' I swallow my sorrow. Æthelwine's a good man. He's devout and fearless, and I don't want him to go to war. I don't want any of the men in this hall at Winchester to bleed their lives into some godforsaken slaughter field. I thought all this was done. I believed enough men had fallen beneath the blades of the damn pestilent Norse. I miss the steadying presence of Lord Osferth. He'd have known what to say to cool these hot heads. Not, I fear, that he'd have been able to stop the inevitable from happening, but still, a voice of reason would have been welcome.

There will always be more Norse prepared to try their luck on the shores of Britain. If I were a man, I confess, I'd welcome slicing open the throats of every one of the bastards.

Cries of acclamation follow Æthelwine's brave words. His brother stands beside him, the pair of them daring others to disagree. They're grandsons of King Alfred just as much as King Athelstan. They mean to fight at his side if Athelstan determines on a military expedition to counter the Norse and Scots alliance.

I glimpse Eadred, my youngest son, and see that even he sits, fists clenched. He's desperate for an opportunity to fight at his king's side, to earn for himself the reputation that his older brother already owns. I close my eyes, listening only to the thrum of the witan. These men and women are civilised, yet they bay for the blood of England's enemies. There'll be no stopping this, not unless Olaf Gothfrithson were to drop dead. And even then, that might not be enough if the alliance between Constantin and Olaf has been agreed, and sealed with a marriage between the two kingdoms, as one rumour states.

England's enemies must be countered. What was agreed at Eamont, a decade ago, has been cast aside by King Constantin. Not even the intervention three summers ago has calmed him. No, King Constantin will not hold to the peace. In fact, he has determined to undermine it, and counter it.

King Athelstan stands. His eyes shimmer in the glowing flames of hearth and candlelight. He's resplendent in his fine tunic, embellished with the eagle of Mercia and the wyvern of Wessex. For all he has no helm or sword, he's the very image of a warrior king. He, who was consecrated with a crown and not a warrior-helm, looks more warlike than his father ever did.

I know this is inevitable, and yet I pray it won't come to a clash of blades, carrion crow screeching overhead, the sobs of those bereaved or wounded.

'My lords and ladies, the men and women of the witan.' Athelstan's voice ripples with conviction. He's come here today to seek the advice of those with whom he rules England, but I don't believe there was ever any doubt about the outcome. 'I've listened to you, and you've listened to me. It's clear that, despite all our intentions, England's enemies are determined to attack her, and even her allies have changed their allegiance or simply refuse to be involved.' I know this wounds Athelstan. He thought King Hywel was his ally, but of late, Hywel has ignored Athelstan's messengers and sent no intelligence to the king. The abandonment by others of his so-called Welsh allies is less surprising. Tewdwr ap Griffi ab Elise and Gwriad, king of Glywysing, were not long reconciled to Athelstan. And Idwal of Gwynedd and Owain of Gwent are both tricky individuals. They both fought against the Scots three summers ago, but since then, their lukewarm support for Athelstan has grown icy.

Belatedly, I recall that Athelstan still speaks.

'And not just with blades and weapons, England's enemies have determined to use words and ancient myth to entice others to join them in combat against us. I would always prefer peace. Enough of our family and friends have died beneath the blades of the Norse, but we can't allow ourselves to be overwhelmed once more. If all the Norse will acknowledge is our blades, then we'll give them what they desire.'

Feet stamp on the wooden floorboards in agreement, satisfaction showing on the faces of all. This is what they want to hear, and I know a sad smile mars my face. King Athelstan couches his words so that no one will think he wanted this. It is England's enemy's fault. Perhaps it's the only way that King Athelstan can justify what must be done. His father wouldn't have made the effort to console himself. King Edward would have ridden to face his enemy without thought for his comrades who might die during the coming altercation. But Athelstan, for all his martial valour, is unlike his father. And I confess, I love him all the more for that.

Athelstan remains standing, taking the acclamation of the witan. Outside, I can hear the news rippling through the waiting mass of the household warriors as well. They want war. They hunger for it, and a war that's not of their devising but which is entirely on their terms is to be welcomed.

I could curse King Constantin of the Scots. He should have bent the knee and then kept his head down as well. I fear what more damage the House of Wessex will inflict against the already wounded King Constantin. And I sorrow for Alpin. Although no one has spoken of him, I doubt he'll survive the coming fight.

But my true rage is directed at Olaf Gothfrithson of the Dublin Norse. He should be happy with what he has. York, or Jorvik as he'll name it, is Saxon, and will remain so. He will not claim back something that was never his in the first place, no matter what he might think.

He's one of the Norse bastards who never take no for an answer, and who believe that their invasion of the Saxon kingdoms isn't something that can be undone. He's very, very wrong.

I only hope that Athelstan, and his warriors, manage to sever his head from his neck so that England can finally enjoy the peace it deserves.

21

937, NOTTINGHAM, THE KINGDOM OF THE ENGLISH

Cousin Athelstan of the English, King Athelstan's ally

Once more, King Athelstan has called the muster to Nottingham. This time, our force is huge, but the lack of any of the Welsh kings and their warriors is noticeable. Although the jarls and ealdormen, holy men and the fyrd, almost make up for the deficiency.

I left my wife and sons at Winchester, along with Lady Eadgifu and young Eadred, desperate to ride to battle beside his brothers but denied doing so, because if the worse should befall our king, and his ætheling, Eadred will be king. Such a burden for the young man. I pity him, although my wife has no such sympathy. Back rigid, she informed me that members of the House of Wessex know only too well their duties to the kingdom. Her coldness astounded me, as did the similarly rigid posture of Eadred's mother. Those women know what's expected of their family. At that moment, it was almost as though I didn't know my wife at all.

My brothers join me. Eadric is the keenest of us all for the coming fight. I'd share his enthusiasm if we had an idea of where the attack would take place.

It's taken us seven days to reach Nottingham from Winchester, using the roadway to London and then Watling Street to head further north, lumbering along with the supply carts pulled by the oxen.

'It'll be to the north of York,' Eadric says with a confidence I admire. 'The Norse won't want to fight far from the prize they hope to claim.'

'No, it'll be to the south of York,' Æthelwald counters with no hint of amusement. 'Any day now, we'll hear that York has already fallen to Olaf Gothfrithson and Constantin, and Athelstan will be forced to entice them from York to have any chance of countering their aggression.'

I shake my head. I'm far from convinced by either argument. We've had no news of the Scots force amassing close to the border at Bamburgh. That either means that it's been overwhelmed or it simply hasn't occurred yet. With York itself reinforced with a contingent of the king's household warriors, I don't foresee that happening. Where, then, will Constantin and Olaf Gothfrithson choose to meet?

I wish I knew. Our journey to Nottingham was reasonably quick, but once here, we've been stuck for another seven days, waiting for credible intelligence to inform us of where the enemy is.

'If King Idwal of Gwynedd was still an ally, he could have sent reports of Norse ships off his coastline,' Æthelwald muses. 'In fact, any of the Welsh bastards could have informed us. And the archbishop of York should have had informants willing to share their knowledge as well. Somehow, we should know where they are.'

'King Athelstan has men seeking the enemy to the north-east and the north-west,' I muse, and yet, so far, we still don't know. If we resume our journey north, along Ermine Street, and the Norse instead come ashore elsewhere, we might lose the battle before it's even begun. Not that I'm panicking. As much as I believe the rumours of the alliance, Constantin and Olaf still need to come to terms with one another. And one thing the Treaty of Eamont taught me is that it's all well and good agreeing to these pacts, but putting them into action is very different.

Now, I stare into the north, eyes squinting against the noonday sun, hoping that the intelligence we need will emerge soon. Feeding the men and horses isn't a problem with the wealth of the king, but boredom and the summer heat are. Already, I've been forced to separate some of my warriors when their bickering became lethal. I'm not alone in that, either.

'My lord.' I face Sigelac with a smirk. He's one of the king's especial warriors, always to be found close to him. I feel a stirring of anticipation.

'Is there news?' Æthelwald interjects before I can say anything.

'The king summons the three of you, my lords.' Sigelac's blank face gives nothing away, and yet I hope, all the same, that this will be the news for which we've been waiting.

Quickly, we follow Sigelac towards the king's canvas, no different to one in which the men of the fyrd might sleep, aside from the sweating guards minding the door.

I offer a smile to the four men, and they watch me so closely I fear I must be suddenly thought an enemy.

Inside the tent, the king waits for his ealdormen, jarls and holy men, and the commanders of the vast force arraigned at Nottingham. Again, I can tell nothing from his face, but Edmund slinks to my side.

'We know where they are,' he exhales, but offers nothing further, allowing his brother to impart the news when we're all assembled. It can't come soon enough as I fidget in the still, hot air of the tent.

Finally, as Flodwin stumbles inside, with Jarl Scule puffing in front of him, the king, Athelstan, faces us.

'Gentlemen,' he begins, then pauses, a faint smile on his lips. 'Our enemy has been sighted to the north of Chester.'

A murmur of confusion rumbles around the room. It's a strange location to choose for men determined to reclaim Jorvik. But perhaps there's wisdom in it.

'They're not sure of their success, then?' Æthelwald whispers the words to me, but there's no need for Ealdorman Uhtred barks the words simultaneously.

'Perhaps.' The king acknowledges Uhtred's words. 'But we should be wary. Those who brought us the intelligence, while not waiting to count the number of ships, believed the number at Olaf Gothfrithson's command to be vast. Ealdorman Guthrum.' King Athelstan turns to face the other man. 'Would you take your warriors north from here, ensure that Constantin of the Scots hasn't thought to split their force, and steal into York while we march on Chester?'

Whether Ealdorman Guthrum is pleased with the order or not, it is impossible to tell. He has a face of stone, even though, if not for him, Athelstan might well have died beneath the blade of bloody Edwin when he thought to assassinate the king.

'Should you find York secure, then hasten to Chester. I will have you at our side if there's no ruse. But inform the ship army sent north to remain, regardless. There are reports that the king of the Danish might be involved. It would be too easy for him to take York while we're distracted with Chester.'

'My lord king.' Guthrum acknowledges the words as a command. He's not been given the simplest of tasks. And, facing the ship army, divided as they have been, so that half sailed north-east and half north-west to counter the threat, will take a strong-willed man.

'For the rest of us, tomorrow we ride north towards Chester. We'll travel along Watling Street. I've already sent word to the ships to the west. They'll shadow our movements.'

'What of the Welsh kings?' Bishop Oda asks in the sudden silence.

A slight grimace touches Athelstan's face. 'As with our old allies to the north, the many Welsh kings have determined they don't need to be a part of the peace accord any more. We'll fight alone, the English, against the Norse, and of course, the Scots.'

'I meant will they join the Norse?'

'No.' Athelstan speaks with more conviction than I'm expecting. 'If our scop, and his subversive tales of a united Welsh, is truly King Constantin's creature, then he's ensured, better than anything I could do, that the Welsh are concerned only with themselves. They have no affinity for the Scots, or the other kingdoms, no matter the scop's words.'

Ever since Hywel spoke to Athelstan in York last year, we've all been alert to the particular song that Edmund is convinced came to the English court when Owain of Strathclyde was in attendance at King's Worthy. It's not been heard within England since then.

'Never fear, my brave warriors. The Dublin Norse and the Scots will not triumph, no matter their beliefs.' And so spoken, the king dismisses us to the many tasks required to move on from Nottingham.

I turn to Eadric.

'York, was it?' I chide him. 'Or south of York?' I continue, looking to Æthelwald.

'Look,' Eadric counters. 'We all know the Dublin Norse are daft bastards. It makes perfect sense to fight for York from the north-west and not at York itself.' Still, he offers me a grin. 'Anyway, I've never been that way before. It'll be good to see more of the kingdom of the English.'

22

937, NORTH OF CHESTER, BRUNANBURH, THE KINGDOM OF THE ENGLISH

Athelstan, king of the English

I rise from my knees before my travel altar, the noises of the busy camp flooding back into my consciousness. Grimacing, I wonder how I've ignored it for so long. Men shout at each other, dogs bark and horses shuffle in their temporary paddocks, the oxen adding their braying to the cacophony. The press of men and animals can be felt in my private tent.

My priest, Beornstan, watches me, his eyes downcast whenever he catches me looking at him. He's not alone. My ealdormen and commanders have spent much of the last week glancing at me surreptitiously, thinking I'm unaware of their scrutiny.

I don't believe they expect me to crumble with the stress and the knowledge of the battle that must come, but they're looking for something. I hazard it's my confidence. And so, I must hold myself firm and not let one flicker of doubt show on my face or in my actions.

That's why I seek the comfort of my lord God. Only to Him can I profess my anxieties. But never out loud. Only when I speak to Him with my mind can I ask the question that taunts me: *Am I doing the right thing?*

Not that I can act any differently, not now. Those who should have sought my protection and my overlordship have tested my patience. They've gone against me. Not all of them, but even those who were my close allies have become distant of late, avoiding my messengers and sending responses that reach me too late to be of use. Even Hywel falls into that category. As of yet, I've heard nothing about the quest to find the scop. Perhaps it was all a means of distracting me from the truth. I've lost my Welsh allies. Maybe I should have tithed them less. I sigh heavily, fearing to acknowledge my mistakes.

Yet the Scots king gave his word. It's Constantin who's broken the pledge. He must be punished. The Scots must learn that the English shouldn't be ridiculed and ignored. We've grown since our near annihilation at the hands of the Viking raiders during my grandfather's rule of the Wessex kingdom. We'll not retreat or run from any who attempts to encroach on our land again.

I'd blame the arrogant Norse king of Dublin for all my ills, but he's not so persuasive that he could have made men act against their true nature. Olaf Gothfrithson is just the excuse the Scots king needed for his current actions.

I've not been ignorant of Olaf's increasing success in his native land. I don't deny that I've been warned that once Olaf felt secure in Dublin, he'd attempt to claim back the land he believes is his birthright, the Viking kingdom of York or Jorvik, as he'd name it, stolen, he'd say, from his father. I can admire Olaf's misguided hopes while acting violently to repel him. There's no irony there. Olaf Gothfrithson will not reclaim something that was never his in the first place. York is a part of the ancient kingdom of Northumbria. It belonged to the ancestors of the English people, the Saxons. We'll keep it or die trying to protect it.

My ealdormen and holy men agree with me. Even the more militant of the holy men have come to fight alongside the men of the fyrd and the warriors of my household troop, as well as the warriors of Mercia.

The only aspect of the coming battle that surprises me is its position. I would have expected the battle to occur near York, close to the heartlands of the kingdom that Olaf Gothfrithson stakes a claim to rule. Instead, we'll meet in violence between the source of his power across the sea, Dublin, and the land he wants, the kingdom of York. It's a strange place to make war.

I consider the reasons behind Olaf's decision to bring his ships to Brunanburh. Perhaps, I hazard a guess, it wasn't his decision at all, but rather Constantin of the Scots. Does he not want Olaf anywhere near his kingdom? That wouldn't surprise me. Constantin, I believe, would rather lose his daughter to the Dublin Norse ruler than allow the Norse into the kingdom of the Scots. A pity he doesn't think the same of his son. Even now Alpin remains a hostage in Winchester. My stepbrother and his mother keep him close, but after near enough a decade, Alpin is more English than Scots. I should have killed him when Constantin caused me problems about the succession at Bamburgh. But I like Alpin. That is my weakness. Not Constantin's.

Such callousness astounds me. I've heard from Constantin's son, my hostage still, that Constantin loves his daughter dearly.

Yet for all the strangeness of the location of Brunanburh, it is close enough to the sea that Olaf might either send for reinforcements from Dublin or the Isle of the Manx or even retreat by ship should we over-whelm them. I'll deploy my men in such a fashion that any of those attempts might be cut off. Olaf isn't the only one to have a ship army to command.

Still, Brunanburh? There was a time when I travelled this way with my aunt. She exclaimed at the location, and ordered one of her many burhs constructed here as a means of deterring the Viking raiders while protecting the local population. Like other burhs she built, it has done what was needed, but it didn't endure for long. Even now, the population is little more than a third of what it was, the walls and ramparts suffering from a lack of men and women to maintain them. After this fight with the men of the Scots and the Dublin Norse, I'll order the place abandoned. There'll be no need for men and women to live close to the scene of such a fight. No, sooner they went to Chester, inside its ancient walls, or even one of the other border settlements, such as Hereford. It'll be better for them all. Brunanburh will be allowed to fall to ruin, provided we win.

Outside, it's an excellent summer's day. A good day for a battle if such could exist. I pray my lord God reveals his support for my actions in everything from the sporadic clouds to the gentle breeze rustling the ripening crops to the light and welcome heat of the sun as the day dawns. We'll be cool when we attack our enemies. Sweat won't quickly bead our faces unless the fighting becomes fierce. It's been a warm summer, but not unbearably so.

I'm fitted out for battle, ready and willing for it to start. My coat, with its closely woven metal rings, fits me perfectly, pulled tight by my decorated belt, complete with pouches and hooks from which my weapons hang: a small, richly decorated seax, a sword made for my hand and height, a carefully constructed piece of workmanship made by the finest metal worker in the land.

I even watched the blacksmith make it, bending the molten metal and hammering it into place, allowing it to cool and then repeating the process, time and time again, until the sword was complete. And then, to top it, the blacksmith added a handle infused with the blessed bone of one of my saints and wound a coil of metal tightly around it so that the blade stayed true to its handle.

If I must make war, then I'll do it with the best weapons possible and with ones blessed by my lord God and holy men.

On the small wooden stool sits my shield, polished, sanded and repainted, the colours bright and gaudy, the reds, yellows and blacks of my wyvern motif easy to differentiate. Any I encounter on the battlefield will know that they fight a man with the blood of the House of Wessex. Those who know me better will also see the eagle of Mercia picked out in the background and know I honour my aunt, and her daughter, too.

My clothing reflects the colours of my shield. A little less bright, perhaps, but it still marks me as a man of England, and many of my warriors dress similarly. My gloves, now safely stowed inside one of my waist pouches, are of the deepest black, better to hide the blood and gore that will cover me before the day's done.

My blonde hair is neatly tied back, secured with bands of twisted hide. For the occasion, I've shortened my blonde beard and moustache a little. In battle, it's important to deny the enemy even the smallest means of killing a man. Without gaining a fist hold on my beard, they'll be unable to grab tightly and hold on, forcing my head into a position of weakness.

King Constantin and King Owain of Strathclyde, who pledged their oaths to me ten summers ago, and King Constantin, who tested me three summers ago in Cait, won't defeat me here. They swore a holy oath. They were both guests at my witan, revered guests no less. Yet they've turned against my gentle imperium and sided with the Dublin Norse. Even Constantin. Once more, he's content to place the life of his son, a hostage for his good behaviour, in my hands. A man less honourable would have killed poor Alpin long ago. But I'm honourable, and as I say, I'm weak in my regard for Alpin. He's a fine man. A shame his father isn't.

But I'll not dwell on the past. We've arrived at this moment, and honeyed words or overtures of friendship won't sway me – not again and not when Constantin and Olaf dare to enter my lands in hostility.

We've been marching north for the last seven days from Nottingham, my troops and the members of the Wessex and Mercian fyrd arranged in a position where we can watch for the enemy should they attempt to rush south, while protecting the slower oxen and the supplies they carry. We know where the enemy are. The forward scouts have seen to that. So, with the help of my ealdormen and leaders of my household troops, and my warrior stepbrother, we hastened north, determined to have the choice of the battle site.

This spot, on a small hill overlooking the lush countryside surrounding the settlement of Brunanburh, is one my aunt once exclaimed with delight at seeing, musing that it would make both a fine muster point and a wonderfully defensive position against any incursion of the Dublin Norse. She knew her enemy well. Had she lived to this day, I don't doubt she'd have instructed me to journey here, rather than believing the focus of the attack would be York.

This will be where I defeat the pretensions of the enemy: Constantin, the old, grizzled warrior, and his underking, Owain of Strathclyde, as well as Olaf Gothfrithson, the upstart from Dublin, and any others who feel that my sway is too great over the lands of the English and that this kingdom is ripe for them to claim.

Beside me, my stepbrother, Edmund, is being fitted with his war gear, his byrnie, weapons belt and thick gloves. He wears the same colours as me, his belt as encumbered with pouches and hooks as mine. Many may think that fighting with a sword is all that's needed, but my brother and I have seaxes, a war axe, a sword and matching shields. We will have spears as well. He looks a little grim, as young as he is, but Edmund's actions are decisive. He's as committed to this battle as I am.

Striding outside my tent, I watch my men with pride. There's purposefulness in them. They share my desires more than when I attacked Constantin's lands three summers ago. Many didn't appreciate my taking the ship and land army away from our kingdom. I can understand their reluctance. They didn't want their land undefended, not when so many enemies surrounded us. They also didn't want more land to defend or people who refused to be ruled by the English added to my kingdom, for they could only cause trouble.

I understand. I don't agree. And I will, my lord God willing, prove to be correct when I triumph over King Constantin and his ungodly alliance with the very enemy of our faith, the Dublin Norse.

23

937, ST DAVID'S, THE KINGDOM OF THE SOUTH WELSH

Hywel, king of the south Welsh

'My lord king.'

I eye the man before me. I know him very well, and a thrill of anticipation churns in my gut.

'I've found him, my lord king. I've found him, and we can apprehend him, tonight. Give me ten warriors, no more.'

I nod, a wolf grin on my face. I sent my warrior to hunt down the scop who's been causing problems throughout my kingdom. That song my grandson lisped to me has entirely undermined my alliance with Athelstan of the English. But if the man is finally caught, it need not do so any more.

'I'll give you a hundred men provided he's caught.'

'There's no need,' Davydd assures me. 'The fewer, the better. I don't wish to rouse his curiosity and have him disappear once more.'

'I understand. I'll order the men now.' Abruptly, the sound of rushing footsteps makes me look up, and I startle on seeing Owain's face, almost white with rage.

'The Dublin Norse,' he gasps. I sit forward, just refraining from standing. There have been many rumours.

'What of them?' I ask, whip-sharp when he still gasps. Where has the fool run from?

'They're coming ashore, to the north of Gwynedd, above Chester. The Scots are there as well.'

I know a moment of relief that their sights aren't set on my kingdom or people. But then I realise what this might mean.

'They mean to take on the might of King Athelstan?'

'Yes, Father, they do. A marriage alliance between the two, Olaf will wed the Scots king's daughter.'

'How do you know this?'

'Traders, from Idwal's kingdom. They just arrived, spreading tales of this.' I look to Davydd, my lips curling in thought. I still want the damn scop. It has just become even more imperative that he's in my grasp.

'Take the men,' I confirm to him. This news changes nothing, not really. But if I can apprehend the scop, then I'll be doing myself a favour, as well as King Athelstan. 'Bring the scop here. Owain, I want three hundred of our best warriors prepared to ride out in two days.'

'You mean to join King Athelstan?' Owain exclaims.

'I mean to be prepared, no matter what happens,' I counter quickly. 'Send word to the coastal settlements. The Dublin Norse might think to try their luck here, if they fail against King Athelstan.' I don't believe I need to say that my kingdom also needs defending. If the Dublin Norse and King Constantin are successful against the English, I wouldn't be surprised to find them overreaching themselves. I think to say something else, but then bite down on my words. Bloody Cousin Idwal hasn't thought to send me word of what's happening, neither has Owain of Gwent. Those two men will face the wrath of the Dublin Norse first, should they determine to march towards England.

'And what of you, Father?' Owain queries. He's caught his breath now, and while Davydd strides from my presence, my other sons have been roused to join me. Rhodri and Edwin adopt the stance of warriors. I'd chuckle to see them in such a way, but I'm pleased to see them keen to defend the kingdom.

'I'll ride with my warriors. You three will have command of the kingdom in my absence. I hope King Athelstan is victorious, but we must be prepared either way. I don't want the Dublin Norse anywhere near my kingdom.'

'I should go,' Owain counters, but I shake my head. I could let him, but he's not the one who warned Athelstan of the scop's intentions. Neither is he the one who swore to uphold a peace with the English king against the pretensions of the Norse.

'No, you remain here. Keep our family safe, and our kingdom safer. Whatever happens, we have more than enough enemies even without the prospect of the Dublin Norse and the Scots rampaging their way south. Look to the north. Rhodri, ensure my dear cousin keeps to his borders. Edwin, you'll keep an eye on the west. The kingdom of Gwent under Owain might think to attack. If you're called upon for assistance from any of the Welsh kingdoms in my absence, don't allow them to undermine you, but we'll send warriors, if they're needed.' I'm thinking quickly, trying to decide what needs to be done, and by whom.

I spare a glance for my sons. They're men grown now, but I know a moment of relief that their sons are still little more than boys. Unlike King Constantin, and the battle at Cait, I don't need to fear for them, unless the Dublin Norse think to invade my kingdom.

'Do you think the Dublin Norse and the king of Scots will triumph?' Rhodri queries, his words perplexed. He knows the strength of the English king. But he's also aware of the news from Dublin. Olaf Gothfrithson isn't a man to be denied when he puts his mind to something.

'I don't know. I hope not. We have peace under King Athelstan. I don't wish to lose that. Peace is needed to ensure we have good laws, and coinage to grow the wealth of the kingdom. The Dublin Norse, and King Constantin, offer none of those things.'

'Perhaps, then, Father, you should fight for King Athelstan,' Edwin taunts. He's been vocal in his agreement of my move away from being a firm supporter of the English king. He won't welcome me fighting on his behalf.

'I'll do what must be done,' I confirm, unprepared to argue with him again. 'I'll do what must be done to ensure our kingdom is secure,' I assure the three of them, meeting their eyes, and seeing a conflict there. Owain is content with my decisions, Rhodri isn't concerned either way, but Edwin doesn't like the English. 'Follow my orders,' I confirm, beckoning my battle commanders to join me as I stride towards the stables.

Davydd is there already, arguing with the stable master. I summon the two to me, and quickly impart my instructions. Davydd nods along with me, but the stable master is far from happy at being asked to provide good horses for a man who looks little more than a beggar in his current garb. But it's been necessary for Davydd to dress in such a way to get close to the scop.

'Do as I command, and quickly. We have a battle to prepare for. Three hundred warriors will need provisions.' Perhaps I should have started with that.

The stable master bows quickly, and hurries away to his task, leaving me with Davydd.

'Bring the scop to me tomorrow,' I instruct the other man. 'He'll be a prize, no matter who triumphs in the battle between the two forces.'

He nods, a faint smile on his face, pleased at seeing the task nearly accomplished.

'Tell me, where's the Englishman Athelstan sent?'

'He's watching the scop. He wouldn't leave him,' Davydd explains. 'Don't worry, my lord king, he's not run away. He was more determined than me to capture him.'

'Very well.' The knowledge pleases me. 'Alive, if possible, but I don't mind how many wounds he carries,' I instruct. He bows out of my presence, and I turn to view the preparations already underway. A trickle of unease thrums through my body. I wish we'd captured the scop sooner. There was never any doubt that King Constantin would seek vengeance against the English king and I wish it had come when the rumours he'd spread had been countered.

I confess, I hope Constantin fails.

24

937, BRUNANBURH, THE KINGDOM OF THE ENGLISH

Constantin, king of the Scots

From my vantage point, I watch the English king with interest, noting the gleam of swords and shields, byrnies and war axes. I suppress a self-satisfied smirk at his precious order and picky ways. We'll show him what a real battle is today.

I'm dressed in equipment similar to the English. I notice it dispassionately. I want to stand aloft from them, completely different, but in warcraft there's not much that separates one warrior from another. We all have swords, war axes, shields and rings of metal around our upper bodies to deflect the sharp points of swords, spears and axes. Gloves of padded leather cover my hands, and they too will ward off initial sword strokes and seax strikes.

Not that I plan on fighting today. I'm too old and too slow. I've sons, grandsons and a son by marriage to fight on my behalf. After all, that was why I gave my precious daughter to Olaf Gothfrithson, a token to seal our alliance. The thought of her, in his bed, forces a growl from my throat. The cost of defeating Athelstan and the English is high. I don't like it, but it's necessary. I spare a thought for Alpin. Athelstan is too weak to kill him, of that I'm sure. All the same, I miss Alpin. He was a good boy. I hardly know what sort of man he's become in the last decade.

But I must dress the part and show that I'm willing to face my enemy. My warriors expect it of me. I'd feel like a fraud if I sat on the side festooned in jewels instead of deadly weapons. It's been hard to admit to my weakness, but to triumph against the English I must let others fight in my place.

King Athelstan. When I think of him, my blood boils afresh. I have to offer words of apology to my lord God. He wouldn't approve of my battle rage, but I can't stop it. Not now, when we've come to this. He's so close. We'll defeat him.

Three summers ago, King Athelstan took it upon himself to run rampant through and around my kingdom by ship, all the way to the far north of Cait. I'm still unsure what he hoped to gain by it, but if it was simply to raise my ire, then he succeeded. King Athelstan may have no lasting token or land gain from that attack, but today, he'll see the budding of the seeds of anger he sowed with such an action.

He meant to impose his imperium over the people of the Scots with his actions, and of course, to stop me from assisting Ealdred of Bamburgh's son in claiming his kingdom. Today, my people will reveal their deep hatred for Athelstan. Ealdred's son will fight with what few men he has. I've not promised him his kingdom, but of course, when Olaf Gothfrithson takes York, he must believe he'll gain Bamburgh. That will depend on how he conducts himself in the coming battle.

Athelstan's audacity in riding through my kingdom, surrounded by his warriors, sending his ships to trail his every move, will be punished. Never, in any of the histories of my people, or the tribes who came before our unification as a kingdom, has a man from Wessex taken such a bold step and travelled through the many kingdoms that now make up that of the Scots.

The old Northumbrian kingdom often attempted to win more land for itself but was stopped every time by my ancestors. Yet King Athelstan just about strolled through my lands, assessing as he went, seeing what riches he could lay claim to, almost as if he meant to stake his claim to it.

My sons met Athelstan in battle, and my grandson bled his last on the slaughter field, murdered by Edmund, Athelstan's stepbrother. I was forced to come to terms with the man and journey to the heartlands of his English kingdom. I had to bend my ancient and protesting knee before him and promise to hold to the accords agreed upon at Eamont, or risk the life of my son, Alpin, a hostage at the English king's court.

I vowed that day that it would never happen again. Never again would an English king inflict such dishonour on my people. With Olaf Gothfrithson's help, I'll erase the stain on our collective memory of Athelstan's attack and win back the love and support of my long-abandoned son, Alpin. No matter that I now know that Athelstan will never kill Alpin, I'm only too aware of the cost of the peace agreed at Eamont. I lost a grandson, my son has been absent for too long and now my daughter must carry the child of one of the Dublin Norse. Athelstan will pay for all of these humiliations.

Today, I'll draw blood and force Athelstan to his knees and drag him back to the heartland of my kingdom, at Scone, or even Dunnottar, where he'll be compelled to accept my overlordship of England. The Saxon warriors will not rise from the battlefield today, other than when their cold, dead bodies are cast into deep ditches and covered with mud thickened with their own blood.

25

937, BRUNANBURH, THE KINGDOM OF THE ENGLISH

Olaf Gothfrithson, king of the Dublin Norse

I narrow my eyes with displeasure as I watch the English king's force before me. He stole my birthright of Jorvik when he defeated my father a decade ago. In the intervening years, if the accounts of that battle are correct, Athelstan has added many more numbers to his force of warriors.

Years it's taken me to mount my counter-attack against Athelstan, my father failing to resurrect his firm hold on Dublin following his defeat outside Jorvik. As such, I might be ten years late, but this is retribution for Athelstan's embarrassment of my father.

I curse my ill luck that I couldn't pursue my claim sooner, but events in Ireland needed my urgent attention, and until my father Gothfrith's death three years ago, that right was his to pursue, not mine. My father was a man who did not succeed in embodying his Norse heritage. That he failed to do so means that it now falls to me and the son of Lord Sihtric's first marriage, Anlaf, to seek victory where my father found only defeat.

Anlaf Sihtricson adds more credence to my claim to Jorvik, as if one was needed. He's a constant reminder that, upon his father's death, King Athelstan stole the kingdom of York from the Dublin Norse, not just from my father but from another branch of the family of Ivarr as well.

As before, the combined kingdom of Dublin and Jorvik can be ruled jointly. I in the more prominent role in Jorvik and the younger Anlaf Sihtricson in Dublin, now that I've subdued the kingdom of Limerick and enforced my will over the Norse who make Ireland their home. Perhaps I can even leave the problem of Donnchad to Anlaf. My brothers have grumbled at this part of the agreement, coming when it's they who've fought at my side, but eventually they appreciated the intent of the alliance. Anlaf Sihtricson and Olaf Gothfrithson. We're both descended from Ivarr the Boneless. We're both owed what he hewed from the kingdom of Northumbria.

But, as I peruse the enemy, I can't deny that the English king is well provisioned. Athelstan has many men in his encampment. It stretches so far south that I can hardly see any of the English kingdom even when I raise my hand to shield my eyes from the brightening dawn.

The forward scouts have attempted to count the enemy during the last day, but they shift and move so often that it's not easy for the scouts to tell whom they've reckoned up and whom they've missed. As such, I dismiss their estimate of three thousand men. I'm sure there are many, but three thousand? I don't believe that's possible.

Still, I imagine that Athelstan has at his command the same number of men that Constantin of the Scots, Owain of Strathclyde and I can rely on. Combined, it's at least five thousand men. This kingdom of the English, now united into a greater whole than ever, is rich and well-endowed with land and coin that I can only hope to have at my command.

I advanced with my scout to observe the English king's camp. It's neat, tidy and massive, with square tents stretching almost to the horizon, their canvasses coloured with the yellow, red and black of the wyvern that the House of Wessex claims. My father had a snake for his motif. His grandfather a bear. I use a wolf, teeth glinting with blood, as my emblem.

The number of horses and ox carts that carry provisions means the English force could stay here for many weeks without the need to leave. My men are in daily need of supplies, and our ships have only enough if we need to make a hasty departure. They carry adequate water, ale and oats to last our return across the sea to Dublin, if it should come to that, which I believe it won't. And they carry just enough treasure to pay my mercenaries, stolen from Olaf Scabbyhead of Limerick. I would wish there were more, but Donnchad took back all I plundered from Clonmacnoise.

But such thoughts try to undermine my confidence. We won't return to Dublin other than as victors. Indeed, I might never return at all, if Anlaf Sihtricson is to rule there. Better if my first wife is abandoned in Dublin. I have a new, younger one, to pluck as I feel is needed. She'll be my queen of Jorvik. The Dublin whore can stay there, where Anlaf Sihtricson will have no need for her either.

I'm mindful that Olaf Scabbyhead's Limerick wasn't as rich as I might have hoped. Even now, much of what I intended to use to finance my reclamation of Jorvik is once more under the command of Donnchad of the Southern Ui Neill and held safely at Clonmacnoise. I need Jorvik's wealth to pay my many warriors as handsomely as I've promised. I know how wealthy the trading settlement is. Once it's back under my command, I need never worry about riches and coins again.

'What do you think?' I turn and meet the gaze of Anlaf Sihtricson as he speaks. 'Do you think all of these men are warriors, or are half of them the fyrd, who don't know their arse from their elbow?' I smirk at Anlaf's dismissive tone. I find I like him, for all we've not long reached an agreement regarding the rulership of Dublin. He wants it. But it's mine. I fought many others for the right to rule it alongside my brothers. But, when I'm victorious, I've determined to return Dublin to Anlaf's care. He can cut his teeth fighting the Southern Ui Neill. With the Constantin alliance, I should have no need to fear an attack against York. Especially as the English will be defeated. Although, well, I might think of taking the Five Boroughs as well. Their populations, I'm told, are more than half Norse anyway. Why would they want an English king?

'I think the English king knows how to make it appear like he outnumbers us. But he erred in arriving after we disembarked. We hold this peninsula. And with a river to either side of us, and the sea at our back, we can overwhelm them, even if we have to call on more of our allies.'

Anlaf twists his face in consideration at my explanation. 'What number do you command?'

'More than enough,' I counter, not enjoying his questions. They imply I might be under-strength.

'And the king of the Scots, and his little pet, Owain of Strathclyde?'

'Again, more than enough. Having the numbers to defeat the English king won't be difficult.'

'Perhaps,' Anlaf prevaricates. I turn, seeking out my brothers or my son, but they're not to be found close by. My son is still angry with me for taking a new wife. And my brothers? Well, Rognavaldr is no doubt sleeping off ale, and Blakari could well be doing the same. The two drank more than I did to celebrate my union with Constantin's daughter. Gothfrith has been left in Dublin. One of us needed to remain just in case Donnchad decided to take advantage of my absence.

'You'll fight for me?' I demand, not enjoying his less-than-effusive responses.

'I will, provided it appears you'll be victorious. I won't fight to the death if your forces are quickly overwhelmed by the English king. After all, you've made it known that I now rule in Dublin. I have somewhere to retreat to, unlike you.'

I feel my body tense at his summary of current affairs. My brothers warned me about Anlaf. Perhaps I should have listened.

'Dublin is only yours when Jorvik is mine, remember that, cousin,' I snarl.

'Perhaps, cousin.' Anlaf smirks as he speaks. I lunge towards him, but he steps backwards, neatly evading my closed fist. 'Careful, cousin,' he huffs in amusement. 'It would be bad for morale if the men saw us fighting.' I doubt that, but I subside all the same.

I must remember that my focus is on winning this battle. I'll be happy with Jorvik for now. And King Athelstan's death. Of course. That goes without saying.

26

937, BRUNANBURH, THE KINGDOM OF THE ENGLISH

Edmund, ætheling and prince of the English

I like this position insisted upon by my brother, King Athelstan. I've argued against it, as all good men of the witan should, fearing it leaves our force too exposed, but I think it's the best option available to us. The Dublin Norse and Scots have the sea to their backs, and two rivers surround them. It could be a slaughter if we're overwhelmed. All the same, I've made my agreement known. I might be the king's younger stepbrother, but I'm also his ætheling and heir. I've fought in his name before, in the north of the kingdom of the Scots. I've killed in his name. I have the reputation of a warrior, even if I know my mother wishes I wasn't here. And I confess, I know a tremor of unease for what I might face. The Scots king's son will want vengeance for my killing of his son, regardless of the fact that it was a fair fight in the heat of a bloody battle.

The might of the Norse and Scots combined will be a skilled fighting force. How can they not be with all their years of experience battling against one another, as well as against the English?

My experience of the Scots is that they fight much as we do. The Dublin

Norse, I've not yet met in combat, but I anticipate that men fighting to the death battle much the same. It must all boil down to one man fighting for his survival against unimaginable odds in the terrible confusion of battle, where it's not always skill with a sword or an axe that determines whether a man lives or dies.

Once our force recovered from the surprise that the Norse of Dublin weren't moving any closer to York, where we'd first thought we'd engage them, all haste was made to reach the western lands from Nottingham. I'm grateful that we were told of the destination. If not, we might have marched on York even as our enemy hurried into the heartland of England. While the intention of leaving my young brother, Eadred, behind in Winchester was to ensure that a member of the House of Wessex would survive the coming fight, it might have been Eadred who was dead while Athelstan and I lived.

The decision of the Dublin Norse and the Scots to force a battle here is an unlikely choice, but then, the Dublin Norse and the Scots, for all that they say otherwise, make uneasy allies.

I imagine that the wily old bastard King Constantin doesn't want the Dublin Norse too close to his lands. Equally, Olaf Gothfrithson must realise it won't be easy to claim York unless he comes as the victorious commander to claim his spoils. Athelstan has been the king of York for too long now. The people who live there have become used to his gentle governance, so unlike that of a Norse ruler. Athelstan doesn't change their lives or alter their livelihoods. He's happy to continue the status quo provided his faith is accepted as the proper one and taxes are paid correctly and on time.

Athelstan isn't a cruel king. He's laboured to stamp out all factionalism and to quiet the voice of my now dead disaffected stepbrother and his remaining followers. But Edwin's few supporters still fester. They wait for Athelstan to make a mistake. York would be an easy mistake to make, and so he governs lightly, with the aid of the archbishop, Wulfstan.

Not that York is alone in this regard. Mercia is accorded the same gentle touch for all that they love and respect him anyway, seeing in Athelstan an embodiment of his aunt, the great Lady Æthelflæd. I've no memory of her. She died before my birth. And yet, when Athelstan and Cousin Ælfwynn speak of her, I can well imagine the kind of ruler she was.

The borderlands with the Welsh are a little more problematic for my brother. In recent years, since his attack on the lands of Constantin, there's been a cooling in his relationships with the subject kings. I believe the Welsh kings, even Hywel of the South Welsh, fear Athelstan and his ultimate intentions. But my brother assures me it is the work of the scop, and his tales of a Welsh force to defeat the English that truly causes the problems. The Welsh have long memories. All these years of trying to show that he simply wants to live in peace have come to this. The Welsh won't stand with Athelstan against Olaf Gothfrithson's determination to take York and Constantin's desire for vengeance. Although neither will they stand against him. At least we need not fear that the Welsh will launch themselves at our rearguard.

It's poor payment for the accord that Athelstan achieved at Eamont and Hereford. The Welsh kings with their belligerence are as much at fault as Constantin of the Scots. All Constantin needed to do was abide by the terms of the peace agreement. Were they onerous terms? Not as I understand it. Even Alpin has told me that his father believed the terms fair, and yet. Well, Constantin has shown himself to be the man he is. He has cast down all attempts to drive the Norse from Britain's shores and, worse, he's allied with them, and welcomed them into his family.

And so, a bitter battle will be fought on the slopes of a small rise in sight of the sea that has brought the Dublin Norse to our lands. This battle site is close to two navigable rivers allowing entry into the heartlands of the English kingdom, but equally, the means to escape to the sea, and back to Dublin. I don't believe England's warriors have failed to note that. The king hasn't. Neither have I.

King Constantin has brought his troops to the same site. Some have come via ship, while others have marched or ridden, collecting the Strathclyde forces of Owain along the way. Our enemy will have an easy means of escape via ship should any live to walk from the battlefield. I doubt they will. The decision has already been made to prevent them from retreating to the sea if possible, and the ship's army is close by, hovering out to sea, but there should they be needed. I imagine those warriors hope they'll be called upon.

Years and years of training will come to fruition here. Men who first blooded their swords on the foray into the lands of Constantin at Cait will get another opportunity for glory and victory. And more will get their first chance. My brother won't fight this battle alone. I'm proud to be here to serve him.

Eadred, my full brother, will not fight in the shield wall. He's remained in Winchester, with my mother. Should we fail here today, which we won't, then he'll be England's king. I pity him. And yet, Eadred's fallen entirely under Athelstan's power. Eadred believes, as we all do, that if England defeats the Norse and the Scots on this occasion, then England can be safe from future attacks.

With decisive moves, I check that my equipment is in place: my rounded shield, painted in the bright colours of Wessex; my sword, gifted to me by my long-dead father; my seax and my war axe. Everything is where it should be and as it should be. I don't feel the same fear that almost crippled me at Cait, but equally, I've not eaten my fill either. I'll not make that mistake again.

And then one of the young servants hands me my leather gloves, and I thank him. I'd have been severely hampered when I went into battle if I'd forgotten them. Perhaps I'm far from as calm as I thought I was.

I walk to where my brother is, ready and waiting, watching the enemy's movements in the early morning sunlight. He's dressed for war, and if ever a man looked like the ideal of a warrior, then that man must be Athelstan with his warrior's garb, and wide stance, the muscles on his arms and legs clearly visible beneath his tunic and byrnie. When he dons his helm, he'll look magnificent.

I'm proud to call him my brother and stand beside him. Today, I'll prove that. Today, great deeds will be done, and tonight, I hope I'll still be alive to celebrate those who've given their lives for England's glory and to know that England is safe from the reaches of the bloody Norse.

27

937, BRUNANBURH, THE KINGDOM OF THE ENGLISH

Athelstan, king of the English

It's still early enough to call one last witan before battle commences. Edmund is grim-faced at my side. Although I know he mirrors himself on my deportment, I childishly reach over and whack him on the back.

He jumps a little at my touch, but on seeing my smile, he impulsively grins back. I love my brother Edmund. Of all my father's children, apart from my full sister, he's the one I care for most.

'Brother, this battle will go well, I assure you.'

His blonde eyebrows rise at my confidence. He grins, although I detect the wobble of his chin. 'Surely it's better to be a little less confident, and then when we prevail, you'll be surprised.' Edmund's tone is as light as mine, the ramblings of men both elated and scared about what's to come. And it's my turn to smile as he flings one of my favourite comments back in my face.

'Ah, today it feels a little different. I think overwhelming confidence is called for.'

Edmund's mouth turns down on considering my words, although his eyes continue to dance with mischief. 'Then I'm glad you feel like this. I'm nervous and apprehensive, but your sureness bolsters me. Especially when it's so rarely seen.'

My brother's right. I'm not one to gloat before something is complete. This righteousness flooding through me, though, is too strong to ignore.

'We'll beat them, Edmund. Never fear that. But there'll be a great slaughter here today, of that, I'm sure. There are too many armed men in one place for death to be avoided. For all my conviction, I command you to keep yourself safe and well. Don't fear to attack, but don't take risks that aren't needed. Do you understand?' My tone grows firmer as I speak. My belief in victory is one thing, but I can't countenance losing my brother to accomplish it. I know he fought well at Cait. I know he killed Constantin's grandson, and yet I still worry for him. I fear for all my warriors.

Edmund sobers at my words, his young face turning serious. I curse myself for a fool until he smiles again, real mirth transforming his unblemished face, apart from where he's cut himself when shaving.

'And I, as the king's heir and ætheling, command the same of you, my lord king.'

I stare him down for a long moment, but I admire his courage. He'll fight exceptionally well, and he'll be doing it for me as his king and brother. At no point will he consider the fight is for his inheritance as well.

'Then I'll do as my heir commands,' I reply testily, my thoughts already on the clash of weapons that I imagine hearing even though the two sides are far from ready for the coming fight.

Other men begin to answer my call to the witan, streaming close to me in dribs and drabs, some calling for swords and others rubbing sleep from their eyes. Some of these men are dressed as we are, with helms under their arms and shields on their backs. These are the men I trust above all others within my kingdom.

The first to join us are the brother lords. Athelstan, Eadric and Æthelwald are vicious warriors who share my deep faith. They wear their weapons and armour with the same ease that they display miniature crosses around their necks.

Edmund greets the brothers warmly. He fought with Eadric and Æthelwald at Cait. They kept him safe and, yet, allowed him to become a man on the slaughter field. It was much the same for me with Flodwin and Sigelac when I was Edmund's age.

The brothers look more alike than Edmund and I, but they're full brothers. Edmund and I only share a father. They have the same auburn hair, intelligent blue eyes and many of the same mannerisms. I've made a small study of them. It's good to know how men think and act, whether they show all their emotions on their faces or mask them and act opposite to how I suspect from their stance or their facial expressions. Edmund might trust them with his life, but I've known the three since my days in Mercia. We were raised together. We're almost as close as brothers.

'My lord king.' Ealdorman Athelstan speaks first as he tugs on his gloves and prepares to meet the enemy. 'My men from East Anglia are ready and keen. I'd request that you let us lead the assault.' His tone's formal, but his eyes glint with the joy of the coming battle. I grin back at him. I'd like nothing more than to give him the command he wishes.

'My thanks, Ealdorman Athelstan, but unfortunately, Edmund has beaten you to that request. Is there another that would satisfy you?'

'No, but I'll be pleased to take the flank beside him.'

Lord Athelstan eyes Edmund with a challenge in his bright eyes as though taunting him; the older man testing the younger.

'It would be my pleasure to fight with you at my side,' Edmund counters aggressively, but luckily Eadric intervenes before I must. I'll not have my men fighting one another. Only through unity can we succeed.

'I think you should both step aside and let me and Æthelwald have that position,' Eadric argues, watching my face to see how I'll react to his efforts to further muddy the waters. Instantly, I feel my temper fray, but then I notice all four grinning at me. They've decided to lighten the mood with their warrior humour.

A smile plays on my lips. It is, after all, expected of me, as their king and commander, to enjoy their attempts to distract me from the coming fight.

'I've a mind to let Ealdorman Uhtred take that position now,' I say to outraged cries of protest. Now it's my turn to cause a little mischief. 'He is, as we all know, a great warrior.'

Edmund scowls, and so does Ealdorman Athelstan.

'Fine, fine,' I capitulate, holding my hands in the air. 'Edmund can keep his place, and Ealdorman Athelstan, you may go on his flank. And Eadric and Æthelwald, where do you wish to station your men?'

Eadric stands silent momentarily, eyeing his brothers and my brother before he speaks.

'I think we'll stand behind the two fools and ensure they don't let the bloody Scots or the fierce Dublin Norse through.' Now it's the turn of the other two men to look irritated. I hide my burst of amusement. Eadric speaks his mind as no other man I know ever has, even if it is, occasionally, unwelcome. Æthelwald nods along in concord with his brother.

'A fine plan,' I concur. 'And behind you all, I'll place the steadying force of Ealdorman Guthrum. He'll make sure that none of you let our enemy advance now that he's returned from York.'

It's the turn of the four to act incensed again at my words, but I know they'll agree with me. After all, this was decided upon yesterday. Now we need only pass the time until the other ealdormen arrive, and it's time to make final battle plans. For, make no mistake, a battle is to be joined today and we all hunger for it.

28

937, BRUNANBURH, THE KINGDOM OF THE ENGLISH

Olaf Gothfrithson, king of the Dublin Norse

My ramshackle collection of allies is far from the assured presence I thought it would be. Olaf Scabbyhead is really my prisoner and the means of ensuring his men fight on my behalf. Ivarr, the prince of Denmark, seems to know little of true war. Even Anlaf Sihtricson, for all his years of warring against me in Dublin, irritates me as I prepare for battle.

The irony isn't lost on me that I ask these men to fight on my behalf and yet entice Constantin and Owain from their alliance with Athelstan. That is how war should be made. Those arguing that his cause is the most righteous and who has the most strength should win. The weaker – well, in my opinion – should die.

In all, I have near enough twenty ships with their men under my command. Added to this I've attracted petty kings and many earls to my cause, more than two handfuls. With each ship carrying up to fifty men, I have over a thousand men at my command.

Yet the kings of the British kingdoms hold sway over far greater territories than do the men of my homeland. I fear as I watch the enemy that they vastly outnumber my force.

But in Ireland, we fight over our land more, demand greater loyalty from our followers, and harshly punish those who go against us. We think nothing of burning monasteries, murdering our rivals and demolishing churches. We may be smaller in numbers, but we have fewer scruples about war. It's dangerous and not at all the grand carnival that bloody King Athelstan of the English has brought with him.

But for all that, I make a good ally and a powerful enemy, as the attacks on Clonmacnoise and Limerick have shown. I'm strong and powerful and have men who'll follow me to their death if need be, and they number more than just my three brothers and son. I can't imagine that Athelstan can say the same about his men.

And the earlier luck of his reign, when he claimed to rule all of Britain while we Norse fought our own battles in Ireland, has run out. Athelstan shouldn't have attacked King Constantin three years ago, even if the wily old bastard was playing him for a fool concerning the kingdom of Bamburgh.

No, Athelstan should have bound Constantin to him more intimately, and what would have been closer than a blood tie, a marriage between him and Constantin's daughter? Not that I'm complaining. I find the girl pleasant enough in my bed, and it's served me far better to be able to marry the Scots king's youngest daughter than to marry another.

Constantin told me that Athelstan stood as godfather to his youngest son and hoped to bind the family that way. What he should have done was arrange a marriage between the two kingdoms. Although, perhaps Constantin would have been even warier of him if he'd suggested that, for after all, that is how Athelstan conquered Jorvik. A marriage that lasted barely half a year, and upon the death of Sihtric, Athelstan claimed my land through the union of his sister to King Sihtric.

What would Athelstan have done if he'd married Constantin's daughter and the old bugger had died before now? Would Athelstan have obtained the land of the Scots too? United all the people upon his island home? I wouldn't be surprised. Athelstan's ambitions are huge and outweigh his skill. And we're about to show him that.

I already have a son to continue my family line. A new young wife to help me govern in Jorvik will be welcome.

The Limerick king, Olaf Scabbyhead, has been bested, taken as my prisoner, and now he serves me here, on English ground. Scabbyhead will endeavour, along with his men, to restore me to the lost realm of Jorvik.

Perhaps, when Scabbyhead's work is done, I might release him from his subservience to me. But it'll depend on how convincing his attack against the English proves and whether he still lives!

'Olaf,' Constantin shouts from inside the huge tent where we will hold our final battle conference. He's finally joined me on this side of the river, his ships at our backs as well. His voice is hoarse and rough with a lack of use. Or age, I consider. Probably age. I stride towards the canvas, hardly looking at where I step.

'Constantin,' I reply eagerly, ducking inside the canvas. There's no need for us to use 'king' or 'my lord' when we speak to each other, for we're equals in everything. I note that his daughter, my wife, stands with her brothers and father. I offer her a smile that she doesn't return. She's an unwilling part of our alliance, but I'll win her regard. Today, I'll prove my worth to her and she can stop stating that she'll return to the kingdom of the Scots with her father. She's my wife, and she'll live with me, in Jorvik. She'll birth sons for me, and in turn, they'll rule Jorvik. A faint smile plays on my lips.

'Are your men aware of what we hope to achieve here?' Constantin's voice, stronger now, is taunting. I glare at him from one side of the tent to the other. He's dressed for war, in his byrnie, weapons belt, helm roughly rammed onto his head so that the horsehair plumage cants to one side. He looks ridiculous. He's too old for this. His legs are stick thin, his arms lack all musculature, while his hair is white and thin, shrouding him as though he were dead already.

A smile plays around his lips. I curb my frustration at his demanding tone. This is simply his way. A little humour and a little gentle teasing.

In those who hate him, it works to enrage them enough that they fight well, even if it is for him. Those who revere him fight excellently, so either way, he wins. Not that I know this first-hand, but my father, Gothfrith, often spoke to me of Constantin, and I listened. Carefully.

'Yes, Constantin, my allies from across the sea know what's expected of them. They'll fight well,' I growl, despite my attempts to dismiss his smirking tone, which questions me.

'They better,' he answers jubilantly. The knowledge that he's annoyed me adds to his enjoyment. I refrain from commenting on his costume. I don't believe in upsetting men who might have to choose between their lives and mine before the sun has set this day.

'And your ally?' I query. 'He, too, knows what's expected of him.'

Now it's Constantin's turn to frown. I hold my mirth in place. It's no secret that Owain of Strathclyde doesn't want to be here. It's also the worst-kept secret that Constantin is hoping for his death so that he can replace him with someone he finds more malleable, Owain's son or perhaps one of Constantin's sons.

'Yes, he knows what he's to do. He'll be in the vanguard as discussed.' Constantin's tone chimes with annoyance at my interrogation of him.

'Is that truly wise?' I counter, all the same. I feel he's putting much faith in a man who's only too aware that Constantin is plotting his death.

'Don't talk to me about battle tactics,' is his hot reply. 'I've been fighting battles since before you were a babe. I know what I need to do to beat the bloody English.'

I bow towards Constantin and narrow my eyes at the sons and grandsons who surround him. They'll hold a position of relative safety behind Owain of Strathclyde, but I still imagine they'll need to raise their swords and axes and engage in warfare before our triumph over the English can be assured. I've also realised that Mael Coluim is conspicuous by his absence. Why, I consider, hasn't the Scots king allowed his heir to march south? Has he left him to rule his kingdom? That would astound me when all know they don't get on. Would the Scots king truly trust Mael Coluim to govern in his absence, or is there something else going on of which I'm ignorant?

His sons and grandsons will also have the opportunity to win through to the English ranks and slay the pestilent King Athelstan. They have the best position and will gain the greater battle glory, but I've held my tongue about my dismay with the battle formation. If Constantin, all white hair, where he has any, and white-bearded, where he has too much, has decided that his age and battle experience make him the expert, then I'm happy to let him think so.

His force will meet the English first. His warriors will suffer the greatest number of casualties.

I'm a victor of sneaking raids and lightning-fast advances and retreats. For years I've fought the Limerick kings and the Southern Ui Neill, sometimes with my father and sometimes not. The Limerick kings have countered my movements. The Southern Ui Neill have done the same. But these skirmishes share one similarity. They're all small and deadly battles. I know the importance of hand-to-hand combat. I know the devious ways of getting an opponent to fall into my trap. I know that I'm far more a warrior than Constantin ever was, despite his victories and battles against Edward, Athelstan's father, and Æthelflæd, his aunt.

'As you will, Constantin. And I will hold my reserve, and only my commands will bring them to the slaughter field,' I announce, determined to rile him. Before he can answer, I continue, 'But when will we let the battle commence?'

Constantin looks surprised. I notice that Ildulb doesn't take kindly to my questions. He's a wild character but fiercely loyal to his father. It's Ildulb who began this process of bringing Constantin and me together. I know that, but Constantin doesn't know I'm more than aware that this wasn't his decision. Not in the beginning.

'When we're well and good.' Ildulb speaks for his father. He, too, is dressed for war, but on him the equipment looks fine. He's a warrior in every sense of the word. He has the build and quick reflexes of a man who's fought for his life before.

'It should be now,' I counter. 'We don't need to posture and make any final demands or even suggest peace. We need to attack.' I notice that my wife watches me with arched eyebrows, my words surprising her. I almost stick my chest out in pride. I'll show her what sort of a man I am.

Constantin scrutinises me while Ildulb's shoulders tense at such a slight against his father. Only then Constantin gestures for another of his sons to come to him. This is Aed, named for Constantin's father.

'Inform my men and Owain of Strathclyde that we'll advance now.'

'My pleasure, father,' he rejoins, bowing low and scowling at me as he strides past on his way towards the rest of the camp. It seems none of my new wife's brothers like me. That's good. I don't want them to like me just because I'm a family member. But I'll win their esteem.

Constantin walks toward me and holds out his hand so I can clasp it.

'May our victory be glorious,' Constantin intones, his voice booming, his dark blue eyes blazing with fiery determination, despite his frail body.

'It will be,' I reiterate, clasping his arm firmly and trying not to notice that his grip on me is so much weaker. 'I'll see you next at the end of the day, when the English king will be dead, and we'll have his kingdom in our grasp.'

Constantin gives me a strained look, and momentarily I worry. Doesn't he wish the same as me? But then the swirl of battle preparation distracts me as I stride outside again. I don't care what Constantin hopes to gain here as long as I get Jorvik.

29

937, BRUNANBURH, THE KINGDOM OF THE ENGLISH

Owain, king of Strathclyde

Bloody Constantin. Bloody Olaf Gothfrithson and bloody Athelstan. Why should I be here now, with my warriors, when their arguments little concern me? I've been asking myself the same question ever since Constantin appeared at my hall, battle-ready and eyebrows raised at my unprepared state.

I'd already informed him, in no uncertain terms, and through Mael Coluim, that I'd not one whit of interest in whatever he'd agreed with the Dublin Norse king. Certainly not after what happened ten years ago, when he chastised me for offering sanctuary to the fleeing Gothfrith, come to claim Jorvik after Sihtric's death, and bid me eject him from my kingdom so as not to upset the English king.

I vowed then that I'd not trouble myself again with the affairs of Dublin and Jorvik. But Constantin has a way with words, a way of persuading a man even against his express wishes.

In the middle of a sumptuous feast to celebrate the marriage of my son to a girl from the Outer Isles, I was well on my way to being more than drunk and enjoying every moment of it. That was until Constantin appeared with his warriors and his damn demands.

Helping himself to a drinking horn and imbibing deeply from it, Constantin glanced at my tastefully decorated hall, eyes alight with mischief. With his white hair spilling down his back and his white beard splattered with my finest wine, his stance and rich warrior's garb made it clear that he was the true master in my hall and my kingdom.

'A beautiful girl,' Constantin had offered, pointing to the bride, dressed in fine cloth and with her fiery red hair intricately braided, dancing with my son and any who wished to swirl and twirl her on the dance floor.

'Pretty enough,' I'd countered, not wanting to upset her father, Jarl Sigurd, at my side, the man as drunk as me. I didn't think her too lovely, but my son seemed happy, so who was I to complain?

'Aye,' Sigurd had interjected, 'the prettier they are, the more other men want them, and the more likely they are to stray. I'm pleased my daughters are all dull.'

We'd all laughed then, drunkenly sloshing our drinks down our tunics and not caring that our best clothes, worn only for state engagements, were besmirched with mead and wine. For the briefest of moments, my dismay at seeing Constantin had lifted. Perhaps, after all, it was just a social visit, despite his warrior's clothing.

'If this is the send-off you give your warriors the day before they march to war, then I must ensure my men don't see how well you treat them,' Constantin had drawled when his laughter had finished. Instantly, I'd sobered. Damn the bloody man.

'My lord, Constantin, I've no plans to take my men into battle. Did Mael Coluim not inform you? Did the messenger I also sent not reach you?'

Constantin's face had turned dark in the flames from the blazing hearth fire as I'd spoken. I'd recognised trouble was coming. We'd known each other far too long not to anticipate one another's response.

'Mael Coluim told me some rubbish, and then I did receive a messenger, but he wasn't very good at delivering the message, or at least not the right message. I punished him on your behalf.'

I'd swallowed and swept a look to the churchmen in my hall, already grimacing at the display of lewd behaviour before them. It wasn't that they were particularly unctuous in their demands for a chaste court, but what was going on amongst the young men and women was too brazen.

I didn't look forward to the conversation I'd need to have with them about why one of their numbers wouldn't return. I'd hoped that the religious Constantin would forgive a man of the Church the words he carried. Clearly, I'd been very wrong. I resented sending the man to Constantin, but then, our usual messenger had been missing for the last three years. Where he was, I didn't know, but it'd caused me to rely on men I wouldn't have usually risked in order to keep in contact with Constantin. And, of course, Constantin had made a game of sending the despised Mael Coluim to my court on his behalf as well.

'Indeed, Constantin. My apologies that the message wasn't to your liking, but it makes it no less true.'

Jarl Sigurd, as instantly sober as I was had become deeply embroiled in a conversation with his wife to my side. I'd wished I could have done the same.

'How long will you need to assemble the best warriors? A day or maybe two? Your kingdom isn't that wide or long. Most should arrive within a day of being summoned by their king.' Constantin had persisted, his words rougher, almost overshadowing the thrumming music of pipe and drum.

'My warriors are here, Constantin, but we've no plans to march to battle.'

He'd eyed me coolly, his displeasure increasing every time I denied his request.

'Owain, once more, I think you forget the basis of our relationship and mistake it for friendship, which it most certainly isn't. You'll do as I command, or I'll replace you, and your sons will never rule in your stead.' Constantin's tone had been bland, almost bored, as he'd looked at the ongoing celebrations.

Damn him, I'd thought to myself. It had always come down to this. Normally a kind master, but one with no compunction about reminding me that I was his creature to do with as he commanded on the few occasions I forgot myself. And it didn't look good beside my son's new wife's father, either. He thought the union was between the king of Strathclyde and his family, not between the king of the Scots' plaything and him.

'Two days at most, Constantin,' I'd heard myself replying, cursing him all the time. I was too old for battle, too comfortable in my hall. Yet I hadn't been able to argue that for Constantin is far older than me. He's a true grizzled stag who doesn't like to be reminded of the horde of grandchildren who overrun his halls even though he wears his age like a cloak of office. *Perhaps*, I'd thought, observing him with a more seasoned eye. He'd looked ridiculous in his clothes that hung on him, revealing where his strength had fled him.

'Excellent. Two days I can spare. We're not due to meet with Olaf Gothfrithson for another six days, so two days I can give you. Especially if there's more mead as good as this,' Constantin had offered, his drinking horn once more raised to his lips.

I'd pressed my lips together in annoyance and fear. I didn't want to go to war. I wanted to enjoy my old age and die in my bed surrounded by beautiful women, not just functional ones.

'I take it you can still wield a sword?' Constantin had asked scathingly as I'd bitten back an angry retort. Not as well as I once had, but I wouldn't confide that in him. I'd have asked him the same, but I'd known better.

'Of course, my men and I train often.'

'Good, I plan on putting you in the vanguard position.'

I'd suppressed a groan at that. Clearly, Constantin had every intention of punishing me for attempting to ignore his call to arms. I may as well have informed my churchmen of my wishes for my body upon my death and which of my sons I expected to succeed me. It seemed pointless to plan on returning.

As I'd pondered this unlooked-for turn of events, I'd noticed that Constantin was watching one of my sons closely, Dyfnwal, and not the one who'd just been married. It seemed that Constantin had determined my successor already. It was a pity I agreed with his choice. A great shame indeed, for it would make my kingdom even more compliant to the wishes of the Scots king.

Two days more at home, drinking and satisfying my needs wherever I chose. *Two days more*, I'd mused, draining my drinking horn and impatiently waiting for it to be refilled.

I'd thought I might as well enjoy myself as I watched the swaying hips of the serving girl.

And I had enjoyed myself, thankfully. For now, arrayed before our combined force is the might of England. No matter how much Constantin, Olaf, and his subordinate kings laugh and joke at the English ineptitude and strut around their tents, talking of how many men they'll kill and how Constantin will be rewarded when Jorvik is recaptured, I'm far more pessimistic.

The plans for my death have, it would seem, by Constantin's determination to send me into the heart of the battle, been made. I accept them. One of my sons will inherit, and so the ruling line will, at least, continue, even if I'm turning to dust in my grave. Constantin will approve my son's succession and dictate policy to him so that he'll be even more of a figurehead to sop the complaints of the people of Strathclyde.

If Constantin lives, that is. He is, after all, a bloody old bastard.

30

937, BRUNANBURH, THE KINGDOM OF THE ENGLISH

Constantin, king of the Scots

I don't trust Olaf Gothfrithson. I know it, and so does he. Allies and enemies are far too easy to interchange at will. He might be married to my beloved daughter, but that doesn't make him my son. Not yet.

The jumped-up little upstart appears to have forgotten who I am and has overlooked that I've almost as many links to the petty kingdoms of his homeland as he does. I was raised in Dublin following my father's untimely death, which coincided with my ill-omened birth. I've allies there. Probably ones Olaf doesn't even know about. One of my sons, Cellach, is half-Irish.

Olaf's kingdom, Dublin, is a tiny part of Tara, or Ireland as many now name it. Amongst his allies, he might count the king of the Islands and the son of the king of Denmark. He might also try and suggest that the king of Limerick, Olaf Scabbyhead, is also his ally. But we all know Olaf's his prisoner, forced to bring his men to fight for Olaf Gothfrithson, for fear that their lord might die before we can reach the battle sight if not.

I might have only one ally, but at least I know Owain of Strathclyde. I know he's mostly a harmless fool. And a coward.

And really, Owain's not my only ally, for I have my sons and grandsons with me. I trust them implicitly. They've no cause to work against me, for if I die here, there's no assurance that any of them will be king after me. Mael Coluim would claim the kingdom, just as I took it from his father. As is the way of our people.

The kingship of the kingdom of the Scots doesn't function in the way of the English kingdom. Just because my sons and grandsons are royally born doesn't automatically make them throne worthy, as the English decree the sons of kings. No, my successor has been nipping at my heels ever since my accession, my cousin Mael Coluim. For the first time in our long years together, I've left him behind to govern in my absence. He eyes my impending death with relish. And that's all to the good because the more he wants my kingdom, the more my sons and grandsons work to keep me alive.

And some of them have already fought against Athelstan. When Athelstan shot through my lands, his forces more akin to the Viking raiders than the sedate English king I see before me today, with his massive tents and masses of supply wagons, my sons and grandsons raced to counter his actions. I count myself lucky that they survived the encounters with the English force. Well, all of them apart from one grandson. I will mourn my lost grandson, Amlaib, for the rest of my life. Why, I think, did I get so many winters and he so few?

Ildulb is the son with the greatest hatred for Athelstan, and he's the son I'm trusting with the most important role of all on the battlefield: keeping Owain of Strathclyde loyal and ensuring that he doesn't run at the first opportunity. Owain suspects me, just as much as I distrust him. This uneasy accord between us is coming to an end. At least, I hope it is. It would be ideal to have Olaf back at Jorvik, and Owain of Strathclyde dead, all from one battle.

If Owain should die, and I confess, I hope he does, by fair means or foul, it's Ildulb who'll rally the remaining warriors. Ildulb is a man who understands the way other men think. They admire and respect him, even when they don't want to. In the press of this battle, they'll turn to him as a drowning man does to the flotsam of the sea.

Ildulb hates Athelstan with the passion all men discover when they lose something they love. Amlaib, a boy of fewer than seventeen winters, lost his life fighting another youth, Edmund, Athelstan's stepbrother.

Since then, for three long years, my oldest son, the brightest of all my sons, has been withdrawn and moody, quick to anger and even swifter to raise his sword against any who go against him. He forced me to this alliance with Olaf Gothfrithson. I might not thank him for it, but if nothing else, this is Ildulb's chance for revenge. I know he'll take it, and I pray to God that it brings him some peace.

'Father.' Ildulb bows his head low as he comes towards me, the top of his head bare as he holds his polished helm under his left arm. As I said, he's a good son, he treats me with honour, and of everyone here, I'm the only one to whom he'll listen.

Ildulb's dressed for the coming fight. Our meeting, when Olaf has already rejoined his men, is merely the final confirmation of our plans. Ildulb's tall and long in the arm and leg, his reach surpassing that of many other men. He uses his length gracefully and chillingly. He knows how to kill. Ildulb is feared by all who know him, be they enemy or ally.

'Am I still to have the honour of fighting at the front with Owain of Strathclyde?' Ildulb manages not to sneer Owain's name. His anger at his son's death has turned him against all cowards. Owain's initial reluctance to fight with me, as our treaty dictates, still rankles.

'Yes, you do. You'll take your warriors and fight amongst Owain and his men. I don't expect treachery, nor do I anticipate him to fight to the best of his abilities. I fear he saw me eying up Dyfnwal when I went to round him up.' I speak with a sneer. I'd sooner Owain had no idea of my intentions. But perhaps I'm not as underhand as I used to be.

'Is Dyfnwal here?' Ildulb queries, his jaw firm.

'No, he's stayed to rule in his father's stead. Dyfnwal is as much a coward as his father.'

Ildulb's hooded eyes lighten at the taunt. I can't deny I'm pleased to see him show some emotion other than anger and hatred. 'He'll make an excellent puppet king once Owain is gone.'

'Then ensure that happens.'

Ildulb nods in understanding but never quite meets my eye. For a brief moment, I wonder if I've miscalculated in taking him into my confidence.

Does he think himself above me, having forced me to the alliance with Olaf Gothfrithson? Surely not. And yet?

'It'll be my pleasure,' Ildulb finally mutters, openly provoking me with raised eyebrows and a mischievous grin. A scar marks the right side of his face, gained from a battle in his youth when he fought with the Viking raider, Rognavaldr Ivarrson, the man who claimed Jorvik before Sihtric, and my father's brother. Ildulb learned much from the wily Viking raider, but still, Rognavaldr's dead, so perhaps he wasn't that good of a warrior after all, like my father. When Ildulb smiles, the scar stretches tightly, making it appear more like a grimace than a mark of happiness.

'Good. It should be,' I respond, but as he turns, I experience a moment of premonition. Before he can leave my sight, I reach out and grab him, smothering this giant son in my arms, unheeding his byrnie that presses into my softening body with cold patches of metal.

My arms tangle in his shield, where it's held in place down his back. I note the colours of our homeland, green and blue with a fleck of purple. I'm grateful he thought to arm all our men in a similar way. They'll be easier to differentiate in the middle of the battle. Ildulb returns the unexpected embrace before walking away, not looking back.

He's my first-born son. My oldest child, and may God help Athelstan if he takes his life. The man will never know peace again if he should harm another member of my family. He's taken too much from me already. A son. My daughter. My grandson. It ends here, now, or I will never know peace either.

31

937, BRUNANBURH, THE KINGDOM OF THE ENGLISH

Edmund, ætheling and prince of the English

The men of the witan are severe and excited in equal measure. This battle must be a victory for everyone in this canvas erected near the boundary of the old Mercian kingdom. For all the joking of the brother ealdormen and Athelstan's good cheer, I know that the weight of this battle rests heavily upon him.

Never one to doubt himself, not once in his thirteen years as king, my stepbrother now looks haunted, no matter how hard he tries to mask it. I glance between Ealdorman Athelstan and his brothers, and they return my stare. They know Athelstan as well as I do, for all that he likes to think he's unreadable and inscrutable.

But there's only one thing for it, to plan and prepare. There's no going back from this battle, and whether Athelstan's scops from far distant lands sing our praises or lament our demise, this slaughter field will be remembered for many long years and talked about for even more. Never before have so many enemies amassed in one place. Not during my grandfather's stand to save Wessex. Not during the fight between his cousin, Lord Æthel-wold, and my father for the throne of Wessex. Never.

Ealdorman Athelstan sidles over to where I stand, slightly behind and to the right of my brother. As soon as I was old enough to attend the witan, my brother instructed me to adopt such a position. It's the only instruction the king has ever given me. Everything else has been gentle guidance so that I act as he hopes. Athelstan doesn't like to issue me with directives. He doesn't wish everyone to see me as his image made flesh again. The king wants me to be unique and my own man.

'Your brother looks keen to engage,' Ealdorman Athelstan offers.

'He is, yes. He has unfinished affairs with King Constantin and new issues to conclude with the Dublin Norse warrior, Olaf Gothfrithson.'

'So I understand. And you? What of your unfinished affairs?'

I tense at his words, for all that they're kindly meant. He knows me as well as his siblings. We're brother warriors, for all they're much older than I am.

'I'll see that I finish what I can and avoid the worst of him.'

'Good, and I'll have my brothers as your constant companions. They'll not let the old bugger Constantin anywhere near you, should he attempt to fight, or his son, Ildulb, who will certainly be warring against the English.'

I look at him in surprise. I'd not expected such care for my person. Ealdorman Athelstan doesn't meet my eye as he speaks, his tone firm, allowing for no argument. Perhaps this isn't concern for me, but a way of ensuring his future.

Angrily, I shake my head. I know that in a case of life or death, Ealdorman Athelstan would give his life for me. I should never doubt his intentions. He's not only my ally, but my cousin through marriage as well, having married Ælfwynn, the daughter of Lady Æthelflæd of Mercia, the aunt I never knew.

'My thanks, Ealdorman Athelstan,' I hear myself say, and I mean it. Athelstan, my brother and king, has taken it upon himself not to discuss with me my involvement in the death of Constantin's grandson three summers ago in the run-up to this new engagement. The ealdorman shows less restraint.

I think the king knows that the king of the Scots, and his son, will be seeking my death in retaliation. I also reason he's decided the safest way to deal with the problem is to disregard it and never voice it. That way, it can't happen. My stepbrother's naivety over certain matters is laughable. Trust Athelstan, his namesake and ealdorman, to think about the matter more. I imagine that it's plagued him ever since he received his summons from the king. I suspect my cousin, his wife, has spoken to him about the potential complications.

In front of us, I sense King Athelstan's shoulders stiffen a little at our words. No doubt he's heard them, and dismay has briefly clouded his face. But he doesn't turn. I step forward and place my hand on his shoulder. He relaxes at the touch.

What a fool I am to think he forgets. More than likely, it's he who's arranged for Ealdorman Athelstan's brothers to stand as my minders again. Equally, it's probably thanks to him that Ealdorman Athelstan spoke to me of it. The king is concerned with even the smallest details of the impending battle. The king knows where everyone should be and when he or she should be there.

The king's hand reaches up and over his shoulder to grasp mine, his grip firm and powerful. And then our focus is on the coming battle. The remaining ealdormen and leaders of the king's household troops enter the tent, expressions ranging from serious to cheerful to terrified etched on to their sleep-drawn faces.

The king has instructed the ealdormen not to send their young sons and heirs to counter the threat from the Dublin Norse, the Scots and the warriors of Strathclyde. But the glory of England is under attack, and it would have been an impossible task for them to keep their sons at home. All those who can hold a shield, sword, seax or spear have joined the expedition north.

Æthelwald and Eadric, Ealdorman Athelstan's brothers, watch me intently. We've fought together before. We'll do the same today. We've joked and laughed on the training ground, and before this meeting came to order. But now all humour has fled Eadric.

Eadric and Æthelwald are similar in appearance to Athelstan, although Eadric is broader and Æthelwald narrower. I wonder if they worried that I'd reject their brother's words and demand he holds them away from me.

And then I consider why they told me at all. Perhaps it was so that my heart would cease beating quite so fast, and I'd stop thinking about my impending death, real or imagined as it might be.

The tension beneath the canvas crackles as though thunder might rumble overhead at any moment. The day is bright, the trill of birdsong impossible to ignore, the salty smell of the sea on everyone's lips. But today will be a dark day. It'll be one of pain, death and sorrow. And it is unavoidable.

Guthrum, whom Athelstan spoke of earlier, is a great giant of a man, proud of his Viking raider ancestry. He's perhaps the most liberal and civil of the men within the small space, excluding the king, of course. Guthrum's older than us all and has been one of Athelstan's ealdormen since the beginning, an early convert when Athelstan was merely Mercia's king and not the king of the English. For all that we joked about Guthrum earlier, I'd be honoured to have the huge man fighting beside me, as would any of us. He's made it to York and back almost in the time it's taken us to arrive here from Nottingham. I knew Guthrum wouldn't wish to miss the battle, when it came. Perhaps he hoped to defeat the coalition, if they headed towards York, alone. Now he's had to race to this place instead, and fight alongside the king and the other ealdormen, bishops and battle commanders.

Guthrum's weapon of choice is his fist, followed by his war axe. He was taught to fight by his father and grandfather, men of direct Viking raider descent in the Danelaw. He can do things with a shield, an axe and his fist that make men's eyes water and emulate at their peril. Even now, he teaches me new techniques to employ, and I thank him every time. I think Guthrum must know a hundred ways to kill a man.

Ealdormen Ælfwold and Uhtred are the two men currently highest in the king's affection. They're as dissimilar as it's possible to be. I know Athelstan values them so highly precisely because of their diverse natures. They speak their minds, always reasoned and concise, but still two sides of the same coin. They have their elite household troops at their command and lead the fyrds. They'll take the difficult positions on the flank of the main attack, and neither will dare to disappoint their king.

Not all the ealdormen are here, deliberately so. Osulf and Scule have been commanded to hold position close to the royal court in Winchester.

Should the worse befall us, they'll stand between any daring attacks into the deep south, either by land or sea, and the rest of the Wessex royal family. My younger brother is ready and able to be crowned king if the need should arise. Eadred took me aside before we left. Disgruntled to be forced to remain behind, I was relieved when he assured me he had no desire to be king.

Other men are here, too, even some of the more aggressive churchmen, with their battle equipment in place and strange half-enlightened expressions on their faces. I hope that God has spoken to them kindly this morning.

Bishop Theodred of London is amongst us, as is Alfred of Sherborne, Cenwold of Worcester and Oda, a man who should have been a warrior first and foremost but who instead is a warrior of God. They're militant men.

Whether the king approves or not, it's difficult to say. I think he prefers the bishops to keep to their monasteries and churches, but their presence amongst us does add another layer of righteousness to our cause. A divine righteousness, and Athelstan believes that our God works in mysterious ways to show approval for his actions.

Cousins Ælfwine and Æthelwine, grandsons of Alfred, just as I am, are in attendance. They're a step or two further away from the ruling family and, as such, not quite throne worthy, although their father was. They're great warriors. Intriguingly, they have the trust of the king, whereby the king's oldest stepbrother did not, but then my cousins don't want Athelstan's kingdom, and never did. They'll happily fight at his side for the good of our people and their kingdom. They wear the colours of the House of Wessex on their byrnies, shields and weapons, the reds, yellows and blacks of the wyvern. They're men of Wessex first and then Englishmen second.

Athelstan urgently calls the meeting to order, but before he can utter another word, one of the outriders races into the tent, barely dismounting in time to avoid colliding with the wooden struts of the canvas. King Athelstan nods to show he should speak.

'My lord king,' the man begins, panting heavily, but Athelstan waves aside his flattering speech. Accustomed to his king's ways, the outrider starts his message. 'The enemy's getting ready. Olaf Gothfrithson and

Constantin of the Scots have donned their battle gear and their men form the line of the shield wall.'

Athelstan takes the words well for all it means he's lost the initiative which he was keen to maintain. He takes a breath and looks at the assembled crowd. We're all so silent, we can hear, from far distant, the sound of the seabirds calling one to another as they fish amongst the incoming tide.

'Gentlemen, we all know where we should be and how to win the coming battle. This meeting was a chance for final words, and we don't need them. Go, ready your warriors and yourselves. Remember, we fight for what's ours against men who don't keep their word and who are fickle in their allegiances. Rid our land of this menace, and do so with our lord God's blessing.' Athelstan's voice doesn't rise as he speaks, but his fierce determination lends a threat to the gently uttered words that shouting them wouldn't have accomplished.

The men cheer all the same, while the holy men add their amens and stride confidently from the aborted meeting. Ealdorman Athelstan grins at me as he walks past but doesn't speak. His confidence bolsters me. Behind, I feel his brothers take up their preferred positions.

I glance at my brother, the king, and he, too, smiles. Calmness sweeps through me. My earlier humour has been masking my fears, but now I'm ready for whatever might come today.

Armed with everything I need, I sweep my shield onto my arm, noticing dispassionately that it's weighted perfectly, with a new layer of paint bright and fresh on its surface. All will know that I'm a man firmly behind the king and a member of his family when they see those colours of red, yellow and black with the wyvern of Wessex depicted on the shield. My chest swells with pride as I step into the brightening day.

All around me, others mirror my actions, emerging from tents, fully armed, with shields, swords, arrows, bows and spears either in hand or around their battle belts. There's a glint of metal from the iron rivulets woven into war coats as the sun climbs ever higher in the blue sky.

Men are silent or quiet as they talk to their comrades. Many know they'll not survive the day but whom those will be is God's doing, so Athelstan has assured me with the confidence born of a man whose life was once saved by the blessed intervention of Saint Cuthbert, and his holy words.

32

937, BRUNANBURH, THE KINGDOM OF THE ENGLISH

Olaf Gothfrithson, king of the Dublin Norse

My allies mill around me in confusion. My frustration starts to boil. What started earlier as the advantage of surprise has quickly dwindled away to nothing. The English are lining up as orderly as they've made their camp. They form up almost silently, the quiet making the men more belligerent to be ready.

If the English would only come in a rush and howl of rage, then I know that these warriors of mine would be ready in the blink of an eye. Instead, the Englishmen's soundless passage has fooled all of my warriors into thinking that this isn't the beginning of a battle, that somehow it's more a display of weapons than anything else. That this is posturing, not war.

My warriors argue and curse each other. None make natural allies. They're too used to being enemies. But they assured me they'd put their differences aside for this attack. Apparently, they bloody lied.

At my side, my commanders, my brothers and son are as silent as the English, for all fury blazes on their faces. They're ready and keen to get on with the fighting. Even Anlaf Sihtricson's prepared. Constantin and his less than reliable ally, Owain, stand ready. I feel their watchful eyes on me. I'm trying not to meet the heat of their gazes. I cannot explain the confusion before me.

Ivarr, the proud son of the new king of Denmark, busily argues with anyone who steps too close to him. He'll be no help in the shield wall if he doesn't allow one of the other kings to fight alongside him. I don't much like him, but he brought great wealth and a full ship of warriors when he washed up on my shore at the beginning of the year. I thought his arrival a sign that my aggressive stance towards the English had garnered the support of the Danish king. I'm far from convinced of that now.

I was loath to turn him away, although now I'm starting to wish I had. Perhaps there was some truth to the later rumours that Ivarr had been sent away by his father, King Gorm, Ivarr's arrogance undermining his father's hard work in the newly conquered kingdom. I see that now.

Even Ivarr's battle wear shouts of his self-importance. His clothing is littered with precious metals. Silver and gold run through his mail rings, even though they're soft metals, more likely to be pierced by swords, axes and arrows. He should be ensconced in iron, not gold. His shield has an enormous gold boss at its centre, and from it sprays of golden rays stretch to its edges. I hope that the gold is just a coating, but I doubt it. I can't see Ivarr surviving the day, but mayhap his father will thank me for ridding him of the menace. Providing I'm still victorious, I can't truly argue with that.

Gebeachan, the king of the Islands, finds the entire situation with the prickly young prince far too enjoyable. Every time that Ivarr looks ready, with his weapons arranged as he wants them around his weapons belt, Gebeachan steps just too close to him, knocking his arm, and the entire debacle starts again. Once more, I wish that the English would just rush across the space between us and launch the attack. But they won't. I imagine they're too honourable to advance before everyone is ready. Bloody fools.

Finally, I can take it no more.

'Deal with it,' I urge my brother, Rognavaldr. He strides towards the two men holding up the formation of our shield wall. No sooner has my brother reached Ivarr, forcing him close to Gebeachan, than Ivarr's angry, twisted face looks my way. But in no time at all, he's lined up amongst his men and next to Gebeachan. The king of the Islands is given no time to smirk at his seeming triumph, for Rognavaldr speaks to him just as harshly. Suddenly, he too is ready and equipped, his men in formation around him, their chosen weapons to hand, as they hold their shields loosely or rest them against their lower legs.

I glower at the pair. If they should live through today, I'll punish them both for their antics. Of all the men here, the earls who serve under me, and the petty kings I oversee, it's these two who have caused the most trouble. There are many men and untried youths but none more challenging than Ivarr and Gebeachan.

Signalling to Constantin's waiting messenger that my allies are finally ready, I avoid the knowing sneer on Constantin's face where he watches from a vantage point to the rear of the coming fight. I eye the quantity of men he has now that I can focus on them. I'm pleasantly surprised at the number. Not only is Owain there with the men from Strathclyde, centred on the enemy and keen to engage, but at least two of Constantin's sons also lead their warriors. Even some of Constantin's grandsons have joined the battle.

Constantin is a man rich in descendants, and yet it's Mael Coluim who'll rule when he's gone. I'd like to change that, have my sons with his daughter, when they're born, rule in place of their grandfather or uncles, but I know better than that. I'm perplexed as to why Mael Coluim isn't here. I understand he's in Dunnotar, or perhaps Scone, ruling in place of Constantin. I can't believe Constantin would trust him, but perhaps Constantin wants his son by his side, more than he'd rather see Mael Coluim dead.

Constantin has his standard-bearer wave the green, purple and blue flag in acknowledgement of my readiness. I finally turn my attention to the amassed English.

What started with us having the element of surprise has dwindled to no initiative at all. The enemy arrayed before us is just as many in number as we are. Our lines stretch along their huge length of over five hundred men, three and four men deep.

I note where the English king is positioned, ready and waiting, but to the rear of the main force. I consider whether he means to fight alongside his men or whether, like Constantin, he'll direct from the rear. I can't see Athelstan refusing to engage.

I also seek out the object of Constantin and Ildulb's anger, the young Edmund. But I can't see him, although I suspect he stands to the front, surrounded by his brother's most trusted warriors.

This is where the main charge from Ildulb and Owain will be directed. Squinting into the growing daylight, it appears the English king has taken more than sufficient precautions. Here, the number of men swells, the ends of the shield wall the weakest elements. But I imagine such an illusion is merely that. The English king has fought many battles in his time.

Behind the English is a line of raised turf, and the scouts have informed us that this is more of a hill than we would at first think from our current position, where the ground lies level. They warn that the ground can be marshy, between the two rivers and with the sea almost at our backs. The hill will be difficult to crest should the English retreat that far because the ground dips low before it. We'll face a steep climb. We must ensure that the battle is over before that happens.

We have a small force of men held in reserve, under the leadership of another of Constantin's sons. If we need them, and time marches on that far, they'll infiltrate the area between the English and this paltry hill. We'll not let the enemy climb out of our reach.

Across the divide separating the two forces, I see a man push his way through the tightly packed English shield wall, surrounded by ten heavily armed warriors. Another carries a banner of the English king, the wyvern of Wessex and the eagle of Mercia intertwined in a riot of bright colours. My eyes roll in frustration. Does this English king have to do everything that's deemed honourable? Couldn't he just let the fight commence without the need to attempt a settlement at this late stage?

At my side, my son's as impatient as me.

'Will this thing never sodding start?' he mutters darkly, his face turned away from me. I can imagine it scowling in contempt. Camman has grown to be a youth with little patience.

'All in good time,' I caution, although, like him, I share the same frustration, and my words are snapped.

A small wave of chanting begins from the rear of the force, started no doubt by my blood-hungry brother, Rognavaldr, returned to me from quelling the argument between my allies. He doesn't fear death and never has.

I raise my arm above my head to show that I agree with the eagerness of the warriors. The roar increases tenfold. Such simple things make the men realise that I'm the same as them. They will redouble their efforts to beat the English, knowing that I fight amongst them.

In between the two opposing forces, the spokesman and his entourage falter. I laugh, the sound echoing around me and magnifying as other voices join. A stray arrow, loosed by one of our few archers, lands quivering in the ground just in front of the feet of the man and his warriors.

For all that they're armed and hold weapons, with helms on their heads, they hesitate at this act of war and look uncertainly back towards where they know King Athelstan directs the engagement. Something passes between the spokesperson and the king, an acceptance, no doubt, that nothing will stop the fight. The man turns without making contact with our combined force, three of his warriors moving to protect his rear so that he can make his way back behind the safety of the shield wall without fearing an attack. Those three men move slowly, shields covering their bodies. It would be good if one of the warriors stumbled to the ground, allowing my warriors to laugh at his misfortune, but there's no such luck.

More and more arrows chase them towards the safety of their shield wall. I shake my head. It's a waste of good arrows.

The noise from my warriors grows louder and louder, the crash of seaxes and war axes on shields, the undulating cry of men who hunger for blood, and suddenly we're moving forward. Slowly but surely, this battle has been joined, and I don't know who finally gave the order, but it's about bloody time.

33

937, BRUNANBURH, THE KINGDOM OF THE ENGLISH

Athelstan, king of the English

My heart's beating too fast. I seek calmness. We're ready for this. Far more prepared than the rabble we face. I meet the eyes of Sigelac and Flodwin, the one dour, the other grinning. Both of them nod, assured in their skills and in mine.

The enemy may well have rebuffed the overtures of peace offered by Bishop Oda, much to his consternation, but I expected nothing else. I warned him, but he wanted to try. Being a most Christian king, I had no choice but to give the word of God a chance.

Now Bishop Oda knows, as I did, that our enemy isn't interested in peace, only bloodshed and victory for themselves. I'll not be giving it to them.

The first arrows have flown from their side. They've not hit any target yet, but their intent is clear.

Purposefully, I've arranged the battlefield so that weak spots appear self-evident. In reality, there aren't any, but I'll use guile to trick them if I must. They think me honourable, which makes me foolish. I am honourable, but I want victory even more than they do.

In front, Edmund commands a combination of household troops and members of the Mercian fyrd. There's little difference between the skills of the warriors. The Mercians are so used to fighting against their enemies that even those who think themselves no more than farmers and would arm themselves with nothing but a hammer or a hunting bow and arrow are more skilled than men trained since birth to wield the weapons of war in the calmer southern lands.

The Mercians are merciless and will fight to the death. As will Edmund, alongside Eadric and Æthelwald.

From behind, I can feel our handful of archers mount the small rise that we might use as a mustering point, or retreat to, or just drag our enemies to so that they perish in the ditch we've deepened from the naturally occurring ones and filled with sharpened stakes of wood. For now, the archers will unleash a rain of arrows onto the heads of the enemy. Hopefully, one or two of the foemen may flee in fear, perhaps causing a rout. The opportunistic arrows may cut down one or two more.

The enemy cheers derisively as their spears and arrows quiver in the bare ground before us. But their cheers quickly turn to cries of fear as the first arrows from my archers whistle amongst them. The raising of their shield wall resounds as an echo of wood and clang of iron, audible long after the action has been accomplished. Now they realise we mean to beat them here today.

We might be more organised than them, but that doesn't mean we're less blood-hungry. Far from it. We've taken the time to train for this eventuality. This isn't an opportunistic attempt to land grab, not like the bloody Scots and the Dublin Norse. We will defend England.

One or two men fall untidily from the long, ragged line of the foemen that face me, arrows protruding from exposed throats and shoulders. My well-trained warriors cheer and shout insults at the enemy. Slowly, step by step, the advance begins. We're taking the battle to them.

Olaf Gothfrithson and King Constantin's men are a strange collection of all shapes and sizes. The colour of their skin varies from the pale white of the northern lands to the darker tan of the native Irish and every shade in between. There's every hue of hair colour and every shade of shield and clothing. I wonder what they think of the uniform shields they face, all painted with the eagle of Mercia and the wyvern of Wessex and its colours of black, yellow and red. These are now the emblem of the English king.

I offer a prayer to God that my brother will fight as well as he can and that, tonight, we'll sit and talk about the day's bloody work together. I pray to God that all my ealdormen, warriors and military bishops will live through the battle.

And I just manage not to utter a prayer calling for Constantin's death. He's a man of God just as I am. As much as I loathe him for his false oaths, I know he acts in the belief that he's doing the correct thing for his people.

Pity he's not as principled as Hywel of the South Welsh in his actions, but even Hywel has been distant of late. He, at least, had the grace to seek me out himself and tell me of his fears and hopes occasioned by the words being spread of discontent between the Welsh and their kings because of the English alliance. While Hywel isn't with me here, I hope he manages to find the man responsible for these problems, the scop with his call to arms for the Welsh kingdoms, being hunted, even now, and for the last year. I would know if his actions are the work of King Constantin or just badly timed happenstance.

When we vanquish our enemies here, I'll not exact further concessions from Hywel but will labour to woo him back to my court if for no other reason than I miss talking to him. He's an intelligent man and has had the luck to travel long distances in his lifetime.

I like to hear tales of his trip to the land of the papacy and the communities he visited along the way. I envy him. I have my mass of relics sent from across the Narrow Sea and collected within the lands of the English, but to have visited the holiest of places is something about which I can only dream.

I console myself with a fragment of the holy cross, with a thorn from the holy crown, but in my heart, it's never enough to sate my religious fervour. I want to see it all.

And the other kings of the Welsh? When I win this fight, and I will win this fight, our alliance will become even more stringent than before. While they unwillingly bent the knee and added their names to the peace treaty signed at Hereford almost ten summers ago, they've grown less and less likely to adhere to the terms imposed on them. Perhaps I shouldn't have ordered Hywel, Idwal and Owain to fight against the Scots in the north three summers ago. Maybe they realised I wasn't to be feared, especially when I took no action to kill Alpin, the son of Constantin and a hostage to guarantee his father's good behaviour. Or perhaps the opposite. Maybe they know to fear me even more than before and now work to shore up their defences against the English. One thing is without doubt: once I'm proclaimed the victor against the Dublin Norse and Scots alliance, I'll impose my wishes far more severely over those who call themselves my allies but have abandoned me to face the Norse alone.

34

937, BRUNANBURH, THE KINGDOM OF THE ENGLISH

Edmund, ætheling and prince of the English

The press of bodies is just as I remember it from the brief battle in Cait. The smell. The fear. And the camaraderie. I fight with men I know and I've previously trained with, the brothers of Ealdorman Athelstan. I'm not in the front line holding my shield above another's head, but I'll be called upon to do so once the fighting is underway. I'm taller and stronger than when I travelled to Cait. I killed then and it took me a year not to see the eyes of the man whose life I took before I slept each night. But I've made my peace with what happened. I'm ready to fight for England. And, if I should be faced with Constantin or his son, Ildulb, I'll kill them too. Or anyone who looks like the two men.

As one, the English shuffle forward, a step at a time, unable to see in front because the man before us obscures the view. None wishes to poke their head high above another's. It would make them an easy target for enemy spear throwers, given the specific task of attacking those foolish enough to make such a mistake. I know we have warriors tasked with the same.

The ground's firm beneath my feet. Here it's far from marshy, as it is close to the small hill. It's been a dry summer, although the land hasn't baked under intense heat. It's been free from torrential rains, not necessarily warm. I wonder if the ground will be sodden with streams of gleaming blood later. I hope so. But I also pray it's not mine or any of these men who've chosen to stand with me.

To my right and left, Ealdorman Athelstan's brothers flank me. They're mean, keen warriors. They look the part. They're men who take their warrior skills seriously. They train every day. They run, spar and devise their own weapons and watch the blacksmith create them. Everything they possess has been made to fit them; no other man can heft the sword of Eadric in the same way he can, for none needs the heaviest part of the weapon to fall exactly in the centre of its long length. No one can grip the handle of Æthelwald's war axe, for his hands are so large that it would be impossible for another to force their hand to meet on the other side.

Around me, my fellow warriors are far from silent. Cries of derision fly from mouths, final words of wisdom from others, and from yet more I hear the softly muttered prayers of those seeking God's help. Not everyone speaks my tongue or with my accent, but we're the English and we fight together.

I remain silent. My resolve is total. I'll not die here, I won't allow it, but I'll fight until I know my death's imminent, and only then withdraw to the safety of the rear of the shield wall. My honour demands it for my king.

The advance ends abruptly as a crashing wave of wood and iron reverberates. The enemy shield wall has been met.

Now, the hustle and struggle begins in earnest.

Before me, the rows of men brace themselves and start to push. Shields protect the head of the men at the front, held there by the men behind them, until my position is reached. A little further back, there are fewer shields and more spears on display, as well as a handful of archers. These men let loose their weapons. As a rain of thunder, I hear them thud amongst the enemy. Some of the missiles crack on wood, but others make a wetter sound. I cheer them, for they've found a target.

A cry from the rear of our attack. All shields rise instantly. Arrows and spears crash down on the temporary shield roof. My arm quivers with the weight of one of the arrows embedded in it.

A further cry and shields remain in place. Another rain thrums down. Beside me, Æthelwald shakes with the blow that's struck his shield.

'Bloody hell,' he shouts, shocked out of his stern demeanour, loud enough for me to hear but no one else.

'Keep it raised until we hear the order,' I holler, knowing he'll instinctively want to lower it and remove the projectile, just as I do.

Nodding vigorously, Æthelwald holds. His shield hovers partially above his head and that of the man in front, sweat gleaming on his face, for all the day is still young.

Eadric hits my arm to get my attention. I glance his way. He's smiling, the joy of battle upon him, as he holds his shield. I see little of his face behind the elaborate helm that covers the top of his head and runs down his cheekbones, covering his nose. He resembles a creature from a nightmare, snake-like, with scales etched into the fine metal. His helm's dull black, the shimmer of iron rubbed away. When he grins, as he does now, his white teeth and blood-red tongue mark him as an animal.

No cry informs us that we can lower our shields. My arm, more used to holding a sword than a shield, quivers under strain. I curse myself for not thinking to work in this position more often when I was training. Perhaps, when fighting Louis, gone now to be the king of the West Franks, we could have ensured our ability to hold in such an awkward stance. I miss Louis. But he's a king now, and I'm a prince. I imagine he has others to do his fighting for him, especially against those who might think to steal his kingdom.

Finally, the cry comes. Almost as one, the men lower their shields, quickly removing the arrows and spears embedded within them. I detach two arrows cleanly, but Æthelwald struggles with the spear in his. It's deeply rooted, and after a few frantic moments, he just snaps the wooden shaft as close to the linden board as possible, leaving the point of the spear behind. He curses loudly. It'll be a bugger to fight with his shield now that its weighting has been disturbed.

Before I can speak, the men in front of me surge forward two steps. I follow to ensure our arrangement remains tight and secure. I spare a moment for the men who must have fallen at the front line and consider how long the battle has lasted so far. It feels as though I've barely taken two breaths, but I know that time moves strangely within the shield wall.

Frantic activity alerts me to something occurring ahead. I watch with a strange fascination as a man's body is manhandled back through the ranks. When he reaches me, I notice the bloody wounds on his face, revealing the bones of his skull and where his sword hand hangs loosely. Red pulses slowly from it, although his sword remains clutched in his other arm.

His pained grey eyes flicker open to glance at me, and a smile stretches across his face.

'You should have seen the other bastard, my lord,' he mutters before his face clouds with agony, as he passes me on his way to where help might ensure he lives. I wonder if the man will live and quickly pray for him. Either way, he's pleased with how he fought. Other men will already be dead, face down amongst the crushing feet of the two sides. We may never know their identities when they're finally pulled free from the mass of broken bones, bloody limbs and concave faces, unrecognisable to friend and foe alike.

I hold out the hope that the enemy has already exhausted their supply of arrows, but I doubt it. They mean to trick us into making a catastrophic mistake. A shout from the rear, and my shield is once more above my head and the man in front. More thudding arrows, more cries of anguish, and a rush forward two steps. Either we're losing men too quickly, or the other side is struggling to hold against us. I consider how many quick steps forward will happen before it's my turn to face our enemy. To meet Constantin's son. To face his wrath for killing his son.

I wish I knew who was winning the opening foray.

Eadric hollers beside me, 'I think we must be cutting them down like wheat with a scythe.'

I admire his comparison.

'I believe you're correct,' Æthelwald roars, 'but they've far more arrows than I thought.'

Æthelwald's accurate. I only hope my brother has noted this development and changed his tactics accordingly. Athelstan thought of every eventuality before the attack began.

A command from behind, and we lower our shields. I didn't hear or feel the fresh arrow sticking out from the top of my shield, but I'm glad for the warning we've been given. Removing the arrow, I force myself not to look above the mass of bowed heads before me. My brother has assured me that if the position looks bleak, as much as he doubted it, he'll pull me out from my place amongst the men. I trust him implicitly and dismiss the thought. This was always going to be a long and tiring battle. The strength of the two sides is similar. We employ the same battle tactics. That's why we need tricks and subterfuge to win here. We could all fight the best we've ever fought, but when men with identical weapons meet in battle, with equal numbers and the same hopes, only a mistake on the part of one of the sides can lead to victory. I need to concentrate and think only of my next move, not what lies ahead. My brother, King Athelstan, has devised his battle strategies, and he'll be victorious.

Another cry from behind. I raise my shield, arms shrieking at the movement before my shield is even in place. I grit my teeth and think of myself somewhere else where my arms aren't being abused in such a way.

Where are all these bloody arrows coming from?

35

937, BRUNANBURH, THE KINGDOM OF THE ENGLISH

Owain, king of Strathclyde

I'm in the thick of it. My men surround me, but we're fighting for our lives, not our kingdom. In fact, my kingdom will be safe and secure no matter what happens here. And anyway, they'll probably be going home, unlike me.

My arms ache with the weight of my shield and sword. I'm more than aware of the scrutiny that King Constantin's son, Ildulb, has me under, but I try to push it aside. I'm not yet ready to die, and while the fighting is so fierce, he has no opportunity to slide his blade into my body. Not without risking his death by breaking up the ordered fighting.

Beneath my feet, the ground's slick with the blood of my fallen and injured warriors.

I came here with nearly five hundred men, and already some of them lie dead or dying. These English are confident and clever warriors. The rumours, brought to me by those with knowledge of the battle at Cait, were true.

We've lost about ten or fifteen steps since our forces first met, by my reckoning, but I imagine we've lost more men than that. I can only see those close to me, not those behind or to the left or right. We need reinforcements, of that I'm sure. I'm far from convinced that Constantin will send any. He hungers for my death, as his determination that I should fight this battle for him has made clear. Never before have I been forced to fight for my overlord. Never before have I been sure that he wished to see the end of me. This'll be the perfect opportunity to bring it about without it being deemed his fault.

A ragged cry from in front of me, and the man who so recently stood there, a man I've known for over fifteen winters, lies bloody and dead at my feet. His familiar face garishly split into two, one side hanging loosely from the thick neck he had, the other pulsing blood all over my booted feet. Grief clouds my vision for only a moment as I offer hasty words of goodbye to him before being forced to abandon him to the stamping feet of the horde of warriors. I doubt I'll recognise his body by the end of the battle.

I step into his place, dismissing the final image of him from my thoughts.

The crash of a sword on wood reverberates up my arm; the whoosh of arrows above my head would be terrifying if I could spare a moment to consider the danger I'm facing. I feel the dull thud of a sword on my shield and remove my war axe from my weapons belt, exchanging it for my sword. I've never liked the sword. No, an axe is my preferred weapon despite its shorter reach.

I lower the shield, curious to know who'll be the object of my death. Dazzling blue eyes face me. An elaborate helm covers the hair, forehead and nose of my enemy, but his eyes pierce me. There's no malice there, just calculation, pure and simple. I take my time to consider my next move and the one after that.

Quickly, I grip my shield. The eyes I saw weren't those of a possessed killer, a man who revels in the thrust of battle, and yet the splashes of blood covering the man's face show me that he's killed and will kill again. But not me. I'll not die at the hands of the English rabble. I refuse.

Another impact on my shield. I lower it and swipe my axe at the man before me. He quickly ducks, labouring to remove his weapon from its temporary lodgement on my shield. He veers away from my wild swing, but

I wasn't as committed to the move as he thought. Expertly, I turn the axe back and smash into his head with the stump of my weapon.

His blue eyes blank. I keep a smile off my face. The enemy never expects me to use the axe's handle. With force behind it, I can quickly stun the best of men in such a way.

The foeman falls beneath my feet, made insensible by my blow, not killed by it. Immediately, another takes his place. I spare no thought for the man who still lives but who'll suffocate amongst the press of feet and other bodies. It won't be a pleasant death.

Hidden behind my shield again, I allow the thrill of the battle to take hold. I'll show bloody Constantin how well I fight.

A crack hums along my arm, but I've not yet recovered my breath enough to make another move. I'll shelter here for just thirty breaths, mindful that I can't stop for long, aware that I need to, all the same.

Either side of me, my warriors face our enemy. I recognise my brother-by-marriage, Donald, and my son-by-marriage, Rhodri. I grin at how well they fight. Their hair and faces are streaked with blood and other men's spit. Rhodri has a slash on the right side of his face that leaks down his cheek and onto his byrnie. He's tried to wipe it away but has merely managed to spread the blood further.

Like me, the pair didn't want this engagement, but they've every intention of walking away with their lives intact.

They slash with their weapons of choice. Rhodri has a bloodied seax. Donald a sword. They lower their shields to pierce the enemy. They aim to strike a limb from their opponent's body or pierce them where blood will flow too quickly to stop. They don't care what they hit as long as they hit something and the enemy falls at their feet.

I feel the surge of the enemy as a fierce wind and brace myself firmly on the damp ground beneath me, my shield securely held in place, hand gripped around the strapping. Only it's impossible. The ground's wet with blood and piss, the verdant grasses flattened by the passage of the feet of the warriors around me.

I place my shoulder against my shield, next to the men beside me on the left and right. With the press of the man behind me, we apply force. Our feet momentarily and unexpectedly hold firm on the ground. Perhaps we'll resist the threat from the enemy. Only then, the man to my left slips, his leg shooting out behind his body. As he slides and works to regain his balance, our opponent pushes against the weakness. I exert myself further, knowing the men behind me do the same.

We push, shove, and the man eventually regains his footing and is quickly back in place, his face covered in sweat and his hands shaking at his near miss.

The enemy continues to press us. My warriors groan with the effort.

'Attack.' A voice from behind – Constantin, I think, or perhaps one of his bloody sons – exhorts us to greater effort. They sound so alike I don't know them apart. All the same, I heave and strain along with those urged to fight better.

Not much longer, I think, my teeth gritted. The enemy won't persist with this tactic. It's too draining to stand shield wall to shield wall in such a way. Better to try something different. More arrows, perhaps. Or even a driving wedge through the heart of the shield wall to sacrifice those at the front to assist the others in surging through the line of defence.

Only then, an axe snakes its way around my shield. It slithers and bangs above the shield rim, trying to pull the shield free from my tightly clasped hand. Frantically, I realise this is a concerted attack. Simultaneously, the same happens to my fellow warriors, as the English attempt to force us backwards. The intent is clear, to use our dead allies and their discarded weapons to hamper us by cutting our lower legs and feet while our attention is focused on not losing our shields. We surge forwards and backwards, unable to look where we step.

The axe on my shield attempts to force it downwards to expose me to the blades of my foemen. I watch the axe with mild interest, trying not to let its closeness distract me. I must stand firm and keep the enemy away, even though my feet are busy beneath me. It feels as though the axe weighs more than two pounds of silver.

Men scream in rage and frustration. I consider why Constantin hasn't reinforced the line. There are surely enough reserves for many more to be arranged behind us, ready to add their strength to our defence.

The axe on the man's shield to my left works its way dangerously close to his shoulder and exposed face. If I were him, I'd be considering ducking away, removing my weight from the shield wall to evade an injury. That he doesn't do so is more to do with his impeccable training than his desire. His face is drained of colour, fear evident in his shaking stance, and still, he holds his ground.

One finger's length, and then another, the axe comes ever closer, rising and falling and crashing against the wood of the shield. I know fear, for if my comrade lets go of his shield, there'll be an opening through which the enemy can pour.

I roar for Constantin's son. Ildulb's name repeats itself over and over. It's he who commands the Scots warriors in the vanguard, and it's he who can decide to send reinforcements. I didn't like being told I wouldn't be the one to command my force, and now I like it even less.

'We need more men!' I bellow. 'Send the reinforcements!' Although others take up my cry, I can't tell whether anything is done about it.

I lose track of how much time passes, so focused on the axe around my neighbour's shield that I fail to notice that I'm also threatened.

Abruptly, pain floods my arm as I feel the bite of metal into my shoulder. My shocked, angry cry is loud.

My eyes should have been on my enemy, not that of my neighbour's.

I stumble, blood pooling down my arm. The warmth of my blood assures me my wound is deep.

Without looking I appreciate that more men have come to reinforce this stretch of the shield wall. I'm more grateful than I should be that Ildulb heard my cry.

I turn to shout my thanks, and at that moment, a great heave of effort comes from the enemy. I'm forced backwards. Holding my shield aloft and in place, I step back, once, twice, wincing at the stabs of pain from my wound. Somehow, I miss the body of a fallen man. With the help of the reinforcements, our defence stabilises. The press from the English force falls away.

They've gained two steps, but we hold our line firm now.

But the tension doesn't abate, and down my shoulder I can feel my blood draining from my body. It needs to stop, but unless someone relieves me, I can't leave my place or staunch the wound.

Behind me, men talk and shout, rough words offering encouragement and congratulations for not allowing the enemy to decimate our line. Whoever shouted 'attack' now demands that we 'hold'. To the left and right, my Strathclyde warriors have disappeared. Straining my neck further, I turn to where Donald was fighting before the English tried to force the battle to a quick conclusion, but he's no longer visible. Did all my men fall in the brief skirmish, and I failed to notice? Have they become victim to the sneaking tactics of the English? Did the axes and twisting seaxes of the enemy find purchase in their soft flesh?

Frantically, I struggle to see, but not one face do I recognise. Not one at all. Well, apart from Ildulb's, his dark eyes gleaming maliciously, blood marring his once handsome face, his teeth stained almost black with the blood of the dead and dying.

Perhaps I should have fallen victim to the Englishman's axe after all.

36

937, BRUNANBURH, THE KINGDOM OF THE ENGLISH

Constantin, king of the Scots

I'm watching from a vantage point, with the river at my back, to see how this first engagement with the enemy resolves itself. I'm not pleased. It's been mere moments, and already I fear for our chances of success. I'm almost grateful that I'm mounted and able to retreat should the need arise. I didn't want this to happen. This was all about success, but fear grips me. I'm an old man, perhaps too old to be driven by the need for vengeance.

My allies seem slow to react to anything King Athelstan and his men attempt. For every three steps the enemy advances, my warriors take four steps back.

I watch the action with disdain. Why I ever thought to trust Owain of Strathclyde with the first attack, I don't know. My dissatisfaction with him blinded me to his faults. Yes, I wish him dead but not at the expense of my victory. I ought to have given different commands to Ildulb, and been more reassuring to Owain. But Owain displeased me and needed to know. Feasibly, though, I should have waited until after the battle to make my stance clear. I've endured the hovering presence of Mael Coluim for all these years. I should have been able to tolerate Owain until the battle was won.

These English have some strange tactics. I thought it would be all shove, shield and sword, but they've more in their arsenal than that. They have spears, bows, arrows, and they've devised a way to ensure that my men always wonder what they'll try next. King Athelstan thinks quickly, assessing any slight weakness in our attack and rushing to take advantage of it. All they need to do now is mount up and attack my men from a saddle, and everything I thought I knew about the English warriors will prove wrong.

Not that I don't have bows and arrows. I do, I have many. My people are excellent hunters and our lands are filled with thick woods and roaming deer. Yet I imagine that for every arrow we've sent flying amongst the shield wall, they've sent double back. I'd hoped this would be a quick battle, our superior skills overwhelming anything the English could attempt. But, apparently, Athelstan has prepared his men for a long struggle. How did he know the strength of our force before even I did?

My archers are far from the fighting, near to me so that I can command them from my mounted position, but they shift uncomfortably. I know they're unhappy to be even this close. Every so often a stray arrow or spear from the enemy passes far too close to where we're stationed for anyone's comfort. The horse upon which I'm mounted has shied more than once, careering backwards and causing the archers to dance out of the way or risk being crushed beneath his heavy hooves.

Realising that I need my men and their arrows far more than I need an immediate victory, I signal the restless archers to retreat. I'll rest them for some time, while the men down at the front of the shield wall do their work. Ildulb is there, amongst the thick of the fighting. He'll force the warriors of Owain of Strathclyde to greater and greater efforts, happy for them all to drop from their wounds before our Scots warriors are bloodied.

I watch as dispassionately as possible, my eyes narrowed against the sun's rays, my feeble heart thundering in my chest. The English are doing their best to gain valuable footsteps forward once more. The men who fight in my name are shouting and offering each other encouragement, but it's clear that they need something more. I look for Ildulb and find him and his men standing to the rear of the attacking shield wall. He's barely even watching the larger arena, his eyes narrowed. I follow his line of sight. He's focused on Owain's efforts and nothing more.

I curse myself once more for making bad decisions and turn to one of my other sons. Aed's younger but wiser than Ildulb, not carrying the anger of bereavement about him like a standard coloured in the bloodiest hues.

'Inform Ildulb that the shield wall needs reinforcing,' I bark, my temper fraying.

A huff of barely contained ire from Aed, and he's marching to where Ildulb stands motionless, his hand hovering over his seax and war axe as though indecisive about which weapon to use to accomplish his wish.

As soon as Aed reaches his side, barging his way through the swaying rear of the shield wall, Ildulb jumps in shock. I see him look to me, apology written all over the parts of his angry face visible beneath his helm. Urgently, I beckon him on with my hand, hoping it conveys that I'm not angry with him. I wouldn't want him to go into battle thinking that his father cursed him. Fatherhood is a double-edged sword; so many mistakes can be made. Not having had my own father to hate or emulate, as seems to be the case with all other men, I often wonder if I'm a father as I should be or whether I'm unsuccessful in fathering my children in any sense more than I helped create them between the legs of their mothers.

Shaking the thought aside angrily, I watch Aed return to me, stamping his way through the dead and dying who've been carried back through the lines of the shield wall. His bright eyes blaze with battle readiness. He's keen to engage with the enemy and would much rather have Ildulb's role than his current one of being a member of my guard.

'He'll do as you request,' Aed mutters, taking up his position next to me on the small command position I've chosen to enable me to witness my victory. Or so I believed. 'Can't I fight as well?' His words are quarrelsome. My tight face cracks with a smile at the childish whining while men take their last breaths before us.

'I need you here with me. Later you can face the enemy.'

Aed snarls in frustration. I lean down to face him and fix his familiar angry eyes with mine.

'Your brother is ready?' I ask intently. I need to know that Ildulb can be trusted with his task, whether I now approve of it or not.

'He's fine. He apologised and said he was distracted for a moment. The thought of retribution is too much on his mind. You should have let *me* go.' The snarl's replaced with conviction. My sons all believe themselves better than one another when it comes to matters of war and inflicting the most destruction on our enemies.

'That's as it may be, but it's too late to make any changes now,' I grunt in return. I wince. It's almost an admission that I was wrong. Aed offers me a wolf grin.

Sighing in exasperation, his anger abruptly dissipated, Aed turns back to view the scene before him. He's unmounted. He has his feet to guide his steps. All the same, he has a full view of the slaughter field arranged before us. It's not only the English who've made use of a small rise to get the better view.

'My new brother, Olaf Gothfrithson, seems overly keen today,' are the next words Aed speaks.

And Aed's correct, for instead of staying back from the vanguard, Olaf's right in the heart of it. I wonder how he expects to extradite himself if the English and their sudden surges against the shield wall catch him out.

'Yes, he battles with all the skill of his countrymen. He's not used to fighting on such a scale. I hope he'll not injure himself or, worse, die here.' Aed smirks at my words, for all that I meant them, they sounded insincere even to my ears. I don't believe any of my sons like Olaf.

A thundering crack of sound reaches my ears. I turn to where Ildulb now stands against the advancing shield wall. Damn the bloody English. They've gained important strides from us. Damn them all.

Aed's eyes blaze white-hot at what's happening. I allow him his head with a flick of my hand. I don't embrace him as I did Ildulb. I know that Aed won't die here. I just know it. He has his troop of warriors, vicious and violent, just waiting to join the fight when I give permission. They'll worm their way amongst my men and Owain's. Hopefully, they'll beat the bloody English back those steps they've gained and even cause a rout. I'd like to see the huge number of English trying to seek solace on their tiny hillock. It'll be their death. I only wish it comes soon.

37

937, BRUNANBURH, THE KINGDOM OF THE ENGLISH

Olaf Gothfrithson, king of the Dublin Norse

Blood streaks my face, and my eyes glisten with the strange combination of joy and rage.

I love to battle, the feel of the weapons beneath my hands, both powerful and sharp. The presence of the strength of the other men who guard my front and rear. If I could cry with joy, I would.

I've forced my way to the front of the shield wall, using my elbows and shoulders to get to the heart of the fight. Sod King Constantin and his tactics and devious ways. A battle should be fought quickly. I want this thing done. I wish to ride into Jorvik in four days' time at the latest. It's been ten long years. I'll wait no longer.

I've already lost track of the number of Englishmen who've met my blade. At least five, perhaps six. They're dead now or will be soon. Five or six fewer English to fight me for Jorvik should they ever recover from the defeat I intend them to suffer. My gloved hands are sticky with blood, my blades are almost welded in place with the stink of the stuff. The English are relentless in their intensity, although easy enough to kill. I don't understand how Constantin allowed such warriors to overwhelm his force in Cait. It should have been easy to devastate them.

The English do nothing but stand there, heaving against the force of my shield. It's enough to strike with a war axe on exposed shoulders and necks and see them disappear beneath the feet of their allies.

My men, my brothers and son, are keen for this battle. They've joined me – Rognavaldr, Blakari and Camman – fighting their way to my side, scything a path through the rear of the shield wall. We're experienced fighters and victors, most of the time, against the Southern Ui Neill and the Norse of Olaf Scabbyhead's Limerick. I don't think of Donnchad's attack on Dublin. I won't let that undermine all I've accomplished since becoming king of Dublin.

The English fight no differently to us, for all their king would have us believe they're stronger and likely to overwhelm us all. They have shields, axes, swords and spears, and some arrows. I'm not sure I approve of the arrows. It seems a coward's way to kill a man without looking into his eyes as I take his life.

An axe hooks itself against the top of my shield. I reach over to slash wildly at the hand of the man who dares such injury against me, growling low in my throat as my axe swings. But my strike flails, and I find nothing but air. Confused, I reach a little further and finally encounter my foeman. Only he does something unexpected, tugging on my hand and pulling my arm further and further forward. My shield's forced down to my knees, exposing my arm almost up to its armpit.

Angrily, I rear back and kick at my enemy beneath the shield, whacking my shins on the shield, as my shield hand aches at the strange angle. The English bastard laughs, the sound derisive, spitting at me. Little shows beneath his helm but his tightly shorn beard.

Without warning, a moment of panic envelops me. I felt so confident, and yet this could be my death.

Glancing around in desperation, I realise that a group of English warriors are trying the same tactic along the shield wall. The shields of my warriors dance precariously close to the ground. In such a position, the man immediately behind my captor slashes forward with an axe to land a blow against the man at my rear. Not just one brave Dublin Norse warrior is exposed, but two.

'Ware!' I roar, hoping my warriors hear the command against the thunderous rage of warriors fighting to the death.

I twist my arm, prepared to break it if need be, as long as it's free from my enemy's grasp. My war axe is almost useless in my hand. Simultaneously, I kick again, jerking my head upwards and forwards, aiming for the nose of the man who holds me immobile, wincing at the stab of pain as our helms collide. The man laughs again, his beard flecked with blood and his teeth black with the stuff. Has he bitten someone? Or has he bitten his tongue?

I feel a flurry of activity from behind, redoubling my hold on the shield, even though I'm still missing my hand and war axe. Stunned, I watch as my fellow warriors are suddenly on the same side of the shield wall as the enemy. I spy my brother, Rognavaldr, and two of his oath-sworn men, Aodh and Dara, their eyes crazed but determined, winding their way through the ten or twelve foemen who've employed the same tactic. Hacking wildly at the English, not one notices before wounds are opened down their exposed back.

'Kill them all!' I roar, snorting at the scene unfolding before me. The English thought to beat us in such a way. But I still don't have my hand returned to me. Half turning, my foeman must glimpse the coming blade, but he dies wearing a shocked expression.

Finally snatching back my hand and war axe, I menace the dead man, my teeth brandished as though a weapon. I force my shield back in position and punch him in the face for good measure with my axe. Devoid of all life, his nose erupts at my attack. He falls back, his body twisted awkwardly, blood pooling down his chin, covering his beard and dripping onto his chest. Hastily, I take stock of my warriors, ensuring they've all returned unscathed.

My men have managed to reform the compromised shield wall. They fight with renewed vigour. These English men have tricks aplenty to play on us, and we must be prepared.

My brother's two warriors, Aodh and Dara, alongside Rognavaldr, slip back into line behind me.

'My thanks,' I call, above the rumble of the battle. Rognavaldr offers me a grin of triumph as he passes me; Aodh's chin is a bloody welter, half of his beard cut away, while Dara's dazed. Not that it stops them. I feel them slip back into position, the jostle of those to either side assuring me we're once more at full strength.

Not to be beaten, the English steadily press against us once more. Here, at the front of the attack, isn't the best position for me. I need a little distance; I must see how we fare and if I need to send in reinforcements yet or not. Signalling to Rognavaldr that he should take my place, I force my way back through the advancing men as they move aside to let me pass with a crash of iron and wood. Cheers greet my appearance, and I clasp hands and shoulders, assuring them that I fight for them as much as they fight for me. As I do so, I keep track of the numbers who still battle. The low number staggers me. How can so many have been lost already? I can't even see Olaf Scabbyhead amongst the crush. Has he fallen to his death? I can't imagine the man being so foolish as to die here.

Moving more quickly, I almost run to the back of the line of advancing men, to where a slight rise allows me to see better. To the far side of it, our camp stretches towards the Mersea river at our back, a shimmering thread of grey on a bright day. Concern makes me incautious over the uneven surface, and I stagger, fall, and then surge upwards once more, trying not to look over my shoulders to see if others have noticed my frailty.

At the front of the shield wall, I felt invincible until the English warrior tried to slice my arm from my body. Now my heart thuds in my tight chest. Sweat beads on my face. I don't risk removing my helm to wipe it. My weapons drip with gore, as do my gloved hands. Yet it's not enough. I can sense it even before I've fully assessed the ebb and flow of the two shield walls.

The sound of the battle is thunderous, as though a storm howls all around us, and yet the sky is blue as far as the eye can see, with no sign of a cloud. No sign of thunder. Just the blazing summer sun.

Spying King Constantin, on his mount, the commander of this battle, I note the apprehension on his twisted lips, all that's visible beneath his elaborate boar-crested helm, the black horse's hair blowing in the slight sea breeze. He sees what I sense.

Turning abruptly, I gaze at the view before me.

A heaving mass of men and shields glint dully on the summer's day, the sound so loud it drowns out all else. The English have advanced many, many steps across the land that was empty space when the fighting began, over which the holy man tried to offer a peaceful resolution, for all we didn't allow him even to speak.

A trail of dead and dying are left in the wake of the English, stretching out to where the English king watches on, his face impossible to see from such a distance, as he sits, mounted, with his bannerman to signify who he is, on a rise that matches Constantin's.

I wince to see some of the English rearguard bending to check whether the stranded men are English or foemen, stabbing and slashing those who don't offer them a response they like. It might be a kindness, but I don't see it as such.

Surely, the English can't have nearly won already. It's impossible. Unless, well, I don't know how long we've been fighting. The sun is high in the sky; it must have been a long time, for all it feels like I've only just woken.

I count the heaving shield wall, seeking out the colours my men wear, white and grey, a wolf's head emblazoned on shields and byrnies. Of over a thousand who first stood, a full quarter must already be wounded or dead. The number of losses sobers me, even as my counting lips assure I'm not wrong.

A messenger reaches me from Constantin: his son, the more intelligent one, Aed, with his flashing eyes and knowing looks, hunger on his face to be part of the fighting. 'Send the reinforcements,' he orders, nodding towards where my collection of allies, Anlaf Sihtricson amongst them, has yet to join the fray.

I nod in agreement. If they don't come soon, I fear there'll be no one left standing. And then I wonder if Ivarr still lives. He was standing next to Gebeachan when the fighting began. Him I'll not miss, and I hope he's dead. I've other allies who're more reliable. I'll have his wealth, but not him.

'Yes, go, give the order at once,' I shout, fear making me forget my position.

'My lord, Olaf Gothfrithson, brother, as you reminded us only moments before the battle was joined, you must give the order.' Nodding at the words that drip with condescension from a man who hates me, I turn to my real brother, Blakari, who's joined me here. These sons of Constantin are tricky bastards, the lot of them.

'Tell the others to come at once. Order them to deploy as we discussed.' Blakari nods smartly, his tongue poking through his lips.

With a swish of air, both men are gone. I'm reeling with shock and fear. The English are far, far stronger than I envisioned. Suddenly, I understand Constantin's rage and failure to counter the attack in his kingdom three summers ago. I've come here and brought my allies, believing that Constantin was outmanoeuvred by a weak English force, but what if I'm wrong? Has bloody Ildulb made overtures of an alliance for this reason? I'll kill him if I live through this battle.

For a heartbeat, my eyes alight on my ships, strung out along the Mersea river behind me, sunlight illuminating the dark grey water. The ships are unprepared to take the body of my army should we need to retreat, something I barely considered as an alternative to my gaining glory on the battlefield. To see them is reassuring, but should we need to run for the safety of caulked wood, they won't be ready to take to the sea.

But no. I'll not run from this field of death just yet. There's still time for this defeat to become a victory. With the reinforcements, we can turn the tide of the English onslaught.

38

937, BRUNANBURH, THE KINGDOM OF THE ENGLISH

Edmund, ætheling and prince of the English

The number of arrows arcing overhead has lessened, allowing me and the brothers of Ealdormen Athelstan to regroup. We need to take the time to consider the best way of forcing our enemy backwards. It's been bloody and brutal, the heave and heft of men sweating, bleeding, dying, pissing themselves in fear, harrowing. And yet we still stand. The fact that I wasn't recalled from the front line by the king, my brother, reassures me that we were never in true danger of being overwhelmed. Such knowledge drives the fear from my mind. I must fight or defend, protect myself or my fellow warriors. I must not fall. I must stand. I am the representative of the House of Wessex. I am a warrior.

Now, in the lull, I recover myself, preparing for what will come next. My arms ache with the weight of my shield. My tongue's dry from licking lips grown salty with my exertions. Overhead, the sun is bright, offering light and gentle warmth. I'd welcome a drink to slake my thirst, but there's no time for that.

We'll force the foemen over their dead, make them lose their footing in the mire of blood, guts and piss that litters the slaughter field, the broken bodies of the dead, as well. Not only will it be unpleasant, but coming face to face with someone who only this morning was alive and well will strike fear into their hearts and have them reconsidering their place here. Will they want to die like the warrior at their feet did? Will they want to die and know that so little respect will be accorded to them that they'll be trodden on, their faces made impossible to recognise, their loved ones never receiving a body to honour and bury?

If we can't drive them back then we need to orchestrate a retreat so that they encounter the slight slope on their side of the battlefield. I was the first to notice it as we crested the incline that Athelstan commands the battle from. It's lucky that I did, for it could do our side untold damage if we blundered into it unawares. Any depression or elevation on the ground gives the opposition an advantage, no matter how small, that they can make use of to gain victory. If we can press them to the slope – caused no doubt by an old building, long since gone to ruin, a stream that has since dried up, or perhaps even an old shepherd's path – then the unexpected bunching of their men will create panic.

Yet the respite must mean the reserve is being called onto the slaughter field. The reinforcements might attempt to rush the front of our shield wall and drive us backwards. If they do, we must stand firm. We're waiting for something to happen, holding our own against the enemy, catching our breaths, and checking that our comrades are hale.

I look behind me for the first time since the battle began, hoping to catch my brother's eye or any of the other commanders who watch our every move, Ealdorman Athelstan and Uhtred to the far extremes. But everyone's looking in different directions.

At my side, Eadric mutters under his breath, effortlessly holding his shield in place, as though it's no more than a feather in his hand.

'We should attack now,' he urges furiously, his chest heaving, blood shimmering on the top of his helm, although how it got there, I don't know. I concur with him. Æthelwald grunts his agreement from my other side. And we're not alone; other men join the cry to continue the advance. We can all feel that, at this moment, the enemy is weak. Whether it's a bluff or not, we should use it to our advantage.

Still, the men are well enough trained not to advance without orders. I risk a look behind me again but can still see no one who's giving any fresh commands. 'Hold,' rings out across the battlefield, echoing from one of Athelstan's commanders to another.

'We should do it,' I murmur to Eadric. He laughs at my cocksure attitude.

'You'll get no disagreement from me.'

'Or me,' his brother echoes, and at that moment I realise that I'm the man on the front line. For all the experience of the men who direct our side and for all that Athelstan has proven himself an able battle commander, I'm in the thick of the fighting. I'm the one who's tasted this fight and learned its ebb and flow.

Decisively, I turn to Eadric, holding myself firm and placing as much tension as possible into the hold of my shield and the grip on my sword.

'Shout the attack. Now.' He doesn't need telling twice.

'Attack!' It's the loudest roar I've ever heard from a man. The shield wall instinctively tightens and begins to advance, my fellow Englishmen adding their voices to show they approve of the tactic.

The enemy's surprised by the sudden advance. I can tell because the hold on their shields is slack, and in the first breath we advance. I focus exclusively on what I plan to do. I hope my brother, the king, and his commanders have seen and will provide the required support for my unexpected strike.

A line of five hundred strong men against another line of five hundred strong men, others pressed behind them in support.

Midway through the fourth step, our momentum's arrested, with a thud of wood on wood as the enemy recovers enough to mount some resistance finally. Now they'll try and undo our advance. I breathe evenly through the pain coursing up my arms as they press against my shield. I look neither left nor right. I focus ahead, hoping that the men who support me mirror my actions. After all, this is what we've trained for since old enough to hold a wooden shield and sword.

Beneath my feet, the grasses are trampled, and the ground has grown sodden. I don't know how close we are to the dip in the land.

A sudden impact jars my shield arm. The enemy reinforcements have arrived. The weight of however many new men is felt as the press becomes tighter, the air in my lungs more befouled by others who try to snatch the same breath. I want to choke on the rankness of piss, shit and mouths polluted by ale.

And then I hear a cry from the rear heralding the arrival of more enemy arrows. A clatter of wood and a huff of effort, and the man behind me shields my head. His breath is hot in my ear, almost the caress of a lover, although in the bloodiest and most public places.

My feet dig into the earth. Strength floods through my shaking body. The shield wall is the hardest place to fight in any battle. As a child, I thought that the shield wall would be the place where heroes were made. I was right and wrong all at the same time. The shield wall forces men to become heroes. The intense fighting might take place there, but it's the perseverance of spirit and soul that's more demanding. To stand knowing that you're but two pieces of wood away from certain death makes men strong and weak. They'll never know what they'll be until faced with the reality of the situation. No amount of training or even experience can tell a man how he'll fare.

The greatest warrior may suddenly piss himself with fear. At the same time, the most insignificant member of the fyrd can suddenly stand tall and take their place beside those mighty warriors of fifty years ago who fought the Viking raiders in my grandfather's lifetime.

Today, the strength of the shield wall floods my body with warmth and renewed vigour. I'll kill many men today. Knowing that, I take a fifth step against the reinforced enemy. My comrades follow me.

Our shield wall is stronger today, enemy reinforcements or not. But it'll be a battle of will as well as strength. We must will them to their death and to their retreat. And to the depression in the ground. One small step at a time.

39

937, BRUNANBURH, THE KINGDOM OF THE ENGLISH

Owain, king of Strathclyde

Any moment now, the English will break the shield wall. The Norse reinforcements have accomplished little. They can't get to the front line because men, more tired than them, hold the shields in place against the enemy. To move them aside will risk the shield wall's integrity, and when some try and force others aside, it ends in bloodied fists and howls of rage. We're fighting amongst ourselves more than against the enemy. The bloody fools. Not that I'm giving up on my position. I hold my shield, for those from the rear will falter. They don't know the rhythm of this battle.

I hear arrow shots resume and know that many spears have streaked through the air, aiming at our enemy, but it's not been enough.

Behind me, I feel Ildulb drawing ever nearer, aware he and his warriors had the task of reinforcing the fallen Strathclyde warriors. I can almost sense his breath down my neck. I'm determined he'll have no part to play in whatever fate I encounter today. If he gets too close, I'll drop my shield and let one of our enemies take me. Anything to disturb King Constantin's plans. As much as I don't want to be killed by the English, I'd rather die at their hands than at those of my supposed ally. Perhaps I should have tried to drive a wedge between Constantin and Mael Coluim. Maybe then I'd not be here now, fighting for my life against an enemy I'm not sure is my enemy.

Even above the noise of the battle, I'm fairly confident that I know who holds their shield against mine. Athelstan's brother and his allies. They fight like devils. I hear the three of them were responsible for the death of Constantin's grandson. I can see why the boy faltered as he did at the battle in Cait.

I've followed Edmund's career with interest, wondering if he'd rise against his brother and attempt to topple him from his kingship. I doubted it. Edmund has only to wait to become king when Athelstan dies. Athelstan has no children and doesn't mean to have any, either. It's the other step-brother, Edwin, who tried to undermine and kill King Athelstan. It was Edwin who paid the ultimate price.

If it is Edmund on the other side of my shield, I know he'll take great pleasure in killing me. The English blame me for the words of the scop that's turned men and women against the peace achieved at Eamont, or so I've been told. Edmund will think it a great benefit for his king. Equally, I'll consider it a great service not to die at Ildulb's hands. I hate Ildulb even more than I do Constantin. I should have brought Mael Coluim to my side, and then I'd be sitting beside my hearth, as Mael Coluim is doing right now.

I ought to have reneged on the agreement between Constantin and me.

I should have reclaimed my father's kingdom from Constantin's grasp.

I strain to hear the words exchanged between my enemy to ensure that I've guessed correctly in my belief that it's Edmund against whom I fight. After all, the Englishmen share a language. It could perhaps be anyone. But it's not. He sounds like his brother, regal and well spoken, every word weighed and tested before it's used, for all he's little more than a child. And I remember speaking to him, many years ago, at the witan, when he demanded to know of the Outer Isles and Iceland. I know it's him.

'Owain, you fight like a young boy who's never taken a kill.' The whispered words startle me, and I hiss, straining every bone in my body to keep the shield in place as I turn and face Ildulb. His twisted face is barely a breath from mine. His foul breath is enough to make me retch. How has he managed to get so close to me?

'Thank you for the compliment,' I retort angrily. I can see my chance of a better death slipping away from me now that he's here. And I'm trapped. I can't go forwards or backwards. Ildulb and his men surround me, and the English are in front of me.

'It was no compliment,' Ildulb growls.

'Then it's as well that I took it as one,' I counter, determined not to let any fear show in my voice. All my weight goes into preventing the English from advancing any further, and in some vain effort to prove to Ildulb that what he says about me is a lie.

'You'll die here,' Ildulb menaces, his attention on me and not on the English. I swivel my head to glare angrily at him.

'And you'll bloody see to that, will you?' I don't know why he hates me so much. I didn't kill his son, but I know who did and also where that person is. But I don't inform him of such. Ildulb sneers as I note his blackened teeth. He doesn't ensure he's clean any more, too consumed with grief and revenge. His clothes are days, if not weeks, old, and the smell of rotting flesh hangs about him even though he's yet to slay any of our enemies.

'I will, and it'll be my pleasure to send you to hell,' he taunts.

'Then I'm sorry to deprive you of that,' I respond, my voice harsh and derisive.

His crazed eyes look unsure, his eyebrows furrowed at my unexpected words. I know he watches without understanding as I lift my shield clear and step against the shield of my enemy. The man opposite me stumbles as the force keeping him upright falls away. The wooden shield, decorated with the wyvern of Wessex and the eagle of Mercia, with fragments of the bright colours of red and yellow still visible beneath the blood, knocks into my face. It jars my helm half-loose, so that it sits back on my head, leaving my face entirely exposed. Quickly, my foeman regains his footing. He lowers his shield to see what's happening, confusion in his bright blue eyes.

Recognition flashes. I imagine the expression on Ildulb's face and hear his cry of dismay. Suddenly, I'm facing my death. Prince Edmund of the English takes only a moment to act, his seax slicing my unprotected face, a well of blood stinging against my beard. I offer no defence as his blade slices lower across my body, my byrnie bursting with the force of the blow. I'd rather die at the hands of an honourable man than a bastard snake.

Pain engulfs me as the grip on my shield and sword slips. I smile, even as I face my death. Behind me, I hear Ildulb's aborted cry of 'No', but it's already too late. I don't know if that's because I face Edmund and Ildulb's only just noticed, or because he's been deprived of killing me.

Edmund raises his seax again for the killing blow. The one that will send me to my God. I don't feel the blood that pours from my many cuts, but I feel my strength waning. I have no remorse, only joy to have thwarted Constantin's plans. That I'll merely be the first significant death of this engagement bothers me not at all.

A flash of shining metal emblazoned by the bright summer sun skims across my eyeline, and an unimaginable pain briefly engulfs me. All I can think of is my heaven. And Ildulb's fury. The smile doesn't leave my lips even as I stumble to the ground, other feet on my body, my eyes closing as though in sleep, and I'm trampled beneath the boots of hundreds of warriors.

40

937, BRUNANBURH, THE KINGDOM OF THE ENGLISH

Athelstan, king of the English

My forces are advancing well, but I perceive the furtive moves by King Constantin and Olaf Gothfrithson to stem the flow of my battle plan. I know they're holding many men in reserve, but I'm unsure of the exact numbers. The strength of my reserve is emblazoned on my mind, making me nervous. I want nothing more than to see these men running for their lives, being cut down by the swords of my warriors as they prevent them from escaping to the ships waiting for my enemy on the Mersea river to their back. They come here with chests swelled, determined to win back Jorvik and shatter my triumphs. Yet they leave themselves an obvious means of escaping. The alliance between the Norse and the Scots, despite the marriage of Constantin's daughter to Olaf, isn't enough to bind the two forces together.

Edmund fights well in the crush of the shield wall. I briefly feared for him, but there was no need. And he must make his name as a warrior, building on the acclaim from the battle at Cait. My aunt allowed me the same when I was Edmund's age. How it must have made her fearful.

Ealdormen Athelstan and Uhtred, on the left and right flanks, are as quick with their commands as I am. They have eyes everywhere, ensuring we press forward, even while protecting our rear. They ensure that the respective ends of the shield wall hold themselves together and don't yield to our enemy. Behind Edmund, Guthrum's ready to reinforce the line should such action be required. For now, his men pull as many casualties clear from the fight as possible, ensuring the English live while the Scots and Norse die. It's to be hoped that some of the English will recover from their wounds. There are men and women with knowledge of healing, and they always amaze me with the power of their skills and exhortations to God.

But I don't watch alone. Up and down my line, I have skilled and well-trained men observing the ebb and flow of the fight. They act as my eyes and ears, ensuring I don't miss any early indication that the battle may turn against us. Periodically, I receive hastily given reports from their messengers. After all, it's too much information for one man to manage single-handedly, just as running my kingdom is only possible with the help of my ealdormen, bishops and archbishops, abbots and members of the witan who serve me in any number of different ways.

I've had my men of letters painstakingly read the Anglo-Saxon Chronicle and the works of Bede and the most learned Asser, who served my grandfather and wrote of his life, for details of other battles as monumental as this one. They searched and scoured the records, but none seemed as impressive as this one here today.

The Battle of Maserfeld, in the shadowy past where myth and fact mix so confusingly three hundred years ago, fought between the Northumbrian king, Oswald, and the native Britons and the Mercians, led by Penda, was far-reaching, but it didn't include as many kingdoms as this one. After all, England was then Mercia, Wessex, Northumbria, the kingdom of the East Angles. There was no England.

The Battle of Nechtansmere, another battle in the legend of possible history, was disputed between the Northumbrians and the Picts. It didn't result in the entire island taking to arms. It did lead to the death of the then Northumbrian king. I've no intention of dying here. The Northumbrian kingdom, or so my scribes tell me, never recovered from that defeat, allowing the Viking raiders to stake a claim to it. I don't intend the same outcome should befall my newly united lands.

The closest my scribes could find were the battles between the Viking raiders and my grandfather. King Alfred united all he could to prevent the threat of the Viking raiders from overwhelming Wessex and Western Mercia. I can't help but think that if the people of this island had united under his rule, as I've tried to join them together now, then the Viking raiders would have found no footing. Our history would have been completely different. There would have been no Norse kingdom of York. No broken kingdom of Bamburgh wrenched away from the other lands of the Saxons. And there'd be no Danelaw, reaching across the eastern side of the once mighty Mercia and the ancient kingdom of the East Angles, peopled by men and women of Danish descent.

No, my scribes assured me and showed me the proof in ancient records and annals that this battle will be the greatest ever fought on this island. It'll be between more peoples than ever before and, for that reason, I'll win it, and then my scops will commemorate the great deed. Our island will be fully united.

A cry to the left, and I narrow my eyes looking for the source of the sound. Near the shield wall, I can see where one of my most skilled warriors has Olaf Gothfrithson at his mercy. I admire his tactic and hope he'll kill my enemy immediately. Without Olaf, this battle will fall apart far more quickly than otherwise. As a warrior king, unlike King Constantin, who was one but isn't any more, Olaf can incite his warriors to greater battle glory than the Scots king.

I eye King Constantin. I see his banners and where he watches the fighting from a low rise to the north, the Mersea river to his back. He's mounted, surrounded by men, and even I can see the shimmer of his battle gear, and the black horsehair that crowns his warrior helm. But he doesn't fight. I don't believe he will. He didn't at Cait. If he strode into the surging shield wall, he'd lose his footing and be crumpled beneath the mass of his warriors.

A cry to the right, and I drag my gaze away from Constantin to another area of intense fighting almost directly in front of me. The men all look the same in their helms and byrnies. I call my squire to me. He has keener sight.

'Who fights there?' I ask him, and the lad, Alfred – named after my grandfather – keenly looks where I point.

'Owain of Strathclyde,' he answers quickly. He has an excellent memory for emblems and faces. That's why I keep him so close. He's invaluable when a crowd surrounds me, expecting me to remember their names. And now, in the middle of this fight, he can see men's helms with far keener eyes than I can.

'Who fights him?' I query, aware that, not far from that place, Edmund and the two brothers of Ealdorman Athelstan battle close to the shield wall, if not a part of it by now.

There's a moment of silence while the boy looks and considers. His slight shoulders are tense, his hair blowing from side to side in the breeze. He has a helm, perhaps the smallest I've ever seen, but he hasn't slid it over his head, believing he's safe here with me, at the rear of the mass of battling men.

'It's one of the ealdormen's brothers, but I'm unsure which one.' He's annoyed, and I offer a non-committal grunt to acknowledge him. I know he'll stay there until he deciphers the identity of the other warriors. 'My lord king.' His quivering voice recalls me from where I instruct one of my messengers to advise Ealdorman Uhtred of a weakness in his battle formation. 'Owain of Strathclyde's dead.'

Quickly, I look where he does. I wish I'd not looked away because I can't find the area of my focus. The thought that Owain of Strathclyde is dead pleases me. Yet this was never really his fight. He was Constantin's to command. I could almost pity him.

Another messenger arrives, out of breath but courteous and concise in his reporting. 'My lord king.'

I wave his use of my title aside. I just want to hear what he has to say.

'Olaf Gothfrithson's withdrawn. Reinforcements are being called in. Constantin's allowing his son, Aed, to take to the field. The forces are in disarray. We'll overwhelm them, and soon.'

'And what does Ealdorman Athelstan advise?'

A cheeky smile lights up the messenger's face.

'Nothing, my lord king, he just wanted you to know that our side is so strong the enemy's forced to send all their strength against us.'

I smirk at the arrogance in his voice, the youth made bold by his master's confidence.

'Tell Ealdorman Athelstan I'm delighted with our success but caution him. I want to know if, at any point, it looks as though we might be in danger. Remind him that we have reserves too.'

He bobs his head and dashes back the way he's just come.

'My lord king, Athelstan,' my squire speaks into the lull in the conversation. 'It was Owain of Strathclyde, I'm sure of it, but now I can't see him. He's dead at the hands of Lord Edmund.'

The news snaps me from my musings. I peer into the mass of men and weapons clambering for attention directly in front of me. The neat and tidy rows of warriors waiting to labour at the shield wall have collapsed amongst the enemy force. Instead, warriors mill around, some desperate to have their turn at slaying my people and some doing all they can to stand to the rear, as far from the fighting as possible, casting longing looks at where the ships wait for them.

'Are you sure? Does Edmund live?' I demand, a solid lump of fear threatening to choke me. I don't want to face his mother if Edmund is dead. Of course, I couldn't promise her son would live through this fight, but I vowed to do all I could to ensure he did.

'I believe so, my lord king, but I'll keep watch.' My fear dissipates instantly at those words. I only hope that they're correct.

'Edmund is well,' Sigelac assures me in a lazy drawl. He's mounted beside me as Flodwin is to the right. 'I can see him. Look, it's impossible to miss Eadric, who fights at his side.' I follow where his arm points and finally breathe freely once more. Edmund's distinctive thanks to his warrior helm, resplendent with a wyvern embellished on its crown, if not for his height, which is why Sigelac indicates Eadric, beside him, first. For a moment, I think I should be with Edmund, fighting at the front of the shield wall. But my place is here. Such a battle as this requires me to command it, not to take part, not yet. I'll fight if the need arrives. I've no fear of facing the Norse or the Scots.

'Good. Ensure Edmund remains so.' There's iron in that command.

Sigelac grunts his agreement, Flodwin licks his lips, eyes never moving from that place in the shield wall. Both men are as eager to engage as I am.

I focus on the dance before me, the slash and crash of swords and axes, shields and spears. Right before my eyes is a horror that a lad of a certain age would give almost anything to witness. I fight the bile in my throat. If only I were young enough not to understand the real costs of this battle, the fatherless children and widowed wives, the lifelong injuries, and the inability to fend for themselves that the maimed will feel.

But I was raised at my aunt's Mercian court. I've been fighting since I was old enough to face men twice my age. I understand what war is.

My gaze sweeps to where Constantin still commands. A flurry of activity, and I know he's trying to correct the imbalance of this battle. He won't succeed. I'll make sure of that.

41

937, BRUNANBURH, THE KINGDOM OF THE ENGLISH

Constantin, king of the Scots

Fear constricts my chest, my breaths shallow and gasped.

I watched as Owain of Strathclyde lowered his shield to become fodder for the English warriors. I saw with disbelief as Owain stepped into the killing blow of the enemy. Now I've lost sight of Ildulb, my frantic gaze seeking him out amongst the bloodied men who war in the distance.

I fear that my men are about to suffer a terrible fate at the hands of the English. With Owain's death, his shield falling to the ground along with his body, the English have poured through into the ranks of my warriors. My warriors don't even realise that they could be fighting with an enemy at their backs. They don't have the clear view that I do.

'Beware,' I roar to my warriors, trying to raise my voice above the thunder of thousands of warriors clattering iron and wood against one another. The beginning of the word falls away so that only 'ware' erupts from my mouth. My warriors must know what's happened. They need to share it between one another, but my voice is too soft. My word, too gasped. I regret allowing Aed to join the fighting.

And Ildulb! I don't know how he fares. I fear for him. He was there, the man closest to Owain. I wish I could rush into the melee, but I can't. My age is too great, my sword arm too weak. I've become a figurehead, no more. I couldn't slay a baby goat if it wandered onto my drawn sword. And still, I can hardly draw enough breath to stay sitting, let alone to shout at my warriors.

Aed too. I can't find him, or my grandsons who wished to fight along-side their fathers.

It's impossible to tell an enemy from an ally, a man from a boy amongst the rough shoving and shrieking. Everyone looks the same. Helms have removed all identifiers, and if I could see shields, they'd be too smeared in blood to determine Scot from Englishman clearly. For the first time in many, many years I know what it is to fear and feel impotent.

Olaf Gothfrithson has at last seen what's happening from where he's retreated. His voice, younger and stronger than mine, rises above the furore. His allies pour into the growing void but only add to the confusion as I frantically search for my family. I didn't want this conflict if it cost me my children and my grandchildren. All I wanted was retribution for King Athelstan's attack three summers ago. Vengeance for the death of Amlaib at Cait. The opportunity to rid myself of Owain of Strathclyde. I should have held true to my reservations instead of blundering into this at the behest of Ildulb. My pride has brought me to this disaster.

Cries of anguish and agony reach my ears, the crash of battle, the wet thud of falling bodies. It fills my senses and unnerves me. I try to control my dread. But there's nothing but panic, as my horse dances beneath me, sensing my terror, smelling the blood, wanting to gallop from this place.

And then somehow Ildulb is at my side, a crazed smile on his lips, blood smearing his face and great slashes of maroon marring his clothing, as he reaches up to grip my arm, startling my horse and me.

'He's dead,' Ildulb announces as if it's the most mundane thing. A lopsided smile crosses my face at the news. I wanted the excuse to have Owain of Strathclyde die. He's become nothing but problematic in recent years. Had he supported me when King Athelstan invaded my kingdom, as he should have done, Amlaib would still live, and more importantly, I'd not have had to bend the knee in humiliation at Cirencester.

I want to enjoy this small triumph, but before me, the swirl of fighting is intense.

'You killed him?' I ask, but he shakes his head.

'No, bloody Edmund of the English did.' His words are filled with disgust and hatred, as I feel his body shuddering as he holds my arm. My horse sidesteps, not enjoying the smell of the slaughterhouse that Ildulb carries. 'I wanted to take Edmund too, but he retreated behind the shield wall, as did all the Englishmen. The influx of Olaf's allies swung the fight back in our favour, for now.'

I watch the scene with narrowing eyes, still trying to make sense of what's happening, hopeful that Ildulb speaks the truth. Slowly, I feel my fear come under control. It's not over. Ildulb lives. Owain is dead. My warriors and those of Olaf Gothfrithson can still overwhelm the English.

Eagerly, I follow the line of the shield wall, where it's stayed firm and true throughout the altercation. As I do so, I see that Ildulb is right. The shield wall is solid once more on both sides.

'And Aed?' I query, while Ildulb catches his breath at my side.

'I didn't see him. Why, is he down there?'

'Yes,' is all I say, searching for my other son, but before I see him, Olaf Gothfrithson's beside me. He's covered with the filth of battle. His beard blood-soaked, wild-eyed. A dark fluid covers his booted feet. He breathes quickly, trying to speak and catch his breath simultaneously.

'Constantin, we must rethink our strategy. The English are too strong. Only the appearance of the reserves forced them back behind their line this time.'

Olaf's voice is ominous and black with meaning. He's trying to place the blame on my shoulders. But I'll not have it. He should have sent more of his reserves in from the beginning instead of just the useless, bickering ones of the king of Denmark's son and Gebeachan of the Islands.

'There's a depression, a gulley in the ground below us. Look, it's barely discernible to our eyes from here, but you can see it if you look for it.'

I see where Olaf's pointing, trying not to focus too closely on his blood-stained clothing and sword that bears the mangled, sliced flesh of his last kill.

'But how can we use it?'

'Let the enemy come racing towards us as we fake a retreat. They won't have seen it, and when they stumble, even just a little, our warriors will overpower them.'

I quickly consider the idea. Olaf suggests giving away a vast swathe of land in the hope that the small gulley will be enough to compel the English from their killing streak. I'd far rather force them backwards, towards the line of the hill that I can see. If the English were retreating up that hill, it would be easy to slice their ankles or sever their feet.

Frantically, I look for any other option, but other than a full retreat, I can see nothing that would give us a greater advantage over the enemy.

'It's a good idea. Arrange it with your men, and Ildulb will inform the commanders here.'

'Excellent,' Olaf barks, already stepping away, calling his men to him as he does so. Only then he stops dead, turning back. 'Is Owain of Strathclyde dead?' he inquires, his eyes on Ildulb, not looking at me at all.

'Yes,' Ildulb growls. 'At the hands of the bloody English.'

Olaf flicks his eyes to mine, his disbelief evident to see. He bows his way out of my line of sight. I watch him leave with dismay. I'd not realised my intentions towards Owain of Strathclyde were so well known. Olaf and I have only known one another for a few days. How has he determined my motivations so quickly?

'Ildulb, inform the commanders. We'll pull back. Make sure the men are aware of our intentions.'

Wiping a bloody hand across his face, he rams his helm back over his unruly hair and strides away without another word. He doesn't like the idea, that's evident from the tension on his shoulders. The fighting hasn't lessened with the re-establishment of the shield wall. If anything, it's become more ferocious, both sides, for a moment, tasting the triumph of victory if they could only hold on to it.

The day has reached its zenith; the sun is high overhead, its heat making me sweat. I consider this has been the quickest morning to pass during my entire life. We began the fight not long after sunrise. And still it rages. At the same time, it seems to have taken weeks to reach this moment. So much has happened in such little time.

A ripple of movement along the shield wall on our side. I appreciate that the men are starting to pull back as orderly as possible. I'm surprised that the ruse looks so tidy. Initially, I smirk with amusement as the English hammer home their victory, taking the advancement as their due, only then, four or five steps in, I notice their advance slow.

The men at the front of the shield wall still move shield to shield with my forces or those of Olaf's, but the rest of the army progresses in a more desultory fashion. They take their time, measuring their pace. Has Olaf underestimated the knowledge that the English have of the landscape? Do the English know of the gulley? Have we just given away the position we've fought all morning to keep for no reason?

A cold dread once more fills my stomach as I survey the slaughter field. There are many dead and wounded amongst our forces. The English shield wall tramples over them with barely a thought. The rearguard watch their backs, checking each body to ensure no life could breathe afresh in the supposed dead, and spring upwards to attack. The English shout to each other as they work, the sight of their opening and closing mouths, not the words themselves, reaching me. A scribe, wearing the robe of a cleric but the byrnie of a warrior, seems to be jotting down details on a scrap of vellum as they do so. Does he attempt to count the dead? Does he try to name the dead? Is he seeking out the English nobles who've perished against the might of the Scots and the Dublin Norse? Does he look for Owain of Strathclyde?

Our shield wall retreats ever backwards, a silver chain of interconnecting rings, the men exchanging sword thrusts and axe strikes. Overhead, not a single arrow flies from the bows of the archers and hunters. It would be too dangerous to let them loose now. They'd just as likely take down one of our men as one of the enemy's.

I notice that King Athelstan has commanded the same on his side.

Our force is within stopping distance of the depression in the ground, so visible to me now that it's been pointed out. Olaf's arranged for the few remaining reserves to lay in wait there. They stand tall and proud, not yet taking part in this battle. They must expect to replace the current men at the front of the shield wall and knock the English back with their greater strength and untested abilities. I think the idea a good one. The English won't be expecting this. No matter if they know about the natural feature, they'll not expect to be greeted with a new force of fresh warriors. For the first time since the planned retreat started, I feel a little glimmer of hope.

We can win this. I know we can. I strain forwards, wishing I could see more, and take my horse into the fray to witness this moment of triumph. The English will fall. They'll be left for the carrion crows circling overhead to devour.

Only then, with a handful of steps left, the English abruptly rush forward, all of them, as if someone has counted to three and said go. And not just the men at the front of the shield wall. No, all those others who've fallen by the wayside as they've advanced so quickly join the rush. Heart thundering in my chest, I understand their actions. They were only taking a moment to ready themselves for this final push, for that's what they'd planned. One last advance to victory.

The sound of the enemy running hits me like thunder during a rainstorm, booming, deafening, blinding the senses. The clatter of iron and wood, the roar of a river in spate as their feet thud over the slick surface.

They run as one. They add their weight to those before them, and they've only one thing on their mind, to force my warriors to the ground. They mean to bowl them over with the force of their speed, pushing them backwards at an unprecedented pace.

I open my mouth to issue a warning cry, but there's no time, and it's too late. The English crash into Olaf Gothfrithson's fresh warriors. Those men slide down into the gulley that they were meant merely to step over in support of the rest of our force.

'Ware,' I cry, 'ware,' but my voice is thin and reedy, and none hears but those within earshot, and those men and women can do nothing to stop the inevitable. A reverberation of metal on wood, a wave of sound as hundreds fall in fear and shock. I watch, as impassively as I can, as men shriek in pain and fear. Although I'd much rather be looking anywhere other than at the terrible destruction being played out before me, I don't look away. These men die with my name on their lips, with Olaf Gothfrithson's name shrieking from their open mouths, but they die all the same.

42

937, BRUNANBURH, THE KINGDOM OF THE ENGLISH

Edmund, ætheling and prince of the English

My mind reeled with incomprehension as to my enemy's actions when he lowered his shield and allowed me to kill him. He put up no defence. His eyes showed acceptance of what was to come. I killed him, as I should, but now I wonder if I was too hasty. Something was happening between him and another helmed warrior that I've not yet worked out. Why did he want to die?

Now that the moment has passed, I know who I struck down. Equally, I've realised who I almost struck down. Owain of Strathclyde allowed me to kill him. Was there truth to the rumours that he and King Constantin were no longer in agreement about everything? If there was, then why did he come here? None of it makes sense, yet I can't stop thinking about it, even as I hold my shield, and batter against my enemy, using my seax.

The brothers, Eadric and Æthelwald, have taken advantage of the free passage amongst the enemy, as have a swell of men behind them. Racing through the gap in the shield wall that Owain opened, I watch as they attack anyone within reach. The enemy on either side of the gap are unaware of Owain's death. They don't know that, as they work to defend their line, the enemy walks among them, killing indiscriminately, slashing exposed backs, hacking at necks, slicing open men's calves and hobbling them. The tang of blood fills the air, and the iron of death and the salt of sweat, fear and piss drench the ground before me.

I stand almost motionless, confused and stunned by what's happened. It seems improbable that I've slain a king, yet the truth is at my feet. But the look on Ildulb's face when Owain met his death mystifies me. Why would he look pleased with the death of one of his allies? I held my seax, ready to fight Ildulb, but then a rush of men surrounded me. I realise that into the void caused by Eadric and Æthelwald's absence, the king has sent men to protect me. There's no need, for I feel as though I could happily slay a hundred men who face me through the hole in the shield wall, but I'm grateful all the same and lower my seax arm as it trembles with the strain.

At my back Ealdorman Guthrum appears, his expression strained when I glance at him.

'My lord, Edmund, where are your men?'

I point to where I can see their backs fighting against the enemy, too exhausted for the moment to speak. Guthrum's surprise quickly turns to fear as our men within the enemy ranks are jostled. I'm unsure why but, at that moment, our warriors begin to rush back through the shield wall, battering me with the speed of their passage. Abruptly, it all starts to make sense.

Enemy reinforcements have arrived.

Ealdorman Guthrum stands his ground, his fierce eyes observing every man, ensuring that none of those retreating through the closing gap is our enemy disguised as an ally. I'm grateful he's there, watching for the tell of our bright yellow and red coloured shields. I can't do everything, and already the enemy is recovering. Their shield wall's strong once more, pressing against my shield, and I can't look to see if Ildulb's there.

'You should retire, my lord,' Ealdorman Guthrum mutters through the side of his mouth, not wanting to order me but seeing my exhaustion for what it is, perhaps fearing that Ildulb is there, waiting to kill me in vengeance for his son's death.

'None of the other men may,' I breathe out.

He glares at me. 'None of the others are the heir to the throne and brother to the king. Get back now, eat, rest, report to the king, and return later.'

The man speaks sense, and grudgingly I relinquish my hold on the shield to one of Guthrum's fresh-faced warriors, my arms heavy and my muscles leaden with fatigue.

The swirl of activity continues around me, but I'm paying little attention. Surveying the ground as I move towards the rear of the fighting, I keep my eyes on where I'm going, not on those who lie mangled and broken at my feet. I see others bending to check whether men still breathe, and I also notice one of Bishop Oda's men, taking note of the names of those who've fallen.

As I reach the rear of the fighting, the king's young squire races to join me, a cup of ale in one hand, the other held out to take my seax, which is suddenly too heavy for me to carry myself. I thank the boy, and he shrugs his shoulders. These are his duties, after all.

'The king would like to speak with you,' his high voice informs me. I nod to show I understand.

'I'll come as soon as I'm able.'

It'll take me just a moment to recover my strength and walk to the spot my brother's chosen as his command post, but long, long moments pass as the battle resumes around me.

Only when Eadric rushes to my side, breathing heavily, his helm covered in the ichor of men, do I find the energy to power my limbs forward.

'My apologies for leaving you,' Eadric grunts, apparently unhappy that he let the glory of the battle take him away from my side.

'No problem. King Athelstan and Guthrum provided additional warriors.'

'Even so,' Eadric says, 'it was wrong of us and against the king's wishes. I'll apologise to him for my failure.' The tall man's winded but strides easily, as though controlling his exhaustion and not the other way around. I wish I had his self-control.

Eadric falls into step beside me.

'Did you slay many of them?' I ask, my curiosity greater than any rancour I might feel for finding myself suddenly alone on the battlefield. Well, as alone as a man can ever be who has command of all the men surrounding him.

'At least five.' Eadric grins, jubilant, despite leaving my side. 'They weren't expecting to have to defend their backs and fronts.'

'And Æthelwald is well?' I ask, looking for his brother but not seeing him.

Eadric pauses a beat in his step and then shakes his head angrily. 'He's injured down the left side of his leg, but only a little. He would be with us, but he can't keep up.'

Stopping abruptly, I turn back to face the path I've just forged. My eyes flicker over the death and destruction I witness, seeking only one face among the many. I see Æthelwald almost immediately, his face sheeted with other men's blood and starkly white against the spray of bright red. He's limping heavily, but his eyes are fixed on mine. I raise my hand in greeting. He lifts his arm in response. I turn away, satisfied that Eadric's telling me the truth.

King Athelstan is stationed half a field away from the front of the shield wall. Able to see what's happening, but with enough space for him to retreat if necessary. In my exhausted state, the walk to him feels onerous. I'd like nothing better than to slump to my arse here and now, and sleep what little remains of the rest of the day away.

But our victory isn't yet assured, although I think it soon will be. Gritting my teeth, I hasten to Athelstan's side.

43

937, BRUNANBURH, THE KINGDOM OF THE ENGLISH

Athelstan, king of the English

I watch Edmund slowly approach me, exhausted and weary but very much alive. I'm relieved. I wouldn't wish to tell his mother her son had died in the fighting. Lady Eadgifu would never speak to me again, for all she knows the risks.

Behind Edmund, our victory is becoming more assured.

New messages have come from Ealdormen Uhtred and Athelstan at the flanks and Guthrum in the middle. The enemy's making an orderly retreat. We can all see it. They hope to trick us into making a hasty advance and have us flounder in the small dip in the ground that Edmund first noticed. They're oblivious to the fact that we know about this gulley and can just as easily use it to our advantage.

I make as quick a decision as possible, my eyes attempting to peer into the future to determine the full benefits of this hoped-for change of tactic.

Even as I watch Edmund stagger towards me, I send messengers to my ealdormen with fresh orders. It's nothing new. We discussed this possibility. I'm ecstatic that we can try such a bold approach.

My eyes narrow slightly as I watch the messengers reach the ealdormen and as the ealdormen circulate the information to their chosen seconds and commanders of the fyrd. Even as the enemy takes the first few steps of retreat, I witness my warriors slowing their movements so that while they still benefit from the staggering backwards steps of our foemen, they do so slowly. Those at the front of the shield wall stand, shield to shield against the enemy, but those further back take a moment, a swig of water from one of the squires amongst them, or just an elongated look at where they stand in relation to where they started, to seek out fallen friends. The moans of wounded men reach my ears.

The English warriors know that the next action they take may well end this battle. Many of the warriors are weary. It's been a long, slow trudge to reach this moment. I feared that the two evenly matched sides would reach an impasse. After all, two groups of men, both as well armed as the other and with the same weapons, will always find it hard for one to be proclaimed the victor. One side needs an advantage, something small or large, such as the death of their leader, to force the side to crumble under the onslaught of the opposition. I hope that this small, two-foot-wide ditch will be the undoing of the Scots and Dublin Norse coalition.

I'd expect the men of Strathclyde to be retreating now that their king is dead, but perhaps no one yet lives. I seek out the bannerman, showing an owl in flight, but I can't see him. Has he too fallen, alongside his king?

Edmund finally reaches my side. He's fatigued, but his keen eyes pick out what's happening on the battlefield from our vantage point. No matter where he looks, he'll see warriors and men prepared to fight to the death to keep England safe.

'Are they falling back?' Edmund queries, exhaustion evident in his slow words, as his chest heaves beneath his bloodied byrnie.

'Yes, and intentionally so,' I reply, eyes everywhere, seeking out weaknesses and hoping not to find any. My squire, Alfred, stands to the side of Edmund, holding his seax, and offering water or ale to swill into his parched mouth.

'Are they going for the ditch?' Edmund demands, his tiredness banished in the face of such a thought.

'It appears so,' I confirm, trying to keep the excitement from my voice but utterly failing.

'Then I must return to the front line,' Edmund murmurs aggressively, reaching for his seax only just discarded on the ground before me by my young squire.

I won't deny Edmund the opportunity to kill another of our allies. 'Take care,' I call after him, not refusing his request, but aware that this is the most dangerous time of the battle. Edmund thinks we've all but won. He won't be alone. My thoughts once more turn to his mother and her sharp words to me before our departure about ensuring her son lived. But Edmund's gone, with Eadric striding along with him, collecting a limping Æthelwald as they go. As Edmund walks, he pulls on his gloves, checking that his weapons are within reach, securing his helm firmly over his head and face. I hope he reaches the front line of the battle before it nears the ditch. When we discussed this possibility in our counsels before the attack, Edmund was keen to force the men to their knees at the ditch. He thought it would give us the quickest way to defeat them.

I, too, am readying myself to join the fight. All morning long, I've sat and watched, biding my time, waiting for the most opportune moment to enter the heat and blood of combat when I can do the most good. My warriors know I'll fight with them. When they see me on the slaughter field, no matter their exhaustion, they'll attack more fiercely. At my side, I have a small collection of warriors and bodyguards, Flodwin and Sigelac amongst them. Some are men I've fought with since my youth in Mercia, and others are newer and younger, just as able to fight as the older men but more lively on their feet. Alfred watches me, ready to take my horse when I dismount, his tongue licking his lips.

They've been standing all morning, battle ready and keen to go at a moment's notice. It's been tedious and thrilling, all at the same time.

But still, I hesitate a little longer. I want some assurance that this is the part of the battle that will be decisive.

The men held back away from the shield wall are barely moving now, but the enemy has nearly reached the ditch. My warriors must be released soon, or they won't gain enough momentum to take full advantage of the enemy's orderly retreat.

I wait, nervous that we'll miss our moment, but I know it's not yet.

A few more steps are needed. I count slowly to five, and then my bannerman signals the ealdormen and commanders, who've been waiting impatiently for my order. Suddenly, hundreds of men are simultaneously racing behind the snaking shield wall as it nears the ditch.

The combined weight of my fyrd and household warriors crashes into the shield wall, driving it closer and faster towards the slowing enemy shield wall, those warriors more intent on where they step than what comes towards them. They don't want to falter in the selfsame ditch that they hope will rescue them and which I believe will cause their death.

A slow smile steals across my face as vast swathes of the enemy fall under the onslaught of pure momentum, the sound reaching my straining ears as little more than a whisper, a complete contrast to the carnage being played out before my joyful eyes.

The enemy trip and fall, rushed off their feet by the unexpected violent attack, entire contingents of men tumbling as though the wind has taken them, one after another, like leaves in the early winter, being shorn from their summer branches. Even those rushing to reinforce them find themselves caught up in the chaos of the retreat.

Those who fall grab for help from those who stand next to them, compelling them to tumble as well. It's like a row of long and deadly icicles falling from the thatch when the weather turns, one part shearing off and then the rest following suit, unable to hold on without its neighbour for support.

The ditch has done much of the work for us, pulled the Dublin Norse and Scots down and into a crush that'll cause the death of those at its bottom while injuring those fighting to escape from its grip. It might only be two feet wide, but I think it's at least four feet deep, enough to lose a sheep or a child on a summer day. Or to kill a man weighed down with his weapons when others fall on him.

And now, it's time for my involvement. With quick words, I dismount, handing the reins to Alfred. With careful steps, I descend the slope, striding through the trail of destruction my warriors have left, avoiding the healers who work their way through the injured or dead. My eyes barely notice the fallen, focused only on making this a decisive victory.

Overhead, the sun continues to blaze fiercely, with no clouds in sight. I squint into the bright light. Sweat quickly beads my face, but I keep my eagle-crested warrior helm, with its red horsehair ridge, in place, my hands free of all weapons, for now. I'll grip them when I decide which I need.

'With me,' I urge my fellow warriors, Sigelac and Flodwin matching my steps while others mirror theirs.

Ahead, Edmund's already rejoined the battle. I see a small line of our men has parted to allow him to reach the front of the shield wall. And I know where the enemy line is faltering, fading away, unable to stand tall against such an unexpected assault. They thought to trap us, but we're the ones entrapping them.

Almost level with the fighting, I can't see the effect of our battle strategies, but I know they're working. I can feel it in the grunts of the men we face and the battle-hungry grins on the faces of my warriors and fyrd men, who see me and raise their voices in acclamation.

Ealdorman Guthrum greets me in the centre of the battlefield, a ghoulish grin on his white face, streaked with dark blood. He holds his sword in his hand, but it's his right hand, glistening with blood, that reveals the fighting he's already taken part in. His nose shows the slightest hint of blood at its tip, visible beneath his simmering nose guard.

'They fell for it, my lord king,' he crows with delight.

I nod as regally as my excitement allows me. 'Now let's win this bloody thing,' I growl. I'm rushing forward, keen to be at the front of the hand-to-hand fighting now that it's finally underway. I've not got my shield in my hand. It would make my progress slower as I dodge around the men who fight in small, tight groups in front of me as the two shield walls disintegrate. I pull my sword into my right hand, and in my left I hold a smaller version of a war axe. I can fight with both weapons simultaneously, even though their weight is very different. My left hand is the weaker, but it can throw wild strikes to split a man's nose and cause his forehead to crumble. With my right hand, I can sever the head of a man. It's not a pretty job, but I can do it. Even those blessed with the neck of a bull.

Those who notice me cheer as I race through them, a huge roar of noise that brings a grim smile to my face. My appearance on the battlefront is working and, God willing, this battle will be over soon now that the stale-mate of the shield wall has been broken.

Quickly, I take stock of the situation. It's warrior against warrior. And the number of enemy fighters is rapidly diminishing.

With a howl of joy, I spy a warrior who must be a king or an earl of somewhere. He's clad from head to foot in ringed mail, his shield newly painted and bright, and a helm covers his head but not his eyes or nose. His weapon looks fresh from the forge. I know him as a man who's never fought for his life. A bully, no doubt. A man who holds his position by commanding others to do his dirty work for him.

I look forward to killing him.

A clear path to him opens up before me. I step into the breach, Sigelac and Flodwin choosing their targets and ensuring they're close, should I need their help. They know I won't, but a king must do all he can to protect himself from the unexpected, especially in bloody battles.

I raise my war axe, moving forward at the same time. The enemy warrior fails to notice me; his attention is focused on something happening behind me. I step over a dead man on the ground, and I'm before him, my axe echoing on his loosely hanging shield as it pierces the fresh wood with a wet smell. Not the strongest of shields.

My foeman howls with rage at being attacked, looking blankly around for those who should be guarding him. But all his men are engaged with mine. He stands alone and unprotected. Not the greatest warrior in the battle, but an easy kill is still a kill when the man is your enemy working to undermine your life's work.

He raises his weapon and pauses for a beat, deciding how best to attack me. Into that gap, I step ever closer, making his sword almost useless in his hand. It can't reach me with its deadly force, as I'm within the man's embrace, making it more likely that the sword will hit him before it hits me.

I yank my war axe free from his shield, wood shattering simultaneously as I drive it forward again, aiming to force the newly made shield down. Shields, like swords, gain from a long life before battle. The extra use and tarnish that must be applied after every practice session and every battle serve to make them stronger and less likely to bend or snap. The wood hardens with the years of use it gets, not weakening but settling into its shape and learning to grab hold of the iron boss that crowns it and holds its tendrils of wood into place, bending it against its natural shape.

The man strains before me, the veins on his neck standing out starkly under his long blonde hair and close-fitting helm. He's holding the wrong weapons, and I'll not give him a moment to change them.

As I force my weight onto the shield, I quickly swap my sword for the seax on my belt, and once more, I raise my axe and crash it against his shield. Splinters of wood fly into the air. The man's eyes bulge at the strength in my left arm. While he tries to hold his own, I use his distraction to slide my seax across his throat. Blood sprays forth, covering my face with a hot wave as I glare into my enemy's eyes, feeling his muscle sever under my hand. I want him to know that he died at the hands of the English king.

He slumps to the disturbed ground, a look of disbelief on his slack face. I kick him to ensure he's fully down. Stepping over him, I move to the next warrior, forgetting about my first kill. I might find out later whom he was, but then again, I might never find the body again. Someone will take the byrnie and weapons, but it won't be me. There are corpses everywhere, piling one on the other, some in the ditch and others just before and behind it. Perhaps, when it's time to bury the fallen here, it'll be best to simply widen the trench and throw in the dead before sealing it above their marbled flesh.

Another steps into my line of sight, a grimace on his hairy face as he tightens the grip on his war axe and battered shield, the paint streaked with death. He's a huge giant of a man. I consider what his weakness will be.

He attacks first, raising his left hand with his war axe to hammer against my chest. Without fear, I grab my sword, using its longer reach to slash with my right hand at the barely exposed left side of his body. Not a natural stroke, but one I've practised before. Before his axe has swung halfway back, my sword impacts and slices open a wound on the unprotected side of his body. It shows red and bloody on this bright summer's day. His mail rings have worked to arrest some of the force, but my sword hits hard enough that I feel the weapon's silky-smooth cut through his skin.

His face blanches, eyes bulging, although he remains silent. And now his axe has reached its full swing. He grins at me, tongue flicking over his lips, anticipating what's about to happen. Only it doesn't.

I raise my axe to meet his. The two weapons meet in mid-air, my hand throbbing with the impact. The eyes of my enemy protrude as a small cry rips from his mouth as the clang of the weapons meeting reverberates down his arm to his bleeding wound. He endeavours to work his shield between us, but his right arm has lost its strength. I just need to decide how best to kill him.

Our war axes remain entangled, the strength of my arm greater than his. But he's not yet prepared to give up. His shield hangs limply between us as I swing my sword back towards him. It's not the most comfortable of moves as I'm too close to raise my arm as I normally would, but with a little strain, I manoeuvre it so that with one slice I might just cleave his head from his neck.

He tries to force the axes down, step away from me and make my movement ineffectual, but he's too weak now. His breath comes in short rasps. I wonder if he was already injured before I came upon him. Perhaps a wound down his back or through the right side of his body. It seems to have been too easy a kill.

I hold my ground, and acceptance comes into the clouding eyes of my foeman. With a heave of effort, my sword comes full circle, meeting the resistance of the man's neck. I exert my strength to cleave entirely through it. I realise I'm never going to complete the move, my blade coming to a shuddering stop stuck halfway through his neck, and the man is long dead anyway.

I let the body tumble to the ground and, using my boot as leverage, force the sword free. Another kill, and I'm feeling strong and keen to fight everyone arranged against me.

The ditch that King Constantin and Olaf Gothfrithson hoped to use to their advantage is filling with the bodies of their warriors. My men step over the dead to face any who still live and have the will to attack us.

Somehow, the order to retreat hasn't yet been called. Have Olaf Gothfrithson and Constantin fallen, and none of their men has noticed, just like with Owain of Strathclyde?

And then another man stands before me, his sword held menacingly high with blood streaking its dulling surface and his shield firmly in place.

I imagine he's watched how I killed the other two men and has no intention of falling victim to any of my ploys.

He's a smaller man, compact and wiry. When he moves toward me, it's with the stealth of a wolf. He's a warrior of much cunning, but I'm happy to find someone who might challenge my skills.

Never one to falter, I move closer to him, making him reconsider such a move. No warrior likes it when you step in too close, and he must decide whether to take a step backwards or meet my challenge by trying to take advantage of my movements.

He chooses the latter, and I smirk at his tactic. We're now so close we could be lovers. In such a confined space, it's difficult to kill a man. Lunging my head forward, I snap it down on his exposed nose with the front of my helm. He howls with anger, blood bubbling from his nose. I wear my helm with a nose guard; he doesn't. Inadvertently, he steps back, licking his lips, tasting his blood and swallowing it down so it won't choke him.

I still hold my axe and sword. He holds his sword and his shield, but he's already bleeding.

'My lord king, Athelstan,' he says through gritted teeth. I note the roll of his words and know that English isn't his first language. He could be one of Olaf Gothfrithson's allies from across the sea in the rough and ready lands of the Irish.

'And you are?' I ask, acutely aware that, around us, other men dance and die while we make introductions.

'Cellach,' he says quickly, and he needs to say no more. He's one of Constantin's bastard sons, not one of Olaf Gothfrithson's allies. An excellent catch if I could kill him. His mother was a woman of the Irish dynasties, and that explains the strong accent which his brothers, Ildulb and Alpin, don't share.

'I've come to avenge the death of my nephew,' Cellach spits.

I laugh, my battle rage roused for all that normally I'm a calm man. 'I didn't kill your nephew. His youth, inexperience and grandfather killed him,' I cry, knowing full well that Cellach will take offence. I hope to knock him off balance and make his anger fuel his moves, not his training.

Cellach's eyes flash with fury. He tightens his stance, but the hoped-for anger doesn't surface. Instead, he abruptly grins and lashes out with his sword, a fast movement that surprises me. For a moment, I'm aware of it hovering dangerously close to my exposed body.

Quickly, I step backwards, moving out of the reach of his sword, hoping I won't trip over a body or a discarded blade.

I rapidly reappraise my next movement. Cellach is imbibed with the stone-cold desire to kill me in revenge for the death of his nephew. Undoubtedly, he'll not turn angry with my words, his resolve written across his bleeding face.

Cellach assesses me with interest, bringing his shield close to his body, holding it loosely, preparing to strike.

My weapons are just as ready, held before my body. It's just a matter of who attacks first.

'Surely it should be your brother who seeks his vengeance on me, and shouldn't it be against my brother? After all, it was he who killed the boy?' I taunt, as though discussing my death is an everyday occurrence.

'You ordered the attack. You marched into our lands. If you'd not, the boy would still live,' Cellach leers. I see he made his mind up about who's to blame long ago.

'If your father had stayed true to his word, I'd not have needed to visit him within your lands.'

A bark of laughter erupts from Cellach, and I smirk.

'You're quibbling over nothings,' Cellach growls, raising his shield into a defensive position. 'I'll take pride in your death, and then my brother will rest easy knowing he's vanquished his son.'

'As you will,' I mutter back. I'm rushing towards him. I need to make the first move, or we'll reach a stalemate, and then he might be the better man.

A slash with my axe across his shield, and it drops just enough that I'm able to see Cellach's neck clearly, but I've already decided not to go for such an obvious move. His eyes watch me impassively, although he steps back on his right foot to brace himself against my attack.

Lightning quick, I pull my axe clear and aim for his sword arm, just below the shoulder. He's expecting me to strike across his body from my left, and instead I reverse the angle of my swing and slash at his right shoulder. My weapon grates across his protective byrnie, loosening the metal rings, and his eyes widen in shock.

Now he bleeds from two wounds, but I know I've barely touched him.

My axe, glistening once more with the enemy's blood, seeks his neck. Cellach jumps back, out of my reach, and fear touches his face. Perhaps, after all, he's not the warrior he thinks he is.

Before Cellach can reconsider the fight, I step close again, repeating my movement of moments ago and then reversing the axe and aiming for his left shoulder. My abrupt change confuses him. His shield is trying to cover his right shoulder while I aim for his left.

I move before his eyes can focus on me, a sharp slash with my sword to his exposed ankles, and he staggers under the onslaught. I imagine he's practised since he was a young boy with his sword and shield, but not how to use both as shield and weapon. A veteran of my grandfather's wars taught me all his most effective aggressive tactics and his defensive ones too, but clearly, I'm the aggressor here.

Cellach's not given up. I watch his every move, and still, he wrong-foots me by stepping towards my axe hand before changing direction, aiming for the arm where my sword points towards the ground. He tries to slash at my side, but my axe counters the move, once more playing the part of a shield. The axe head, close to my shoulder, stops his sword. Cellach holds it there, hoping to force my left hand against my body and wrench his sword free.

While Cellach focuses all of his strength into pressing his sword against my axe, I lazily move my right arm, my sword not quite tight in my grasp, but enough that I'll be able to strike him with it if I can just force him backwards.

Cellach's hot breath is on my face, and his crazed eyes bore into mine. The sounds of battle have faded to nothing, and yet I know no fear.

With a roar of rage, I apply all my strength to my axe, first letting it fall a little, as though my arm's weakening and forcing him off balance. As soon as that's done, I retreat half a step, just enough room to swing my sword. It strikes the side of his head, his close-fitting helm almost of no help against such a near blow.

I see his eyes lose their focus as bone grates on my blade. Then he's gone, my sword digging into the side of his ear just above his neck, not cleaving his head, but playing havoc with the lifeblood that flows there. He's dead before he hits the ground. A growl of real triumph erupts from my throat. Flodwin watches me, a glint in his eye. Sigelac pants loudly, holding his side, and I wince to see the dark stain there, relieved to see he's steady on his feet. Flodwin and Sigelac have been my shield brothers for years. I wouldn't wish to lose them now.

Breathing heavily, I judge the situation now that my enemy is dead. The shield wall's gone, wasted to nothing as men face each other, one on one, but occasionally two to one, or even three. My English force outnumbers those of the Dublin Norse and Scots combined.

I hear Ealdorman Guthrum's deep voice.

'A good death,' he rumbles. I meet his eyes, and nod. I'd almost forgotten I was the king, so intent on my altercation.

'My thanks, Guthrum,' I breathe, trying to determine how the battle's proceeding.

'Your brother's fighting well,' Guthrum offers, pointing with his bloodied sword to a press of bodies on our side of the ditch. Edmund's there, I can tell by his helm and byrnie, but other than that, the men have all merged into a brown mass of living, thrashing beasts, the only identifiers their eyes and voices.

'Good, but there are still many of the enemy?' I query, chest heaving, hoping he's a little more aware of what's happening around us.

'Yes, but you've rid us of Cellach, and over there, Edmund and Eadric face Gebeachan, king of the Isles, and the few men of his who remain. And over there' – Guthrum points towards the flank of the original shield wall, where Ealdorman Athelstan had been commanding his troop – 'Olaf Gothfrithson faces your cousin, Ælfwine, and his warriors.'

'And Constantin?' I wonder if the old bugger has deigned to get off his horse and join the fighting.

'He still sits and watches,' Guthrum confirms, indicating with his head where a solitary horseman can be seen on a faraway rise in the land.

'He's unprotected?' I query, surprised by the apparent confidence or desperation.

'It appears so,' Guthrum confirms, and I know what I want to do now.

'Then we must make our way towards him.'

Ealdorman Guthrum nods in agreement. 'A bold plan, my lord king, and one I'll happily accomplish for you.'

'No, but my thanks all the same. I wish to confront him. Knock him from his horse and have him face me with his sword.'

'As you will,' Guthrum accedes without further argument. Now isn't the time to argue about who should have the privilege of killing the lying Scots king.

But before I can take even one step, attempt to cross the ditch that has been my enemy's downfall, a wild-eyed man steps into my line of sight from the far side of the gulley. He looks like the man I dispatched moments ago and my eyes betray me and glance to the dead body on the ground. It's not moved so this must be another of Constantin's by-blows.

'Bloody Athelstan,' he growls, his eyes flickering over the corpse and showing remorse for the death.

'And you are?' I ask, feeling Guthrum tense at my back.

'Your worst nightmare,' the man chuckles, his back suddenly protected by a small collection of bloodied warriors. Not one of them is devoid of another man's blood. Abruptly, I recognise him: Ildulb, the father of the boy Edmund killed at Cait. His rage emanates from every muscle.

Ildulb runs toward me, leaping over the ditch, the dead and dying who lie there, axe raised. Fumbling, I replace my sword and scoop a discarded shield from the ground. If Ildulb's been watching me fight, I need to change my methods.

Ildulb smirks at the shield, throwing his to the ground. I consider what sort of fool he is to defy me so openly. And then I know. He's a man who thinks enough to try and force me to a bad decision, just as I've sought to do with those I've already slain.

Calmly, I raise my shield before my body, my axe in my left hand, my back covered by Guthrum, Sigelac and Flodwin. This altercation could end this battle if I kill Ildulb. I can't imagine the old bastard Constantin fighting on if two of his sons are dead, and God alone knows how many of his grandsons.

Behind me, the cries of other men calling my name alert me to the fact that this might be more a spectator event than I'd have liked, but then, my men deserve to see me fight and win. That is after all why they're all here.

The ground's damp with blood and piss, but I step confidently into Ildulb, noting once more how much the Scots seem to hate this tactic.

Surely someone has taught them the advantage of constricting the opposition's actions, forcing them to consider their every move?

My axe streaks through the air, landing cleanly on Ildulb's head, the blunt force knocking him sideways. But his countermovement has already started, his sword sneaking its way past the shield, and grazing my chest. He pulls it back, as I do my axe, and then I strike again. My blow aims to draw blood, not just stun. In mid-air, I twirl the weapon so that the sharpened edge is aimed at Ildulb's hand loosely holding his axe. Ildulb doesn't even attempt to defend himself, instead using my moment of temporary distraction to force his sword even closer to my chest, hoping to catch me with the sword's sharp edge. He succeeds, and I feel the impact as a brief quiver up my side.

Changing strategy, I drop my shield, knowing that it's hampering my attack. My seax to hand, I fend off the third attack of his sword with my seax, ensuring the two hasps tangle, his sword the longer of the two and harder to extricate. As Ildulb endeavours to pull his sword back, I aim again with my axe, this time for his arm where it crosses his body.

The weapon bites deeply into the gloves he wears, but I can't tell if he bleeds or not. The leather is good, and it might just have stopped my strike.

Ildulb's sword, finally released, shines through the air, aiming for my neck. I step out of its reach. He's a strong man, plenty capable of severing my neck if I give him the opportunity.

Behind Ildulb, his warriors glare menacingly at me. I consider when Guthrum will command the men who protect my back to attack. I'd like it to be sooner rather than later while Ildulb's men are distracted by their lord's fight to the death.

Ildulb laughs derisively at my avoidance of his sword and readies himself to swing again, thinking that I'm scared of his sword without my shield. Perhaps, after all, he didn't watch me tackle his half-brother and the other men who now lie lifeless on the ground.

I decide I'd rather bring this to a rapid conclusion. Once more, I step forward, my foot rising off the ground and tensing to strike his knee with as much weight as I can muster. He grins again, perhaps thinking that I've tripped. I push my weight onto my back foot so that I can raise the other off the floor, and the blunt force hitting his kneecap knocks the grin instantly from Ildulb's face. He staggers back. My axe is behind his other knee, my head level with his sword hanging lifelessly in his hand, and the sharpened edge of my axe digs deeply into his shins.

I step back quickly. I need to follow up this advantage. I raise my sword to do some more serious damage, to slash at his arm snaking down his shin.

A howl of rage erupts from my mouth as another man rudely pushes his lord aside, sending Ildulb tumbling to the ground, where four men protectively surround him with shields. Another stands, war axe menacing, in the place of Ildulb.

The new warrior roars with fury. I use my already in-play sword move to attack the giant. As I do so, warily watching the man's next move, Ildulb's escorted from the battlefield, for all he batters against his saviours. I can't determine his words, spoken in the tongue of the Scots, but I can imagine he demands to be allowed to continue the fight. Anger floods my actions. No matter the size of the man, I don't want to waste my time on him. I want another son of Constantin. I'll dip my blade into yet more blood of the Scots king. I thought Constantin a warrior of great renown, a man worthy of being my ally in peace, but in war he's shown himself to be beneath my contempt. He sends others to fight his battles.

My axe slices the air, first biting into the flesh on the warrior's left shoulder and then on his right before scoring across his waist, and all before he's got a shield in place for protection. He eyes me with anger mixed with pain. I spit in his face. Sod him and his interfering ways.

'You'll die for that,' I roar, aware my wrath makes me irrational, but I've been denied an easy kill. A short, sharp tap on the man's nose with my seax forces blood to well, and my axe is buried deep within his chest. I yank it harshly, watching dispassionately as blood and bone join my axe. I walk away in disgust. The warrior's dead or will be soon. I hope it was worth his while to die at his lord's expense.

I want to go after Ildulb, but the men who protected him have run from the slaughter field, and more of our foemen converge on me.

'We need to spread them out,' I shout to Ealdorman Guthrum, only now noticing that Edmund has joined my attack.

With steps akin to those in dance, every warrior standing chooses an opponent and taunts them into moving onto more open ground. With more space between them, it'll be harder for them to protect each other's backs, and any reinforcements who race to help them will have to take valuable time to decide whom they should protect.

I'm disgusted with Ildulb's withdrawal. But I know that the battle is, for the time being, here on the slaughter field and not with the orchestrator of this fight.

A howl of battle lust leaves my throat. I eye the men coming to fight me with interest, determining who'll be my next victim.

44

937, BRUNANBURH, THE KINGDOM OF THE ENGLISH

Olaf Gothfrithson, king of the Dublin Norse

It didn't work. That's all I know. My great ploy to hack the Englishmen to pieces using the location of the ditch has faltered. Now, in the thick of the fighting, I'm aware that one wrong move and I'll be dead. This battle is a bloody mess.

I'm back with the dismembered shield wall, my men surrounding me, the cries of my allies reaching my ears although I'm unable to run to their aid. The sodding English are everywhere.

And yet, a cold realisation settles over me. I can still turn the tide of this battle, single-handedly if need be. All I need to do is face the English king, for my man saw him enter the fray and now I'm searching for him, praying that I find him and that the honour of slaying the robbing bastard will fall to me.

I feel stronger than an ox, able to beat any who step before me. Even as I consider where I'll find bloody King Athelstan, my sword's raised, shield to hand, as I fight a stringy little man with only half my attention.

Resolved, I slice him cleanly through the stomach, watching with disinterest as I pull the sword through his body, leaving a bloody gaping hole through which I can see the red and grey of his insides. He howls in agony as I lower my sword with the weight of his body and let him slide to the ground. A kick to the face and his eyes shut, his knees on the ground. His head won't be upright for much longer.

King Athelstan, where will I find him?

A shout from one of my men, and I follow his sword to where he points to a nobleman, dressed in the finest battle gear I've yet seen and surrounded by men fighting as valiantly as he does and as well dressed.

I've not met the English king before, but this must be him. No one else would fight in such equipment, the helm crested with brightly coloured horsehair, the nose and chin guards etched with writhing beasts, no doubt the famous wyvern of Wessex.

With determined strides, I slide past the sharp swords and hacking axes of any I meet on my journey to stand before him. My feet slip and slide through the dead and dying, the occasional crack of a bone failing to distract me.

The men surrounding King Athelstan of the English shout and jostle each other, making him aware of my presence. A brief grin lights his face beneath the intricate helm. My temper rises and then falls instantaneously. To kill this man, this great power of the English, I'll need to recollect myself to the here and now and not think of my gains of tomorrow.

Done with dispatching the warrior against whom he battles, he looks me squarely in the face.

'And who might you be?' he spits into my face, the saliva mixing with the blood already covering me.

'Olaf Gothfrithson, my lord king, Athelstan,' I crow. 'King of the Dublin Norse, and soon Jorvik as well.'

He chuckles at my words and a cheer ripples through his men. He throws his head back, exposing his throat. His arrogance astounds me. I wonder at his laughter, but I'm too busy preparing my sword and readying my stance to think more of it. I hope a few sharp stabs of my sword will have him on his knees, as Rognavaldr and his warriors rush to attack any who might think to protect Athelstan. For all his flushed face, and battle-bloodied weapons, he looks no more kingly than I when we're so close together. I've been his equal, and I'm about to prove that I'm also his superior.

I swing my sword across my body, my limbs loose and eager to obey my commands. He quickly covers his body with his once brightly coloured shield, daubed with the blood and grey of his kills. There's a crash of iron on wood, but I'm already retracting my arm back for another swing. The impact barely registers.

Before I can complete the curve of my stroke, I feel a sword crash into my shield. It knocks my stance, sending my sword arm flying wildly to the side. Disgruntled, I glare at King Athelstan, noticing that his bright blue eyes are composed. Irritated, I raise my arm again, swinging with less force but more quickly.

His shield blocks my path. He's changed his weapon, holding an axe in his hand, which he drives against my shield. His massive strokes dent it. Chunks of wood fly free as the boss crushes the stretched linden board into my hand, where I grip the handle. I grimace but keep my grip. Using his axe has brought him closer to me. I can use my sword or my helm to inflict some serious damage.

I lunge forward, trying to knock his head with mine, but he dances back, his axe wedged in my shield and a slight grin across his bearded cheeks.

I wonder what makes him smile?

With a yank of my shield, I force his axe free. It's my turn to dance backwards, careful not to trip over any obstruction on the ground, my shield in front and free from the uncomfortable weight of his weapon.

I weigh my sword in my hand. I want to give a wounding shot, perhaps down the side of his leg or his arms. Somewhere where it'll hurt and make him lash out in pain.

His thoughts mirror mine. I watch him attempt to switch his weapons again. Before he can complete the move, I knock my shield into the arm that reaches for his sword. His axe falls and drops at my feet, the edge embedded in the muck of the churned ground.

Frantically, Athelstan reaches for the sword on his back, but still, he smiles. I grin back at him, confused by his carefree manner. He doesn't seem to fear me at all, even though I'm halfway to overpowering him.

As Athelstan fumbles, he advances into my shield, knocking it with his and forcing me off balance and to my left. By the time I've righted myself, Athelstan holds his sword and has resumed his attack. One, two, three crashes of his weapon against my shield. I hear the roar of my brother, the shrieks of those he kills and yet, I catch Athelstan's ragged breathing. He's not such an accomplished warrior as his allies would have me believe. A few moments of close combat, and he seems done.

Another crash on my shield, and it's my turn to hesitate before lowering my shield and sprinting into the space between us, my blade slashing wildly from side to side, its sharp tip seeking the flesh of this warrior.

With a satisfied smirk, I feel the iron pierce the byrnie and then the man's skin when I strike him down the unprotected right-hand side of his body. He exhales into my face, his spit merging with the blood and sweat. Angrily, I turn my head and wipe my eyes clear. At that moment, with my shield in hand, and my shoulder raised to my face, he knocks the shield, causing it to clatter against my front teeth with the metal rim, and I'm sure some of them come loose.

Anger strengthens my arm as I slam my shield into his and force it down and away from his body. The injury weakens him. I can feel his strength waxing as I apply more and more pressure until I have almost all my weight pressed down on the shield.

A glance to ensure that no one's coming to his rescue, and I stab forward into his already bleeding wound. His face twists in pain, but he doesn't cry out. Instead, he takes the time to grab his sword and slash wildly at the side of my neck. As his guts spill over my hand, a momentary flash of heat runs up my arm. I crow with delight. I've done it, I've attacked the bloody English king, and he kneels, even now, dying at my feet. Jorvik will be mine. Damn my feeble father. I'll restore that which he lost.

A sting of pain clouds my vision. I feel rather than see his sword slicing down the side of my face and across my neck. I jump back in shock, looking at the man who's forcing my sword deeper and deeper into his body, twisting it as it goes in to hasten his death. I watch with horror as he opens his bloodied mouth, his teeth red-rimmed.

He garbles, and I lean forward to catch what he says. 'My name's Ælfwine. Ælfwine,' he repeats, voice wet and choking with blood, and then a chuckling, gurgling breath pours forth with a welter of pink blood. 'I'm not the bloody king, Olaf, and you'll never kill him.'

I look about in confusion. Not the king?

'Then who the fuck are you?' I shout, angry that I've wasted my time.

'The king's cousin, you arse,' he laughs, his death almost upon him. 'But thanks for the enjoyment of watching you not kill the king. You jumped-up little turd.' And with that, his eyes shut, and he slumps to the ground. Suddenly, five men advance towards me, menace in their eyes. Only one of them looks just like Ælfwine. Where did they come from? Why hasn't Rognavaldr killed them? Where's Blakari? Where's my son?

'Who the bloody hell are you?' I shout, not wanting to make the same mistake again.

'Whomever you want me to be,' the similarly dressed man calls unhelpfully, his sword raised, lips curling and his blue eyes clear with vengeance, as he eyes the body of the dead man.

He rushes at me, four warriors behind him, and I'm alone. Rognavaldr has, from the corner of my eye, rushed to help a knot of Dublin Norse trying to escape over the ditch, crowded with the dead and dying. I snap my shield against my body, sword back to my side, not caring that blood and skin still dangle from it, or that my arm's tiring and my back aching.

He crashes into me, deciding to use his weight, not his sword. His attack rebounds up and down my fatigued arms. I feel a moment of genuine anger. Growling, I reach for my axe and snake a quick strike at his shoulder, where it's still held up against my shield. I catch his ear through his helm, and he rages in anger but quickly recovers, stabbing forward with his sword into my shield, uncaring of the blood pooling down his neck. I wish I knew if this was the king or just another of his bloody cousins. I didn't know he had cousins. I thought he was only blessed with too many brothers, and they all – apart from Edmund, whom I saw fighting earlier, and some small child – are the only ones who remain.

My foeman steps backwards and swings his sword wide, raising his shield simultaneously, attempting to knock my face with the reinforced metal edges of his shield. I've already lost enough damn teeth, but if I duck my head away, I'll step more fully into his swinging blade. Instead, I hold my ground, allowing the sword to graze me ineffectually as the shield knocks my nose, and momentarily blinds me. Blood gushes into my mouth, and I spit aside the taste of salt and iron.

The man I face grunts in annoyance that I've not fallen for his ploy. As he does, I repeatedly hammer my sword into his scarred shield, not giving him time to react other than to hold his flimsy piece of linden wood out in front of him.

My arm starts to vibrate with the strain, but I'm not stopping until he falls to his knees under the blows of my frenzied attack.

Over and over, my sword crashes down, always from the right side, and I hope it's weakening my enemy, whomever he might be. I need to kill him, and then I need to find King Athelstan and kill him too. And I must do it before the enemy forces us to retreat. Already I know that some men have made a run for the waiting ships. I'll ensure they're punished when I turn this battle aside. They should have more faith, even in the face of such overwhelming odds.

The man I fight grows noticeably weaker. With each stroke of my sword, I feel his shield drop slightly, and a grin fills my face. This old man is easy to kill.

I slow my sword strikes, sucking air into my body, ready to take the final blow and watch the light of life fade from this warrior's face.

Only when I think he should be weakened and unable to go on, he raises his shield, using it to knock my sword away. It's I who struggle with the weight of my weapon. The pounding I've given his shield has left deep gouges in its surface, but not in him. He seems stronger, if that's possible, and I'm weaker from my massive strokes with my sword.

He looks at me with a smirk.

'Still wondering who I am?' he taunts, stepping into my space, coming too close to me as my sword's resting its tip on the ground while I fight exhaustion and try to find the will to resume my battle against him.

'No,' I shout defiantly. 'You're one of Alfred's or Edward's by-blows, and I'll be pleased to kill you before I move on to your king.'

His grin remains as he exchanges sword for war axe, which until now had been lost on the muddy ground.

'And I'll have the joy of killing you, Olaf Gothfrithson of the Norse, desperately trying to claw back land your father lost to my king in a fair fight. I wish you luck with that.'

And he's upon me, his axe against my shield, trying to work its way behind it so that he can sever my hand or my neck or simply form a deep gouge down my right-hand side. The power of his attack is astonishing. With every crash of his weapon, he laughs loud and long, a terrible cry that I'll not quickly banish from my memory if I survive his frenzied movements.

His attack is as violent as mine, only he has nowhere else he'd rather be. He wants to kill me. I just want to kill him to move on and find the real King Athelstan. Frustration warring with my fear, I realise that I can cower behind my shield, or attack him and be on my way.

His allies have found other battles to fight, rushing after my brother to prevent my Norse warriors from escaping.

Growling with anger and rage, I thrust my shield aside, taking his axe, embedded deeply into the wood, with it. He's left standing without a weapon or shield. I grin in delight at my ruse, and with a slow and steady step, I bring my sword around and ram it into his hard iron chest, forcing all my weight behind the move and hoping it'll work.

His eyes never lose their joy in the battle, and he laughs the whole time I work my weapon deeper and deeper into his body. As the man before him did – his brother, it seems – he grabs the sword and twists it first one way and then the next, hastening his inevitable death.

As blood streams from his open mouth, staining his teeth with the bright fluid, he spits in my face.

'Go to hell, you robbing bastard.' And he falls at my feet, my sword deep in his body. I know I'll not retrieve it now.

Without further thought, I reach for his sword and pick my shield up, working his axe free.

Now I just need to find King Athelstan, wherever he's bloody hiding.

45

937, BRUNANBURH, THE KINGDOM OF THE ENGLISH

Constantin, king of the Scots

The shield wall is long gone. Now it's one man against another. The voices of any commanders would be ignored no matter what they ordered, apart from 'retreat'. I think retreat might still be heeded. But only just.

This has become a bloody battle to the death, but I think the men aren't yet aware that we've lost so catastrophically.

I want to call the men to withdraw, but I've lost sight of all three of my sons, and I can't get a message to Olaf Gothfrithson, who likewise is invisible in the massive scrum of men before me. I can hear harsh cries of anger and rage. I can listen to the scrape of weapons on metal and flesh. But they won't listen to an old man such as me above so much noise. We're being slaughtered like pigs, and no one other than myself seems to be aware. My archers have gone. They ran at the first chance. For a moment, I consider how they'll cross the Mersea river at our back, but maybe they'll take one of Olaf's ships. I can't see he'll have the men to use them all again. Even my archers should be able to direct a ship across the Mersea river, where much of my encampment, including my daughter, waits for our triumphant return.

Owain of Strathclyde was right, after all, when he wished to refuse to fight at my side. King Athelstan wasn't an enemy I needed.

And before Owain, Ealdred of Bamburgh was correct as well. He called on me from his deathbed to ensure his son inherited his kingdom. I failed to act to support his son and make myself a friend once more to the men and women of his land. Now King Athelstan has a firm hold on the kingdom of Bamburgh, and the men there see me as an enemy, not an ally.

I'm in two minds as to whether to withdraw or stay. Should I flee the battlefield while I still can and ensure my survival? I can't turn my back on my sons, not while I hope they still live. Ildulb, Cellach and Aed. They're all fighting on my behalf.

Neither can I bear to watch the massacre unfolding before me.

Messengers no longer come to tell me how the battle progresses. They're all dead or too busy fighting for their lives against the English warriors. I don't need their words anyway. I know this battle is lost. I shouldn't have allowed Ildulb to convince me of the merit of an alliance with Olaf Gothfrithson of the Dublin Norse. I should have continued to undermine the alliance of Athelstan with the Welsh kings. That would have been enough to stop Athelstan from ever stepping foot in the land of the Scots again.

My plan to undermine the English king's alliance with the Welsh was already succeeding without this Norse alliance. Indeed, not one of the Welsh kings is here with the English king, not a single one. Even Hywel, his long-time ally, decided against the move, and it's not just because they didn't want to fight Olaf. No, it's because they fear a backlash from their people should they realise how close their links with the English have become. The enemy who marched across their lands four hundred years ago and stole their wives, their farms and their prosperity, forcing them to the hilly lands of the far west, east and north. The people haven't forgotten that, no matter how much the kings might like to.

Every Welsh king has taken a huge step back. None has attended the English king's witans for the last two years. I should have been happy with that success and continued to drive a wedge between the English king and his one-time allies by using the words of the scop. That would have been more than enough to ensure the freedom of my people and the eventual independence of Bamburgh once more.

I only hope that I'll be able to rebuild the trust of my people after this debacle. I hope the losses I fear I've suffered today don't cripple me for the rest of my days.

Resolved, I turn my back on the battle. I'll not be doing my people any more favours if I die here, no matter how hard it is for me to leave. If the kingdom of the Scots loses its fighting men, it will not thank me for allowing Mael Coluim to rule over it. I left him behind because I couldn't trust him on the battlefield. But now, with defeat a certainty, I can't allow him to meddle with my kingdom. For all I'm a failure twice over, I am a better tactician than Mael Coluim. The fact that I yet live will allow me to rebuild. I'll have my daughter, and those of my sons who yet live to support me. And of course, in Strathclyde, a new man will rule in my name, and he'll do everything I command him to do.

None of my warriors surrounds me, only boys and my youngest grandsons remain at my side, and I tell myself it is also for them that I must leave. They shouldn't die here, not like young Amlaib in Cait. They have many, many long years of their lives still to live.

I can see the men slowly starting to understand the futility of the fight. In dribs and drabs and then in more sustained numbers, they turn and run back towards their ships on the Mersea river. I don't blame them. I'd have done the same had I been a member of the fractured shield wall.

I hope they make it to their ships, but just as quickly as I note the men are running with their bloody weapons and shields, I also watch the English take barely a breath before they race after them. More of these men will die as they attempt to escape, and as much as it saddens me, I can't blame the English for this brutal attack. The men, after all, have decided to run for their lives.

And then I see one of the Englishmen fix his gaze on my grandsons and me. The time for thought and inaction is over. Calling to the ragtag collection of ten boys and youths, I direct them to race with all haste away from the field of slaughter. I only hope that we make it to the safety of one of Olaf's ships before the English catch us. We need only get to the far side of the Mersea river. We don't need to face the fleet of English ships waiting for the Dublin Norse on the sea. No, the kingdom of the Scots is some distance away, but with swift horses beneath us, we'll make it there before the English can intercept us.

46

937, BRUNANBURH, THE KINGDOM OF THE ENGLISH

Edmund, ætheling and prince of the English

The shouts and screaming batter my head as I fight, almost without thought. I can taste our victory, but it's not yet absolute. Something could still unhinge our greatest success.

I watched Athelstan fight the men he killed dispassionately. I watched a great warrior at work. I tried to determine his next move, and I marvelled at his prowess without fear or worry. Athelstan would never enter a battle he didn't know he could win.

Ildulb's hasty departure from the battle line has caused unease to run through the enemy. I know that Olaf still fights, for I've just seen him take the lives of my two cousins, Ælfwine and Æthelwine, but Ildulb and Constantin are conspicuous by their absence. We must take advantage of that before all the men still standing turn to flee and leave us with nothing but a mass of stinking bodies to bury and the memories of how close we came to total victory.

Not that the English haven't suffered losses. As I said, my cousins are dead; grandsons of the great Alfred like myself have bled to death on this battlefield. I know they were pleased to do so. They might have held only the slimmest chance of ever attaining the crown of the English, but they still protected it with their lives, proud of our shared heritage for all that they kept quiet lives on their estates.

My brother, King Athelstan, remains fixated on Constantin. I walk past him, my mind resolved to gain some vengeance for my dead cousins. Olaf Gothfrithson needs to feel the slice of English iron on his skin to know that his actions here are deeply, profoundly wrong.

Eadric stays close to me, but we've sent Æthelwald on his way. He's fought well, but carries an injury, and with the battle so nearly won, he needn't fight on to his death. I hope the healers will work on his deep cuts and gaping wound. I'll celebrate this great victory with him when he's well.

The number of men still fighting has dwindled far more quickly than I thought possible, but Olaf Gothfrithson continues to fight on, no matter how hopeless it is. With delight, I see him trying to make his way towards me, just as I'm striding towards him.

I imagine he's looking for the king.

But he's found me. I'll kill him for the work he's done here today. I'll be amused to see what happens to his precious Dublin when he's dead. The great-grandsons of Ivarr are violent thugs. Those who yet live will fight to the death to get their claws into Dublin. And all the while, Athelstan's hold on York will become more secure.

Abruptly, I stop before Olaf, and he does me the courtesy of looking surprised. As he reaches for his weapons, I'm pleased he perceives me as a threat.

'Olaf, son of Gothfrith,' I begin, 'were you looking for me?' It's a taunt, and a question all rolled into one.

Lazily, he replies, his hands far more tense than his voice implies. 'No, but you'll suffice for the time being. The more of Alfred's bloodstock I kill here, the greater the peace will be in my restored kingdom of Jorvik.'

A burst of laughter jumps from my mouth at the cocky words of this upstart Viking raider. He doesn't have the blood of real kings in his veins. No, he's the descendant of a self-made Viking raider who stole the land he ruled and named himself king, just as Olaf Scabbyhead of Limerick has done. There's no honour in such an act.

'I wish you luck with that,' I counter, deciding I'd rather fight than talk. I swing my sword forward and crouch a little, ready to strike or defend, depending on what he plans on doing first.

'I don't need your luck, I've already killed your cousins, and it'll be your brother after you.'

Without pause, I step into an attack position, my sword and shield ready. I don't want to listen to another word this man speaks. His breathing the same air as me offends me. I want him dead more than anyone in my entire life. Still, I hold my anger in check and use it to fuel my aching arms and tired legs. It's been a long day of battle, and it's far from over, the sun still blazing overhead. I've sweated and sweated. I lick my dry lips. I'll drink when Olaf's dead.

Surprised that I don't wish to duel with words, Olaf isn't prepared as I launch my first attack, my sword crashing into his shield, causing it to bounce shakily in his hand. When he speaks, his voice sounds whistly. I've already seen his mouth filled with blood and crushed teeth. I hope my cousins did that.

Before Olaf can recentre his sword, I smash into it with my sword, gritting my teeth against the sharp pulses that race up my shield arm. I know I'll have wounded him more than myself, but I can't deny that it hurts.

Angry words erupt from Olaf in a stream so fast I can't make them all out. I laugh. Whether he's upset with himself or me, I don't mind much, but I must make his anger count.

My entire body floods with renewed vigour. I've gone from feeling invincible to shaky more times than I care to remember during this fight, but I know it happens to all warriors. The joy of the fight can be quickly replaced by fear of it. A true hero of the shield wall must learn to master those twin emotions: fight the fear and use the joy. It's a skill as important as how to use a shield, sword and axe.

Olaf steps out of the attack and quickly lunges for me. I'm ready with my sword, hammering it onto his already beaten shield. He's made much use of his shield today, and I remember that fact. He's a man who must like to cower and wait for his opponent to be exhausted and then take advantage of his greater strength. I'll not be making that mistake.

I allow Olaf to circle me. Let him think that he has some advantage to be played, but I'm watching his hands and feet, waiting to see which telltale sign will give his next move away first. And it's his feet. He stumbles on them, sorting out his balance before he dances forward two steps and attacks my right-hand side, trying to slide his sword between my shield and body.

Olaf's eyes gleam with the ease of it all. He doesn't notice that I'm exchanging my sword for my axe while he tries to worm his sword closer and closer to my byrnie.

Only then, something in my movements must give me away. His surprise shows just before my axe slashes a wild strike at his exposed neck. He moves aside a fraction, but it's enough to have my axe connect with his solid shoulder. My hand, with its firm grip on the weapon, buckles at the unexpected resistance it encounters. My fingers only just keep themselves wrapped around the wooden handle.

Olaf steps away from me, unhappy that he thought he was winning, and his arrogance almost cost him his life.

Behind him, I see his men torn between watching their lord and their desire to leap over the ditch of dead and dying and flee to the safety of their ships. The river's a forbidding grey on the horizon, its surface offering the allure of safety and home. As I take a long hard look at the retreating men, I recall myself to the here and now.

'Eadric, get the men running after those cowards. Don't let them reach their ships.'

Eadric jumps to attention at my shouted words, which have the desired effect on Olaf. His back to his ships, he doesn't know how many men are going. Is it a mass exodus or just a slow trickle? His head whips around, and with his attention elsewhere, I race toward him and knock him to the ground with my shield.

He squirms in the mud and muck of the battlefield, his one hand resting on the head of a dead man, his fingers sliding inside the open mouth and into the pools of crimson eyes. He shudders at the horror of it and attempts to stand, only I'm above him, my axe at his neck, and there's nowhere for him to go. If he moves his head back to watch the lines of retreating men, ants across a sticky surface, he'll slice his neck, and I'll not have to do anything other than claim his death as my victory.

So focused on Olaf, I don't realise that my men have run to do my bidding, and another, an ally of Olaf's, now has his weapon levelled against my back.

'I suggest you move away from the king,' a deep voice booms. I turn carefully to meet the eyes of a stranger, but one who shares the look of Olaf. They must be brothers.

As much as it angers me to do so, I act on his words. It's my fault for sending Eadric away.

Warily, I take three steps away from Olaf and feel the blade of the seax come away from my back as I do so. The man before me watches keenly. He's festooned in blood. His own or his foes, I can't decide. He doesn't seem as robust as his voice implies. Is he already dying from a wound, and this is his final stand?

Olaf looks from me to the man, not exactly happy, but relieved.

The enemy steps forward and offers him his hand, and Olaf grasps it and stands. 'Thank you, Rognavaldr.' His words are breathless.

'You need to follow the men,' the voice says urgently, his eyes on me, seax to hand, while Olaf sweeps his gaze from the sanctuary of his ships to the slaughter field.

Few men remain from his side, but the English are still advancing.

'Aren't you coming, Rognavaldr?' Olaf queries, his drooping body revealing his acceptance that this battle is lost.

'No, not yet. I'll follow.'

And that's that. Before my eyes, I watch Olaf bend and grab his weapons and turn to break into a loping run that has him out of reach in mere moments. I could cry with anger and rage, but he's not heading towards Athelstan any more.

The warrior watches me intently as I hold him with my eyes. His body sags as soon as Olaf's out of sight. As he drops to his knees, I see the large slash of red across his belly. The injury could take days to kill him as it slowly drains his lifeblood.

Without further words, I raise my axe, cutting through his neck with

one mighty stroke. His eyes close at my action, but as he crumbles to the
floor, I realise he intervened not to save his king but to hasten his death.

And now I'm even more livid and race to find Eadric and the rest of my
men. There's still a chance I can catch Olaf Gothfrithson before he climbs
on to his bloody ship and sails away to Dublin.

47

937, BRUNANBURH, THE KINGDOM OF THE ENGLISH

Constantin, king of the Scots

Stunned by my defeat once more, I arrest my horse's rapid canter and gently turn him around to face back the way we've just fled while my grandsons hasten to commandeer one of Olaf's ships to take us over the Mersea river. The enemy didn't have time to retrieve their horses, rushing to strike down the retreating warriors with only their weapons and shields. My escape was easily achieved, for all that I feel as though it were I who died on that battlefield.

Men will write of this day within our land, their grief will make words flow from mouths. Their quills will flow with blood, and my arrogance brought my people to this. My sorrows may mean that the outcry is slightly tempered, but I want the anger of my people to hit with the force of a blunt sword, and strike my head from my shoulders, my arms from my body, my hands from my arm. It should have happened here today. I should have fought beside my men, sons and grandsons. I shouldn't be alive to flee the field of slaughter.

My sorrow and soul lie behind me, discarded where I fear my sons fell. My remaining grandsons and I must take a moment to collect our thoughts and say our goodbyes. I doubt the English king will send the bodies of my dead home for burial. They'll lie on the slaughter field until picked up by the victors and tossed into an anonymous mass grave with their friends, allies and enemies alike.

I know what will happen, for I've ordered the same when victorious.

I wish I'd acted differently, but winning such victories twisted me and made me a vicious and unfeeling bastard. Victory made me invincible. Always invincible. Only abject failure has wiped that confidence from me.

The sun's almost gone, the light bleached from the land even without the carrion swirling around the battlefield as though night itself.

I fear my sons lie there. Dead.

I fear my friends, my allies, my enemies lie there. Dead.

I fear those whom I thought allies but became enemies lie there. Dead.

In defeat, I am desolate, and also resolved. I must return to my kingdom. I will ensure that I rebuild all I've lost. I can't allow the kingdom I've ruled for nearly forty winters to fall under the command of Mael Coluim.

With no consolation to be found from my failure, I abandon my horse and, with the aid of my grandsons, scramble onto one of the ships, its prow pushed out into the flowing river. Those who live and those who are injured, but who hope to live, hasten to add their strength and join me. But we're a band of weak old men and injured young fools. I offer a brief prayer that King Athelstan will be content for now with his total victory. If his men follow me and try to attack our small host, I'll offer up my throat for the killing stroke. I've little enough to live for now and would welcome the respite from my all-consuming grief.

A cry in front of me, and I turn my dull, grief-filled eyes to the young man who shouts. He's streaked with blood, his nose knocked askew, his lip and chin covered in dried blood. He looks like a messenger from hell.

'My lord king,' he cries again, just as the ship is about to leave the shore, and I focus on him, trying to summon enough enthusiasm to hear and see. And the sight that greets me is a balm for an old man's aching heart.

A warrior staggers towards me, his helm gone, his face reddened as though bleeding from eyes, nose and mouth. My mouth twists. Why does the boy shout me? Who is this man to me? And then I truly see.

Ildulb.

He lives.

Ildulb. One son has been rescued from death.

48

937, BRUNANBURH, THE KINGDOM OF THE ENGLISH

Edmund, ætheling and prince of the English

The ground's awash with discarded weapons and bodies. None have stopped to pick up extra weapons, every man fleeing as quickly as they can across the blood-soaked grasses.

The ditch where our enemy stumbled doesn't bear close examination, so I manoeuvre my way around it, mindful of sharp objects, and then I'm one step closer to the retreating men.

And then I remember who I am and what I'm supposed to be doing here and stop abruptly, calling for Eadric.

He stops his forward rush and looks back to me.

'What are you doing?' he calls with exasperation, seax in one hand, his axe in the other. Killing men by striking their backs can be done far more efficiently with a smaller weapon.

'I need to check that the king's protected.'

Recalled to his duties as well, Eadric squints along with me into the distance, and then he points. 'Yes, see, his standard-bearer is with him, and a few of the men. And look, Edmund, none of the enemies remains stand-ing. They're all dead or fled.'

I realise Eadric's correct, and content that my brother won't be harmed in my absence, I turn and begin to race after the retreating backs of the enemy, quickly joining Eadric.

My limbs are tired, and my weapons are heavy. I can't help wishing I'd thought to retrieve my horse to race after these men, but I'm too far gone in my pursuit now. It's as far to return to my horse as it is to reach the river and the ships waiting for the defeated warriors.

Already I can see that one of the ships has made its way into the river channel while men row with all the energy they have left, and others try to raise the sail to take advantage of the stiffening breeze now that I'm close to the water of the Mersea river. To the left, the sea is far from inviting, rolling violently, and yet, if it's that or death, I'd take my chances as well. I pity them. Those who make it on board a ship will have to face the wrath of Athelstan's ship army, which they probably don't even realise is there, just waiting to play their part in this mighty defeat of our enemy.

'How many men in a ship?' I huff to Eadric. I know the answer, but I want him to confirm it for me.

'Up to fifty,' he pants. I look with narrowing eyes as another ship begins to force its way into the channel. I notice another one trying to strike out across the Mersea river. Who's in that one? Is it men who don't know how to sail, or is it the Scots? Escaping northwards to where their encampment lies? I can't help thinking that Constantin lacked belief in this fight. If he'd been convinced of the win, then why is his camp still over the river?

'So that could be well over a hundred men already who've escaped,' I shout, trying to force myself to run faster while offering some incentive to the other tired men from the English side who are mirroring my actions. Ahead, others rush as well, those who were quicker to realise what was happening.

'Yes, a hundred or more, if they've had the balls to wait until each ship is full. Let's hope that, instead, the men are jumping in any old ship they can find and pushing themselves off even if there aren't enough men to power the craft. It'll make it easier for our ship army to attack them.'

I like Eadric's thinking. It adds to my impetus to reach the riverbank. I want to kill as many as possible. I want the river to run with their blood. Not a single soul will ever set foot in their homeland again.

We're racing through the campsite the Dublin Norse and their allies have inhabited for the last few days. Smouldering fires, discarded clothing and possessions are littered everywhere. A few women and children huddle together, crying in fear. I ignore them and hope my men do as well. They're not our targets here.

And then, forcing my way over a falling tent, I happen upon a man with his back to the ships, blood dripping from a wound on his forehead, working his axe backwards and forwards in the soil beneath him. I know what he's doing, and he's a bloody fool. Better to escape with his life than with his buried hack silver.

Eadric takes one huge swing of his axe and aims it at the man's damaged head. The foeman's eyes glaze. He tumbles forward, his arms falling into the mud at his feet. I hope he died clutching the silver he thought was so important.

We're still racing onwards. The distance I thought was only short from the ditch is much, much further.

Slowing, because I can barely breathe, I see a small collection of men down a slight rise. Quirking my eyebrows at Eadric, he follows me as we investigate what's happening. The men are shoving and fighting, unheeding the menace at their backs. Abruptly, one of them turns and, seeing us, darts away from the others, running towards the safety of the ships.

The man next to him looks up to see where his friend has gone and likewise dashes away eyes filled with fear, bloody gashes on his arm showing he's fought in the press of the shield wall. I shake my head. This group of men rob their dead lord before making their escape. Another bloodstained man startles up and makes a run for it. Where he's standing, I see the naked body of a man while five men are arguing over arm rings and jewel-encrusted clothing, their voices shrill.

I don't know whom the dead man was, but he must have been out of his mind to come to a battle with all of his wealth so prominently displayed on his elaborately decorated byrnie, shimmering warrior's helm and arm rings over which the men bicker rather than running for their lives.

Without pausing for others to make their getaway, I step forward and slice through the exposed neck of one while Eadric does the same to another arguing about the armbands. Words die on their lips as blood pours down their backs. The remaining three men stumble to a run.

Bending down, I pull one of the dying men from the body and gaze at it in interest.

'He looks like a Norseman,' Eadric says matter-of-factly, although his chest heaves with exertion.

'A very wealthy and stupid Norseman,' I counter. Eadric smirks. He's bruised and battered, but I think he could still endure the battle all over again.

'It must have been that bloody fool Ivarr from Denmark. King Athelstan heard rumours that he'd been banished by his father and was looking for a more suitable place to call his home.'

'Well, he's bloody dead now and robbed of all his wealth. Come, I still have the urge to face Olaf again.'

Eadric grins at my determination. We continue to beat the path that the retreating host has taken.

Now we walk, grown tired from our activities.

'How many men do you think you've killed?' I ask Eadric, curious to know what wild accounting he'll give.

'At least fifteen.' He smiles with joy, and not a little self-importance. 'And you, my lord?'

'At least bloody thirty,' I say, laughing loudly, my relief that this battle is almost over and we're victorious making me giddy.

'You're not serious?' he says, his eyes losing their good humour. Now I can't stop laughing.

'Of course not, but it was good to see the disappointment on your face.'

He smirks again, and now we're walking amongst another battle line. The shoreline of the Mersea river has been reached. Here, the English attack the Norse, who try to retreat to their ships while the English hack at them. Men's cries are desperate and pitiful, some abandoned by their fellows in sight of safety, their wounds making it impossible to get them on the ships without risking their own lives.

I seek Olaf Gothfrithson. I want to make sure he dies, but up and down the shoreline, there are at least twenty ships, and I can't see Olaf on any of them. Eagerly, Eadric and I walk the line of ships, ignoring the fighting unless a Norseman walks into our ready weapons as we search for the bigger prize. I know that Athelstan would like Olaf alive or dead, but probably more dead than alive.

Some of the ships are set on fire by our men – better to have them burn than escape – and still, I can't see Olaf Gothfrithson, the growing pall of smoke making it even harder to see.

If the damn bastard has escaped, he'll return to these shores one day. The thought drives me onwards, despite knowing it's hopeless.

Even though I had him at my mercy, Olaf Gothfrithson has escaped my wrath.

49

937, BRUNANBURH, THE KINGDOM OF THE ENGLISH

Athelstan, king of the English

My breath's harsh in my ears, my anger slowly dissipating.

I stand virtually alone on the battlefield. Everyone has fled.

In the distance, I can see fires starting amongst the line of ships that the enemy hoped to use to escape. I doubt many of them will make it home and I'm pleased with the overwhelming success of this battle. For those who do make it to a ship, they must still evade the reaches of my ship army. They know what to do. My fleet commanders will hunt down our enemy.

While I remain fuelled by the joy of battle, I walk amongst the bodies, looking for any I might know, hoping I don't see them.

It's no joy to come across my cousins' bodies, both dead from various wounds. I signal to Alfred that these bodies should be gathered and returned to our campsite. They'll need a burial fitting of their royal ancestry. I know where that will be. I won't submit them to the cavernous under-crypt of the New or Old Minsters in Winchester. No. I'll have them close to where I'll one day be buried. I might be king because of my birthright, but

Wessex is not truly my home. And so I'll seek burial elsewhere, closer to Mercia, the kingdom that nurtured me, and made me a man.

I walk further from the ditch where so many met their deaths. I look, as dispassionately as I can, at the faces of those who've died here. Young, old, thin and fat, every size of man and boy has perished, but as yet, I feel no remorse, only joy in the victory.

I didn't ask for this battle. I didn't taunt my allies to bring about a great rift between us. In fact, my alliance of ten summers ago was designed specifically to prevent a battle on this unprecedented scale from ever happening again. My peace was intended to keep the Norse from our island.

I was wrong to think that a man's word has more force than his sword.

50

937, BRUNANBURH, THE KINGDOM OF THE ENGLISH

Olaf Gothfrithson, king of the Dublin Norse

As my ship's readied for the open sea, I look back in shock and dismay at the site of the bloodiest battle I've ever seen. The only one I've ever lost. I don't count Donnchad's raid as a battle. That was merely a raid. Quick, only intended to retrieve what I stole from Clonmacnoise.

That I'm escaping with my life is a miracle, and I realise how great that miracle is when I see the king's brother, a huge warrior at his side, probably searching the coastline for me. Edmund truly intended to kill me before my brother intervened. I consider where Rognavaldr is. Does he still live? Fear turns my chest tight. I can't imagine he does if Edmund is here.

I'm bloody, bruised and broken in places. There's no joy in running from the battle like a scolded child.

All my hopes and dreams of the last ten years lie shattered and ruined. Where's my son, Camman? Where's my other brother, Blakari? Do they live? I wish I knew.

I want my kingdom back. I want to unite Dublin and Jorvik, but this English king is too great a warrior. He's accomplished what I didn't think possible, and the fact that as many of his men as my men must have perished is no consolation.

King Athelstan had only the support of his countrymen. I came at the head of an army of allies. I had kings' sons and earls by the handful, and still, he beat us. I forged an alliance with the Scots, and took a new wife, lost to me for the time being, and still, I run from this place, grateful to be alive.

As soon as we hit the open sea, I slouch into the swaying hull of the ship. I'm exhausted and worn out. Those men who power the ship are in no better condition, and yet I owe them my life.

A horn of mead is offered by one of them. I don't want to take it. It should have been to toast our victory, but I'm thirsty, hungry and bone weary.

I grab the drink and gulp it without tasting it.

The mead hits my empty stomach, forcing a belch. Now I taste my lost victory gone sour as well.

Aggrieved, I stand and throw the horn into the crashing waves around the ship. As I see the few straggling ships leaving the English shore, I note the mighty blazes engulfing those that didn't make it, the coming grey of a gathering storm after a day of bright sunlight. I fear a storm will chase us home, so rare for this stretch of sea, and the calls of my fellow survivors assures me that we're not alone out here. The sea isn't yet the haven I need it to be, as the bright red and yellow of Athelstan's warships appear as if from nowhere.

Breathless, I stand, issuing hasty instructions to my exhausted warriors, praying we can evade the reach of these ships, as I rush to add my failing strength to one of the oars without a man to power it.

Harsh shrieks fill the air, more akin to the birds overhead than man or beast. Some men weep for those they've lost, others sob for wives and children abandoned amongst the wreckage of the encampment, and yet, somehow, the ship changes course, surging through two of the English king's fleet and striking out towards the growing storm. I'd sooner take my chances there.

But I can't ignore the cries of those less fortunate than I. Tears leak down my face as I think of all I've lost, only to be replaced by burning anger. I'm beaten for now. But I'll be back as soon as I can. Dublin is still mine. Whether Anlaf Sihtricson lives or dies, it's irrelevant. Dublin is mine, and despite this loss, men and women there will still answer my call to seek revenge against the English. They hunger for Jorvik as much as I do, and the mass of orphans and widows created today will ensure their rage is firmly directed at Athelstan and Edmund, and not at me.

I have land to claim and an English king, and his heir, to kill.

51

937, BRUNANBURH, THE KINGDOM OF THE ENGLISH

Athelstan, king of the English

Exhausted, bloodied and bone-weary, I watch with pride as my men continue to chase the enemy from our land. There are few enough of them left, and fewer yet will reach their ships. And those that do have no assurance of reaching home. Black clouds far out at sea assure me a storm rages there. Those who flee towards Dublin must beat the sea, and my ship army, waiting, desperate to play their part in this victory.

The slaughter field is a sea of broken and bloodied bodies, horrifying in its contrasts of bright red, dead white and dying grey, but a necessary evil. As soon as the enemy's confirmed as fled or slaughtered, I'll allow my priests to walk amongst the dead men and offer prayers for their souls. They can fight the circling carrion crows for the honour.

Edmund is gone, chasing the enemy. My ealdormen are gone, chasing the enemy, but I remain looking at the triumph we've earned today. If I weren't so convinced that I laboured with God on my side, I'd be in peril for my soul. The destruction of so many men in one place has placed a heavy burden on me. When I return to my court, I'll arrange for grants of land to my favourite monasteries, and I'll amend my will. More men will be needed to pray for my soul when I'm gone. I must ensure they have enough funds to do so for all eternity. Without their intervention, I may not make it into God's heaven. Not now. Not with the deaths of my beloved cousins on my hands, as well as so many other good Englishmen. I hope my bishops yet live. I've not seen the military holy men since the fighting broke up into skirmishes.

The day has become quiet and calm, the gentle breeze caressing my skin as the sunlight slowly bleeds from the sky, dark clouds starting to coat the land. At my side, young Alfred hands me a horn of mead and a lump of bread and cheese. I swallow hastily and eat as quickly as possible. I'm starving and thirsty in equal measure. Warmongering makes a man hungry.

In the distance, I discern the noise of a troop of men advancing. Frantically, I look around me, pulled abruptly from my reverie. My men are all dispersed either back to their tents to tend to their injuries or gone to ensure no more of the enemy reach their ships. I stand alone, ruminating on my victory, all apart from young Alfred leaving me to my thoughts.

For a long moment, fear stills my heart. I'd thought my enemy run away towards their ships or retreated over the Mersea river using some of the Norse ships. Only then do I discern the man at the front of the rapidly approaching force. My body relaxes, all tension draining away. I'll not have to fight for my survival again today. My arms ache, and my head rings with the cries of dying men.

Before me sits Hywel, king of the South Welsh, on a magnificent horse of deepest black, a smirk across his uncovered face, lined and illuminated by the lowering sun as his gaze takes in the same scene I've been considering.

'I see I come too late, my lord king, Athelstan,' he calls jauntily as soon as he's within earshot.

'Yes, you do. The enemy is vanquished. Hundreds, if not thousands, lie dead before us. See.'

I hide my surprise at Hywel's arrival at the head of up to three hundred warriors and point towards the field of death. I watch with some satisfaction as he gulps at the all too visible scene of my greatest success.

'My lord king, Athelstan, this is a great victory for you, and now I'm even more aggrieved that I didn't arrive sooner,' he says with all seriousness.

'Is that why you're here? To join the battle?' I ask with interest, but hopefully, not too keenly. It would be rewarding to know he changed his mind about supporting me before this great victory was won.

'Yes, my lord king, of course,' he quickly assures me, his voice remaining serious. 'I realised the error of my judgement. Our island has grown quiet under your guardianship, and I shouldn't have turned ambivalent at the thought of proving my loyalty to you.'

I'm too tired to mask my surprise at the words. Hywel starts to chuckle, his sombre expression evaporating in the face of my obvious joy at his words.

'I mean no disrespect, my lord king, but it's the first time I've ever truly seen you speechless.'

'I won't deny that you've shocked me. You have my thanks for making the journey.'

Hywel sobers at that, looking out at the field carpeted in bodies.

'You had an overwhelming victory?' he queries, more statement than an actual question.

'It was a hard-won victory after a day of fighting. We must count the total number of dead and reckon up those we've lost on our side.'

'I imagine that'll take some time,' Hywel mutters cynically. I smile: a small, sad thing that spreads across my face, turning it from winter to summer's day at the thought of those I've surrendered to the battlefield. They all died for me, but they wanted to, and they had good deaths, if such can be said. All of them.

'It will, and there will, of course, be many graves to dig.' The reminder of that unhappy task turns me even more solemn.

'My men are good at digging graves and looting a little as they go, I can't deny that, and so I won't. If you allow us, my lord king, we'll set up camp and help with disposing of the dead.'

'That would be most welcome. I imagine my men won't look with joy upon the task of preparing the dead for burial, not when they might fear whom they'll discover next and whether they're kin or enemy.'

Hywel bows low at the acceptance of his request. 'You have my thanks, my lord king.'

'And you have mine. I've missed your company.'

A commotion behind him, and Hywel's impetuous grin is back on his face. 'I almost forgot,' he announces, his head turning to where a ragged man is being led forward between two men, one a man I recognise. I sent him as part of a small force to aid Hywel in tracking down our meddlesome scop. The man is beaten, although not too much; dried blood streaks his nose and his clothes are muddy from where he's been forced to march while Hywel and his men have ridden. But his eyes are clear and his face clean other than for the caked, days-old blood. 'I found something for you,' Hywel continues.

I narrow my eyes and look at the man a little more carefully. I'm wondering if my guess as to his identity is correct. I'm sure I recognise him.

'This, my lord king, Athelstan, is your scop, the source of much of the discontent within the Welsh lands. And we were right; he's told me every-thing. His most famous scop song was constructed on the orders of King Constantin of the Scots, a little something to worm its way into the minds of all those intelligent enough to interpret it.'

I was right. I'm overjoyed that Hywel has gone to all the trouble of finding the man responsible for me losing my Welsh allies, that, when combined with the honeyed words of Olaf Gothfrithson, has forced all my allies to remain at home during this fight. I'm equally relieved to know that my assumptions have proven to be correct and ecstatic that Hywel has returned to me. Hopefully, the other men of the Welsh kingdoms will follow suit in the coming months. If not, I might just have to assist Hywel in his desire to overwhelm his cousin and claim Gwynedd for himself.

Hywel grasps my arm firmly. I return the greeting wholeheartedly. After the day I've had, it feels good to have this further evidence of the right-eousness of my kingship and overlordship.

'Repeat those words, now, scop,' I demand from the dazed man. I think he'll refuse, and I feel Hywel tense at the command. 'Repeat those words you composed for the defeated King Constantin of the Scots.'

The man looks at me, his eyes struggling to focus. He coughs, but stands proud, as he begins to speak.

'And after peace, commotion everywhere,
Brave, mighty men, in battle tumult.
Swift to attack, stubborn in defence.
Warriors will scatter the interlopers as far as Cait
The Welsh and the men of Dublin, the Scots and the Norsemen,
Those of Cornwall and Strathclyde will reconcile as one.
Kings and nobles will subdue the interlopers, drive them into exile,
Bring an end to the dominion, and make them food for the wild
beasts.
There will be no return for the tribes of the Saxons.'

'Will there be a return of the Scots, the Dublin Norse, and the Norsemen?' I demand from him, his words dying away like the cries of those who might still draw breath. Abruptly, he sags, defeated, and that's all I need to witness. I don't yet know what I'll do with him, but the scop, alongside Constantin's son, Alpin, will be more than enough to ensure the meddlesome old fool keeps quietly to his kingdom from now on.

'Come, my lord king, I'll get my men to set their camp, and then we'll begin our grisly work.' Hywel speaks in the reverberating silence.

I look bleakly out at the field of destruction and death; the blood-churned bodies, the early evening sun dully shining on discarded swords and shields. Scraps of bright clothes catch my eye, the occasional glimpse of a pale upturned face, eyes now forever staring. I hear the harsh caw-cawing of the black, flapping cloud overhead.

'Tomorrow will be soon enough. There's no need to rush.'

And with that, I resolutely turn my back on the slaughter field.

Brunanburh.

The name fills me with pride and disquiet in equal measure.

Brunanburh.

I know it'll be remembered for a thousand years to come.

The Norse have finally been banished from the shores of my kingdom. May that last for a thousand years as well.

AUTHOR'S NOTES
934–937

First things first, no one actually knows where the Battle of Brunanburh took place. No one. There are a number of different sites that historians have suggested from the one I've chosen, Bromborough in Cheshire, Brinsworth in South Yorkshire and Burnswark in Dumfries and Galloway. As one historian has commented, more discussion has taken place about where Brunanburh was than about its actual historical significance, which is often seen as much less important in the grand scheme of later events. In recent years, and, indeed, before I wrote the initial drafts of this book and its predecessor, there has been a move to accept the Wirral as the possible location. Bernard Cornwell has been instrumental, as have an archaeology group based in Wirral, in trying to find corroborating evidence for this. The results of the work can be found in *Never Greater Slaughter* by Michael Livingstone.

In my role as writer of historical fiction, I chose the site that I thought offered the best opportunity to develop the storyline and the one that intrigued me the most. After all, it does sort of make sense that any battle for York would have taken place close to York, but equally, why would the Dublin Norse have sailed all the way around the tip of Scotland to get to York from the east coast? If they used one of the portage routes overland then, again, we must ask why. And so, I opted for the position which would be the closest way of them stepping foot on English soil.

An accounting of the Battle of Brunanburh survives as a poem in the Anglo-Saxon Chronicle A version, an almost singular occurrence in a prose piece of writing (there are four such occurrences, the one concerning the Battle of Brunanburh, King Edmund [twice], and the coronation of King Edgar, who was Edmund's youngest son), and this, I think, shows that it was deemed to be very important at the time, and certainly worthy of composing a poem. Below is some of the poem.

> 'Here King Athelstan, leader of warriors,
> ring-giver of men, and also his brother,
> the ætheling Edmund, struck life-long glory
> in strife around Brunanburh, clove the shield-wall
> hacked the war-time, with hammers' leavings,
> Edward's offspring, as was natural to them
> by ancestry, that in frequent conflict
> they defend land, treasures and homes
> against every foe. The antagonists succumbed,
> the nation of Scots and sea-men
> fell doomed. The field darkened
> With soldiers' blood...
>
> There the ruler of
> Northmen, compelled by necessity,
> was put to flight, to ship's prow,
> with a small troop. The boat withdrew,
> saved life, over the fallow flood.
> There also likewise, the aged Constantine
> came north to his kith by flight.
> The hoary man of war had no cause to exult
> in the clash of blades; he was shorn of his kinsmen,
> deprived of friends, on the meeting-place of peoples,
> cut off in strife, and left his son
> on the place of slaughter, mangled by wounds,

young in battle...

Never yet in this island
Was there a greater slaughter
of people felled by the sword's edges,
before this, as books tell us,
old authorities, since Angles and Saxons
came here from the east,
sought out Britain over the broad ocean,
warriors eager for fame, proud war-smiths,
overcame the Welsh, seized the country.'

— *THE ANGLO-SAXON CHRONICLES*, M.
SWANTON ED. AND TRANS., PP.106–110

Pauline Stafford, who has written an extensive account of the actual writing of what we know as the Anglo-Saxon Chronicle (which survives in nine recensions or versions, all with slightly different details and emphasis), states that the Brunanburh poem was a retrospective addition, probably written in the twenty years after Athelstan's death, and certainly before the death of the last son of King Edward the Elder, in 955. Some have suggested that Edmund may not actually have been present at the battle but that it was deemed expedient to assign him a part in it, perhaps after his death, to show the sons of King Edward working together for England.

However, other than the knowledge the battle lasted all day and that, in the end, Constantin and Olaf retreated, nothing further is known, although again, the battle is mentioned in Welsh, Scottish and Irish sources as well. It was deemed to be significant. The Chronicles of the Kings of Alba gives a very brief account: 'And the battle of *Dun Brunde* in his xxxiii year in which was slain the son of Constantin.' While the Annals of Ulster tells us: 'AU 937.6. A great, lamentable and horrible battle was cruelly fought between the Saxons and the Northmen, in which several thousands of Northmen, who are uncounted, fell, but their king, Amlaib, escaped with a few followers. A large number of Saxons fell on the other side, but Æðelstan, king of the Saxons, enjoyed a great victory.' (*From Pictland to Alba, 789–1070*, A.

Woolf, p. 169) Amlaib was an Irish version of the name Olaf. A later source, that of the *Historia Regum Anglorum* by Symeon of Durham, tells that 'Onlaf' came with 615 ships. There are also many later sources that tell of the Battle of Brunanburh, the distance in time to them being written tending to add more and more details which can't be confirmed with any accuracy.

The size of the force is impossible to determine. The figure given by Symeon of Durham is no doubt wildly exaggerated. Much time and effort has been spent trying to determine the size of Norse forces attacking England and elsewhere. It's believed that the population of England at this time was about two million. This article may be of interest concerning numbers and the logistics of the campaign: *A Long Walk South: Constantine's Route To Brunanburh* by Dave Capener, free to read on Academia.edu.

Affairs in Ireland at this time were complex. Dublin was largely a Norse enclave, involved in almost constant warfare with the Irish clans. Claire Downham has written extensively on this period. 'The rivalry between Limerick and Dublin marks an important chapter in the history of vikings in Ireland. The number of viking campaigns recorded in these years rivals any other period of Irish history. The influence of the vikings is reflected in the range of their campaigns across the island and in the involvement of Irish overkings in their wars.' (*Viking Kings of Britain and Ireland: The Dynasty of Ivarr to A.D. 1014*, C. Downham, p. 41) Affairs in Ireland fall far outside my expertise, but I hope I've correctly portrayed what events are known from this period and which concern Olaf Gothfrithson (you'll find his name also written as Óláfr Guðrøðsson and Amlaib), Olaf Cenncairech – Scabbyhead (a wonderful name for the man – again my thanks to C. Downham for including this in her work) – and Olaf's brothers and sons.

Athelstan's foster son and nephew, Louis, was indeed returned to West Frankia in 936 through the aid, we're told, of Count Hugh and Count Arnulf, according to the Annals of Floadoard, an account written at Rheims throughout this period.

> Louis's uncle, King Athelstan, sent him to Frankia along with bishops
> and others of his fideles after oaths had been given by the legates of the
> Franks. Hugh and the rest of the nobles of the Franks set out to meet

Louis when he left the ship, and they committed themselves to him on the beach at Boulogne-sur-Mer just as both sides had previously agreed. They then conducted Louis to Laon and he was consecrated king, anointed and crowned by Lord Archbishop Artoldus (of Rheims) in the presence of the leading men of the kingdom and more than twenty bishops.

— *THE ANNALS OF FLODOARD OF REIMS, 919–966*, B.S. BACHRACH AND S. FANNING ED. AND TRANS., UNIVERSITY OF TORONTO PRESS, 2004, 18A (936).

— *ATHELSTAN*, S. FOOT, YALE UNIVERSITY PRESS, 2011, P. 168

Again, I'm not expert on the words of Flodoard, but without him, and those who continued his annalistic tradition, we'd know much less about affairs in West Frankia at this time. It's an appealing source, for it is contemporary, although the copies we have of it aren't. I've made little mention of the marriages of Athelstan's sisters in this book. I'll return to them, when they become more relevant. Whether or not Hakon, the son of the king of Norway, was also one of Athelstan's foster sons is a little more open to interpretation. I've taken it as fact for the purpose of this story. Not wishing to confuse my readers with side stories, I've not made much mention of Alain of Brittany, who also returned to his birthright at a similar time to Louis.

Since writing *King of Kings*, I've discovered that Osferth was named in Alfred's will, so feel I should clarify that he was a historical figure. What is difficult to determine is who he was. He was clearly an acknowledged member of Alfred's close family, as were his wife, daughters and Æthelred, the husband of Lady Æthelflæd.

Camping, I hear you cry. Yes, camping. John Blair has recently addressed the issue of camping in his *Building Anglo-Saxon England*, with a determination that, because much of the lives of the Saxon and then English kings were peripatetic, it seems quite possible that there were canvas tents, and some slightly more durable but temporary buildings as well, some of which have left their marks in the archaeological record.

Affairs in Bamburgh at this time are much less confidently attested than I've portrayed them. Again, the focus of this tale is on the Battle of Brunanburh. We aren't told that any one from Bamburgh took part in the battle, but that doesn't necessarily preclude them.

The poem quoted as being invented by Constantin and the scop did exist, and almost as much controversy surrounds it as the Battle of Brunanburh itself. It has been used variously by many historians for different reasons. For the purpose of Brunanburh, I took the suggestion of Nick Higham (and others) that it was a poem devised in Wales from 930 onwards to show unhappiness at the links with the English. It was written in Welsh and you can easily find translations of it online. That Constantin had a hand to play in it is my own invention, although you just never know!

I'm indebted to a military history book (the name of which escapes me) I read about the Battle of Hastings for making me understand just how important small landscape features could be in a battle of such magnitude.

The irony of Brunanburh is that it was the greatest battle to take place in the British Isles before the Battle of Hastings in 1066 and yet, before I researched the time period between Alfred and my Earls of Mercia series, I'd never heard of it and nor, more than likely, have most of the people reading this. I hope that this novel resurrects the battle for some of my readers and gives Athelstan his final wish!

ACKNOWLEDGMENTS

Huge thanks to my editor, Caroline Ridding, for believing in my desire to retell the story of Brunanburh, the events that preceded it, as well as the battle itself. It's been quite a wild ride so far.

As ever, I'm indebted to my wonderful copy editor/proofreader, Ross, for his eagle eyes, Gary for stepping in to help and to Susan and the team of proofreaders and copy editors who work for Boldwood.

I'd also like to thank the entire team at Boldwood Books. Your enthusiasm is infectious. And a special shout-out to Claire – I hope you get to use a lot of (fake) fur in the promotion images for this one 😊.

I would also like to thank EP, CS and MC who particularly believed in my story of Brunanburh and continually supported me through its many iterations over the last decade. A shout-out as well to Amy McElroy and Stacy Townsend who are now my author buddies as well as my readers. And another shout-out to my author buddies, Kelly Evans, Elizabeth R. Andersen, Eilis Quinn, Peter Gibbons, Donovan Cook and JC Duncan for your support. And to Shaun at Flintlock Covers for helping me with the map and to my cover designer for working such magic with both *King of Kings* and *Kings of War*. And finally, to Matt Coles, narrator extraordinaire. I never make it easy for you.

And to my readers. Thank you as ever for journeying with me to Saxon England.

MORE FROM MJ PORTER

We hope you enjoyed reading *King of War*. If you did, please leave a review.

If you'd like to gift a copy, this book is also available as an ebook, large print, paperback, digital audio download and audiobook CD.

Sign up to MJ Porter's mailing list for news, competitions and updates on future books.

https://bit.ly/MJPorterNews

Explore exciting historical fiction from MJ Porter:

   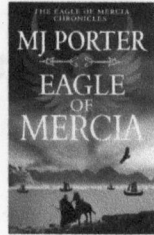

ABOUT THE AUTHOR

MJ Porter is the author of many historical novels set predominantly in Seventh to Eleventh-Century England, and in Viking Age Denmark. Raised in the shadow of a building that was believed to house the bones of long-dead Kings of Mercia, meant that the author's writing destiny was set.

Visit MJ's website: www.mjporterauthor.com

Follow MJ on social media:

twitter.com/coloursofunison

instagram.com/m_j_porter

bookbub.com/authors/mj-porter

Boldwood

Boldwood Books is an award-winning fiction publishing company seeking out the best stories from around the world.

Find out more at www.boldwoodbooks.com

Join our reader community for brilliant books, competitions and offers!

Follow us
@BoldwoodBooks
@BookandTonic

Sign up to our weekly
deals newsletter

https://bit.ly/BoldwoodBNewsletter

9 781837 511877

Milton Keynes UK
Ingram Content Group UK Ltd.
UKHW041324290324
440100UK00002B/16

9 781837 511877